A Daughter's Wish

For my school friend, Mary Lascelles,
the kindest woman I know

A Daughter's Wish

Elizabeth Gill

QUERCUS

First published in Great Britain in 2009 as *Paradise Lane* by Severn House Publishers
First published in eBook as *A Daughter's Wish* by Quercus in 2016
This hardback edition published in 2023 by

QUERCUS

Quercus Editions Ltd
Carmelite House
50 Victoria Embankment
London EC4Y 0DZ

An Hachette UK company

A CIP catalogue record for this book is available
from the British Library

HB ISBN 978 1 52942 801 8
EBOOK ISBN 978 1 78429 258 4

10 9 8 7 6 5 4 3 2 1

Typeset by CC Book Production
Printed and bound in Great Britain by Clays Ltd, Elcograf S.p.A.

Papers used by Quercus are from well-managed forests and other responsible sources.

Author's Note

Those who know the Garden House Hotel on North Road in Durham City may be aware of who owned this in 1902 and assuredly it was not Mr and Mrs Hatty but I did want to make use of a place which people know so well and maybe those who enjoy such ideas would see it and think that perhaps Mr and Mrs Hatty just might have lived there at some time.

The Durham newspaper which I knew of was the *Durham County Advertiser* and I could not resist making the newspaper premises in my story in Saddler Street where the *Durham County Advertiser* was lodged some years ago and where I had my first glimpse into the journalistic life. I wanted to make sure that my research was accurate and discovered from the librarians in the reference library that there were two newspapers at the time of which I am writing. I had no idea of this but had already put them in my story. The *Durham County Advertiser* began in 1814, the *Durham Chronicle and County Gazette* in 1820. They both eventually ended up at 64 Saddler Street.

I have made use in several of my stories of the County Hotel and cannot help but imagine when I go there that one or another of my characters is staying in a room just above which looks out over the river or drinking Martinis in a cocktail bar before dinner.

Prologue

Al had not been able to go out that day. Such a little thing to make such a difference, Sarah thought when she looked back at it. It had been a lovely day, one of those spring days in March which you rarely got and which this time had come in number. There had been more than a week of warm sunshine. People took off their coats as they walked by the river, and lingered there in the winding cobbled streets of the small city. The shopkeepers left their doors open. She had wanted to go for a picnic. The daffodils were beginning to show yellow, the crocuses were purple and white on the roadsides and the snowdrops were just about finished.

She had been desperate for a free day because she worked so hard at the dressmaker's in the back of the shop in the marketplace. She hated the work there. In winter she had to strain her gaze and furrow her brow to see at all during the dark days because Mrs Cheveley who owned the place would not provide the light which her workers needed and all day they sat there in the little light there was and she watched over them so they should not stop.

It was Sunday. On Sundays she had to go to chapel with her parents, was allowed to do nothing, in fact it was just as boring as the rest of the week and she had finally rebelled and said to Al that it was lovely weather and they should run away just for an hour or two and take the consequences and then Al had had to work, that was what he said anyhow.

But that had not been the start of things going wrong. The beginning had been when Fergus Seaton saw her and she saw him. Until then she thought she had loved Al but she fell in love with Fergus. She knew that it was stupid, she had not known that she could do such things, she thought stuff like that only happened in stories but he was so dark and brown-eyed and good-looking that she couldn't help herself. She wanted to be with him all the time, she wanted to run to him at every opportunity. She lay in bed and thought about him and she knew that she would never love like that again. They were meant to be together. She could not think how she had come to be as lucky as to find him, nor he to find her.

She could not believe that he had noticed her. He was a fine man from London, he owned pits, had come there, he said, to see how things were going as he occasionally did and he had seen her in the street and he had taken a shine to her and when she stopped in the middle of Elvet Bridge he had gone up to her and very politely told her his name and asked for hers.

She knew that she was very pretty, many men had noticed, many men had come up to her but she had always brushed them off and then she had met Al and he was respectable, he was better than the rest but he was not like Fergus. Nobody in the world was like Fergus.

Sarah had gone into hiding, down here in Paradise Lane. What a name for such a place. Perhaps once it had been green fields but it was right in the middle of the city so she could not think why it was named in such a way. She had lived in the city all her life and never seen this part of it and it was not a big city but only the likes of thieves and prostitutes and those so poverty-stricken that they had nothing lived in such a place and she had dreaded the knowing of it, never thinking that she would end up here.

The name was so ironic and yet everybody in Durham knew of it. She remembered her mother saying to her when she had behaved badly when she was little, 'Anybody would think you'd been dragged up in Paradise Lane,' and yet every Sunday the minister would talk of paradise and say how people who believed in God and Jesus would end up in such a place where there was no pain or suffering, the sun shone all day and there were wonderful things to eat. In fact, she had thought then, it would be like Christmas when the house was decorated with paper chains and everybody got a present and a big dinner or Easter Sunday when she got new summer clothes and she and her sister would decorate hard-boiled eggs with their paint boxes and brushes and roll them down the hill in Wharton Park.

But Paradise Lane was the place where people went to when

there was nothing left. Her mother had found her being sick and she had said it must have been something she ate and her mother scoffed and said, 'What, two mornings running? It's that man, isn't it? I've heard of him and I didn't believe the gossip, I didn't think that you would do such a thing, I thought you had more sense but I should have known that no good would come of it. I was so proud, I thought I knew my daughters. Wait until your father finds out.'

She listened to their raised voices when he came home in the late afternoon and he had not said anything though his face changed as she had not seen it change before. All he had done was take her by the arm and walk her to the front door, put her out of it, close it and lock it. She stood there for a long time sure that they would think better of their action and let her back in. She could not even remember what her mother had said, her voice high and shrill, and her brother and sister had gone upstairs for fear they should somehow get the blame just by being in the room. She had had to go away, the neighbours had heard the noise and people were surreptitiously at their doors, peering out at her and going back in, taking another look and then another until she could bear it no longer and was sure that she would not be let back inside and she thought about trying the door and hammering and shouting but she had known that it would do no good so in the end she walked away.

When you had nowhere to go, that was the worst feeling in the world. Because of the condition she was in and she did not doubt even for a moment that her mother was right, nobody, neither friend nor relative, would take her in, they were too afraid of the shame being somehow on them as well and they would not dare to trespass on her mother and father's decision because they would be sure that it was right. She had been respectable, that was the word for it. She had not realized what a small way it was from that kind of respectability to this. She had had her head turned, that was what they called it.

She thought of the comfortable little house under the viaduct on the hill above the town. Her parents and her sister would be sitting around the fire now. It was only a few minutes' walk away yet she would never go there again. They had been so ashamed of what she had done. The worst thing a woman could do was to become pregnant when she was not married and her parents were good chapel-going people.

She could not even think now how she had got herself into such a predicament. You did hear of loose women but it seemed to her that they were just unfortunate and that men had made them so. Fergus had certainly done so to her. He had lured her to a shady spot by the river on a fine day, they were going to have a picnic and then he had kissed her until her body was on fire.

What had happened after that had not been something she had wanted to happen but neither had he forced her. She had not known what he was doing, she was carried away by the feel of his mouth and hands.

It seemed amazing that people should have to pay such a high price for something which felt so good and so natural and she – it made her laugh bitterly to think of it – she had thought he would marry her, that having done such a thing any man would marry the woman, why else would he want to be with her that way?

She had not known that there were men who did such things and had no honour, that all they wished was their own pleasure with no thought for the consequences and he knew what could happen and he had gone ahead anyway. He had not thought about her, he had only thought about her body.

She had dreaded her thoughts. She had imagined the horror which came upon her when her monthly bleeding stopped and her breasts hurt and the sickness began and her clothes began to tighten. At first she had lain in bed and thought God could not visit such things upon her but gradually it became obvious to her what was happening.

Fergus was not interested, she finally admitted this to herself, he did not care, they no longer met. Once he had had her half a dozen times at various secluded places he had lost interest, he spent time with other people, no doubt with other women. She was astonished that men of money, property and pit-owners, could do such things.

She had been brought up to believe that they were right, that they knew better than the people who worked for them. Fergus was so important that he had agents to run his pits, he didn't go near them most of the time, yet having come to the town – and how she wished he never had – he seemed reluctant to leave and stayed there in a big house just outside the city with friends and went fishing and shooting and away for the weekends: he had told her of these pleasures and she had envied the people concerned – but he had never thought of her like that, she was just there for use.

The time spent with her, the picnic which she had packed so carefully went uneaten, the beer which she had brought undrunk and he had left her there, he said he had somewhere to be, she could not even remember where it was.

She tried to tell him that she was having a baby and he made a joke and asked her how many other men she had pleasured and she had been obliged to hide her condition as well as she could for as long as she could and it was not long because the sickness was so bad almost from the beginning.

When she mentioned marriage he had laughed and said he was married already so she couldn't catch him that way and she said her father would kill her and he said he was sure that nothing of the sort would occur, such things happened every day, her family would take in the baby and they would get over it, just like everybody did.

She left. She knew that there must be some place in the small city where she could hide successfully, where people lived who were cut off from respectable society, from those who went to church and chapel.

She had no money and only the clothes she had left in and it rained and the other girls on the street corners down there had done nothing but laugh at first and then she knew that all the women who went there ended up on the street just like they did, enticing men to dark corners for money. She stood in a shop doorway for a while, unable to believe what had happened, and she tried to get work. She had gone to the shop where she sewed but somebody had already told Mrs Cheveley because she came to the door, pushed Sarah back out of it, locked it – she heard the key turn – and told her not to come back.

'I'm owed wages,' she protested.

'Sluts are owed nothing,' Mrs Cheveley said and that was when Sarah realized that she had become the subject of gossip all over the town. This was confirmed when she went to the offices and shops to ask for work and it was like she had a sign on her saying that she was expecting or could they see it in her face? She was turned down everywhere.

When the day grew dark and cold the owner of the shop where she was sheltering from the rain came out and told her to move and gradually she drifted, as no doubt, she thought, many of the other girls had done, further and further away from her house and the respectable places in the town. The poor and the abandoned and the hopeless congregated down by the river here.

The shadows of people waited in the doorways, the women made themselves visible as the light died from the day.

A man found her beneath Elvet Bridge when the river was running swiftly and offered her a small sum so that what she had once thought she was doing for love she now did for money. It was the same and it was different and then she saw herself somehow reflected in the dark shadows. She had never thought of herself much at all, they were not encouraged to look into mirrors, beauty was something of a sin somehow. Humility was the thing. Loveliness brought on sins of the flesh and that resulted, she knew very well now, in degradation.

Each girl had her spot and men soon got to know hers. Under the bridge she earned her money and she found a room nearby in a back alley. It was not a lot of money but that plus a hot pie or two from the nearest pub was what she could afford and as the weeks went on and she got bigger the men objected to paying as much so they got her cheaply.

She made no friends though the other women were friendly with one another. She was too ashamed to speak to anyone and she found that she had nothing to say.

She deliberately didn't look at the men. She did not know whether they were young or old, how they smelled. She turned her face from them when they got that close. To taste them would finish her off, she thought. And the feel of them. She held them as lightly as possible while they did what they wanted and only seemed to let go of her breath again freely when it was over.

She eked the money out day after day and each day she felt more worthless and despised herself more for getting herself into such a state. Often and often she almost went to Al but she knew that he would be unforgiving, what man could forgive what she had done, what man would take another man's child and if she did not tell him that she had had to give her body in return for money – what would happen then?

It was a long, long time before the baby was born and each day she hid there in the room which came alive with insects at night. If she was there they dropped on her when she slept, making her scream so at least during the daylight hours she did not have that to endure but the nights, especially the cold nights with the wind blowing off the river, seemed to last forever and there was always a fat ill-dressed man with rough hands and breath she would turn away from as he took what he had paid for.

When the baby was born, after what seemed like years the woman from upstairs heard her screams and came down and helped her.

She had been glad of any help she could get by then, the pain went on and on. And now the baby was born and there was nothing else for her to do. She had taken a note to where Fergus was staying. She thought he was there still. She tucked up the baby as best she could and took a last look at the room which had been all her home during the months after she left Atherton Street and then she slipped on her coat against the weather and left the house.

Everything had changed now. She had tried to think what she would do. She could not take the child with her when she went to what she thought of as work. Nor could she leave it alone in the room. She ventured up the grimy broken stairs to see the woman who had helped when the baby was born but she had known it was no good. She went through her explanation and already the woman, older than she was with a deeply lined face, was shaking her head.

'Please help me, there's no one else,' but the door was already closing.

She had been in that one room with her baby for almost a week and the money had run out. She suspected that her milk was not enough for her child, who screamed constantly. She thought about going home, about the little house where she had been brought up and the job she had hated so much. She thought back now to all the things that she had had and could not believe she had thought herself unhappy. It seemed to her now like paradise indeed.

She wondered whether she should leave the baby on her parents' doorstep and go somewhere different but it seemed like such an awful thing to do. She had the feeling they would not take it in and then what would happen to it?

That was when she made her decision. There was nothing else to do. She would take a note to the house where Fergus was staying.

It was a long walk and she made sure that she went in the dim light. She did think of leaving the baby there but then everybody in the house would know and perhaps he would even refuse and say it was not his and would not take the responsibility for it. She could not guarantee that he would come to Paradise Lane either but it was the best that she could do.

There was even a very bad moment when she considered taking the baby with her. What if he didn't get the note, what if he ignored it? What if her baby was left in that room alone and died? Would it not be better to make an end to both of them? A risk. She could have smiled – had she had the energy left she would have. Even at this stage she was prepared to take a risk?

None of this was the child's fault. Should she not have even a small chance? Otherwise this would be a total defeat. The baby slept inside her shawl, quiet for once as Sarah trudged all the way through the town towards Shincliffe, the little village which lay just beyond the city. Fergus had been staying at the big house just to this side of the village. They would know where to find him.

The front of the house was in darkness. At first as she trudged up the drive she thought it was just because of the trees, because it was totally without life. She panicked. What if he was not here? What if they had shut up the house and would not be back for weeks, pleasing themselves with sport and parties as people like that did, she thought savagely, but she went on and up the long wide stone steps and she pushed the note through the letter box in the front door.

The first part of her plan was completed and now that she had put it into operation it seemed to carry its own momentum. She was glad of that, it was as though she did not have to make any decisions, it was all done. She went wearily back to the room which was the only home she had known in almost six months and there she fed the baby for the last time and held her until she slept and put her down and wrapped her up for comfort and warmth and then she slipped out of the building.

Even the whores had gone home, the weather was so vile. It was freezing and foggy, she could barely see the pavement and when she reached it she could only just see the river.

They said drowning was an easy way to go. She thought people only said it because they had not done it but there was nothing else for her now. She found stones down there and filled her pockets with them, her coat and her skirt, and then she walked towards the black, oily water.

It was so cold, worse than she had thought it would be and

the bottom was uneven as she had not imagined it, there were rocks and lower places and the fog seemed to come down even further to meet the water.

Above her she could hear the sound of three o'clock as the cathedral bell struck and she imagined the great shadows of the castle and the cathedral. In the morning the sun would come up, maybe it would even get past the fog, it would rise round and golden but she would not see it. She would never see another day. It was such a relief to think she would not have to worry any more.

One

1902 London

Annabel Seaton had been expecting Thomas Grant to ask her to marry him. That sounded awful. It wasn't like that, it was just that she couldn't think what she might do other than be his wife. It was right, it was meant to be, it was their future together. They had been best friends since they were children and it was the most important friendship of her life. Somewhere in among all that was her sister, Millie, less than two years younger than she was, it had always been herself and Millie and Tom, somehow she could not leave out the sister who was so precious to her.

It was winter, it had snowed and they had spent a silly morning firing snowballs at one another across the park, running away and coming back and helping various children to build snowmen. At one point Millie had even gone home and come back with five round pieces of coal, three for his buttons and two for his eyes, filched a scarf and red woollen hat for his neck and head and they had given them to the children and watched the snowman take on an appearance so real to Millie that she hung on to Annabel's arm for a second or two and laughed, still breathless from her trek into the house and said, 'Oh, dear, I'm afraid that he is real and will come to us in the night and scare us half to death.'

To which Tom had said, 'I don't think there's much chance of that, it's thawing already.'

'Don't spoil it, Tom!' Annabel said.

'It's true,' Tom insisted, 'he'll be nothing but a puddle by morning.'

They went back as the day grew dark and in the late afternoon the icicles in the guttering at the top of the houses began to drip but later the relentless cold came down again across London. Annabel and Tom were sitting over the fire and when Millie had gone Annabel was not quite sure where he took the opportunity to say, 'Now that we have some privacy there's something I want to say to you.'

'Hurry up, then, she'll be back in a minute.'

And he hurried. He said, 'Will you marry me?'

She stared.

'I'm of age, you know,' he said.

'Yes, I know how old you are.'

'And so are you. There's no reason why we shouldn't and damn it, Bel, our families expect it.'

Still she was so taken aback that she couldn't think of anything to say.

'And is that why you want to?'

'No, of course not,' he said impatiently and he got up and did a little bit of a turn around the room as though he was embarrassed and wished he hadn't said anything.

It was not what she had thought he was going to say; she had thought it was some silly secret of one of their friends which Millie was too young to hear. She stared at him for a good long while, thinking that he was making a joke but it was only because, she realized now, that she had always expected they would be married and it seemed strange that he should have to ask her. She couldn't say that, of course, it would sound so stupid and so forward as though she had assumed what she was not entitled to assume but it was just that she could never see her future without him. She didn't know what to say.

Tom looked deflated. His shoulders went down. He was almost beetroot in the face. He turned around and looked her in the eyes and she reflected that he was all she had ever wanted in a man, he had pale yellow hair the colour of straw and bright blue eyes and wore his expensive perfectly fitting clothes beautifully. He was a catch and she knew it, but to her he was her other part, he completed her. 'All right. I've always cared for you very much and I want to marry you. Please say yes.'

She hesitated for just a second longer. She had imagined that when she was asked to marry there would be music playing and there would be a moon and they would be in Venice or Paris, anywhere but here, but it was right to marry him, what else would they have done? She thought she could hear Millie's footsteps just beyond the door so she said, 'Yes!' and he came back and clasped her into his arms as the door opened and Millie stood upon the threshold, still with surprise.

*

He would have to ask her father of course and he went to do that. And her mother must be told but her mother had gone visiting friends and was not there and there was no harm in his going to see her father who had come in just a little while since and would be toasting his frozen feet by the fire as he had come back from his club and would no doubt be thinking of his dinner.

She watched anxiously from across the hall even though the draught was a serious business. Her mother came back only in time to dress for dinner but her father was closeted up there with Tom for so long and then with her mother that Annabel despaired. Whatever could be taking so much time?

Finally Tom came downstairs and she flew across the hall, only to find that he guided her into the little sitting room which was in darkness and had no fire and there in the dark Tom said, 'I don't think they were very pleased.' He looked uncomfortable. Annabel hesitated, unable to understand and upset for him that her father had made him feel like this. She tried to take it in. 'Your father wanted to be pleased and he seemed stunned, which amazed me . . . and your mother . . . I think she positively dislikes me.'

'She can't do that.' Tom had run wild about their house since he was a little boy and she and Millie had done the same in his house.

Tom was obviously at a loss as to what to say next and it was freezing in that room, she knew particularly because she was dressed for dinner and had no wrap. He sounded injured and it was not surprising since he was one of the most eligible young men in London, his family were not just rich, they were respected and well known, so it was not astonishing that he seemed grieved.

'But he did give his permission?' she said.

'Reluctantly, he did that. My father would be really annoyed if he knew.'

'You told him first?'

'I would hardly come here and ask you to marry me without. He's my banker,' Tom said flatly. 'Your mother looked particularly angry. You'd have thought I'd done something wrong, though what in heaven's name it could be I can't think. My politics are to be sure a little different but my father thinks like they do. My parents were delighted, they couldn't have been more pleased. I really haven't done anything wrong, Bel . . .'

His voice faded off as he went through the past weeks and months in his mind, she could see by his expression and his creased brow, in case he should discover anything that had let his family down, anything that might have disgraced them. If things hadn't been so difficult Annabel would have laughed. Tom was the most upright of young men. He was not like many, running after women, and getting drunk and ending up in jail and deliberately taking opposing views to his family.

'I had better go,' Tom said, rather stiffly. He nodded and left and it was only then that she made her way across the hall and into the dining room where her parents and Millie were now gathered. None of them looked at her, there were no explanations, there were no congratulations, it was as if nothing had happened.

The dinner was almost an hour late and when they sat down it was obvious that it had been a very good meal, now it was somewhat dry and not as hot as it should be. Annabel could taste nothing. She didn't know what she was eating and she didn't understand what was going on. It was only later when the meal was finished that her father called her into the study and said, 'You are to be congratulated, my dear, Tom has asked me for your hand.'

She looked at him but he was not watching her and she went to him because all she could think was that if it was not Tom then it was her.

'Have I done something?' she asked softly.

That was when he looked at her and he made her uncomfortable by it. Her father was a difficult man and she had always been a little afraid of him. He did not like women's company, she thought now, at least not women like herself, her sister Millie and her mother. She had heard, she knew that he liked very well the company of other women.

'What could you have done?' he said and in such a way that it made her nervous.

'I don't know but it can't be Tom. We thought you would be pleased.'

'Why should you think that?'

She didn't know what to say and was inclined to stutter or to run from the room. It had not occurred to her that her father would not be pleased when she had been offered marriage by one of the most eligible young men in London.

'I didn't think you would marry,' he said.

'Not marry? Why not?'

'Because you're not the kind of young woman that men want.'

She looked at him. She had long been aware that her parents did not approve of her and she had tried to pretend that it was not so. She couldn't think of anything to say but it didn't matter. Her father said, 'Men want obedient women, not those who voice their opinions at the supper table, not women who care little for how they dress and less for how they act, they want pretty obliging women like your sister.'

She wanted to deny these things. She didn't think she had ever voiced an opinion in front of him, he would never have suffered her to do it and she was too afraid of his temper to do such a thing. He was given to shouting even in front of the servants if he chose. She knew that she had a certain careless-ness about her dress. She was not pretty like Millie and her mother and neither did she want to try to compete, it seemed easier to let them shine, she would stay in the background.

'Tom cares about me in spite of this,' she said, her throat constricting so much she was afraid she might cry.

'Apparently so. Your ungainliness, your lack of manners, your want of interesting conversation seem not to bear with him, I cannot think why, unless he has lost his wits, but it seems that we are to be rid of you and I will be happy to pay. And your mother and I will be happy to host an engagement party for you here so that all London can be as amazed as we are.'

If there was a reply which suited this Annabel could not

think of it and she left the room, when he dismissed her, without a word.

Over the teacups beside the drawing-room fire, when the servants had gone and she was alone with her mother – it was only then that her mother said, 'Your father told me that Tom had offered for you.'

Annabel knew better than to say anything since the interview with her father. Her mother looked down into the pretty white, gold and red teacup she held in her hands. And, not understanding at all as the silence went on, Annabel blurted out, 'Why should he not?'

There was a slight pause before her mother said, 'I thought Tom loved Millie.'

Annabel could not believe it. Was this the problem? How could they have imagined such a thing? She didn't understand it. She couldn't drink her tea and she wished she hadn't eaten the little she had managed at dinner because she felt sick.

'I think he does,' she said.

'Then why did he offer for you?' Her mother looked at her in such a straight way that she could hardly breathe.

'Because his love for Millie is the kind he would have for his sister if he had one.'

'Millie is beautiful,' her mother said. 'She is the kind of woman who could make a man happy.'

Annabel felt as though she had been turned to wood. For years she had denied to herself that Millie was her mother's favourite, it was only because she was young and looked so vulnerable, because she was slight and pretty, with a pink and white complexion, shiny yellow hair and startlingly blue eyes.

'I'm the older sister. Did you not think that I would marry first?'

'Perhaps, but not to Tom. There are plenty of other men. It did not occur to me that Tom preferred you, that's all. He dances with Millie, he spends a great deal of time with her—'

'That's because Millie and I are so close.'

'Are you sure that's all?' Etta, Annabel realized with surprise, was still hoping that her younger daughter would marry the most eligible man in the area.

'He could have asked her and would have if he had wanted to marry her. You aren't pleased, then?'

'Of course I'm pleased for you, it just wasn't what I was expecting and I think you will find that Millie doesn't share your joy,' her mother said.

Millie had gone to bed. Annabel had not noticed. As soon as she could she went upstairs and banged on Millie's bedroom door. There was no answer.

'Millie? Millie, let me in.'

After a long time in the draughty corridor the door finally opened and her sister turned a tear-stained face to her. Annabel went inside despite her sister's obvious reluctance.

'Why didn't you tell me how you feel about Tom?' she said.

Millie shrugged and suddenly looked older. 'There's nothing to tell.'

'You should have. I didn't know. I didn't mean to hurt you.

The last thing I would ever want is to cause you pain. You're my only sister and I love you.'

Millie broke down and cried at that but refused to let Annabel comfort her.

'I'm silly. Tom has always loved you. I think it's just that I have always known him and he's kind, he was always kinder than other boys, he never made fun of my toys, pulled my hair or avoided talking to me so that he could run away with the other boys. I couldn't imagine us being apart. There's always been the three of us. I just can't bear the idea of you and Tom going away and living somewhere that has nothing to do with me.'

'But we wouldn't do such a thing. There's no question of it.'

'Yes, you will. You'll want a house of your own and to have Tom to yourself and I'll be left here with no one but Mother and you have to say, Bel, that she is the most disagreeable woman on earth.'

That made them both laugh and the tension eased.

'I won't go anywhere without you,' Annabel promised. 'I won't go off with Tom and most of all I won't leave you with Mother, I swear it on everything I care for. I don't suppose I'd be going any further than Tom's house because his father and mother would not let him out of their sight and it's the biggest house in the whole world and you shall come with us. I wouldn't leave you here with Mother, she would swallow you whole.'

Millie laughed again at that and Annabel was so pleased to hear her do so and felt so much better.

She didn't say that Millie was already, because of her beauty and position in society and her father's money and reputation, the young woman that the majority of young men wanted to marry. Millie didn't know what it was to want for a partner at dances, they pushed to be near her and Annabel had no doubt that within the year Millie would marry somebody much more glamorous and exciting than Tom.

It was only that she was shy and did not put herself forward like so many young women and Annabel knew that she stayed around her sister and Tom because she and Annabel had always got on so well and could not bear to be parted. Tom was not the right man for Millie but they would always be there for her and Annabel swore to herself that as soon as they were married they would hold a ball in honour of Millie's next birthday and it would be the most wonderful party ever.

Two

Durham City

There was a noise in the back of the old building which housed the *Durham County Chronicle*. Ned Fleming turned around quickly as a tall bulky figure came into sight out of the gloom, taking up half the doorway of the editor's office and then relief warmed Ned's body and he broke into a smile.

'Bert, it's you.'

'Indeed,' Bert said and smiled his crinkly smile and Ned was transported back to his childhood, the sound of the machinery which printed the newspaper, the smell of ink and paper and his uncle sitting at the big desk there, his pipe was still on top of the desk and the place still smelling of his special tobacco. Bert was in charge of printing the newspaper.

Bert wore a shabby suit but he wore it with distinction. He moved like a gentleman and spoke like a local and Ned thought once again of what his father had said, that the newspaper business was nothing to do with gentlemen and that it would never be profitable and that it was a ridiculous venture for his uncle to have got into in the first place, Jasper being the younger son and therefore unimportant, he had for some reason had no share in the three big pits along the coast which their family owned.

'For a minute there I thought we had intruders,' Ned said.

'Nothing for them to take,' Bert observed and said by way of half-apology, 'I wanted to come back here after the funeral. Somehow I feel closer to him here.'

He didn't say 'Do you know what will happen now?' but the words hung in the air as if he had.

They stood and the silence between them became awkward until Ned was inspired. 'Let's put the stove on and the kettle.'

He began, as he spoke, crumpling old newspapers and lifting up the top of the pot-bellied stove which warmed the place usually, throwing them into the huge space inside and after them sticks from the wood basket beside the hearth and when that started to catch he fed small pieces of coal in as well and then put a small very dry log in there too and then he put down the top and watched in satisfaction through the glass at the front as flames began to lick and pull.

Bert went to fill the kettle and when he came back put it on top of the stove and he said, 'When is the will to be read?' as though he had not been able to resist voicing his worries any longer.

Ned had been dreading the question. If his uncle had left the newspaper to his father, and considering there was no money to fund it he probably had, since Ned's father was the rich member of the family, it would be closed down. How often had his father said that one newspaper in the place was enough and that there was nothing wrong with the *Durham City Echo*?

Ned was not unwise enough to say that there was nothing for ordinary people in that newspaper but his father was of the opinion that the ordinary people were there to work, had nothing else to do with important matters such as the running of the country, and since many of them could not read, the newspaper which Jasper had struggled to make a profit at for so long and failed was unnecessary. Ned could not say any of this to Bert. The newspaper was Bert's whole life since his wife had died some years earlier.

It had been his uncle's whole life too. He remembered coming past the place when he had been out to some boring function or other with his father and seeing the lights burning late and knowing that Bert and Jasper were sitting over the fire in the front office or in Bert's smaller office at the back, drinking whisky and talking about their favourite subjects, cricket and football and the state of the government and their own plans for the newspaper, none of which could be put into action because there was no money.

His uncle had stuck it out to the end and he had not come to his elder brother for financial help, much as Ned thought he might have liked to. He had always known that he would not be helped, even though Tranter was so very rich.

Tranter had inherited everything from his father and it was understandable because he was such a good businessman and had run the pits so that they made a huge profit. Ned was ashamed of his father but he knew that very often people who had a lot of money were on a different level and could not conceive of how distressing it was to others when they had so little.

Jasper had given away what he had to people who had less, Ned knew that. He had always admired Jasper so much, could not believe he was dead.

He was forever taking people into his house, giving out food and money and taking on what Tranter called 'hopeless cases'. 'Another of Jasper's hopeless cases', was all he ever called them. Jasper had never married. Ned had gained the impression that he could have married to suit his parents but he would not and after that he was regarded as a failure in the family but Ned did not think that Jasper regretted his life.

They drank their tea when the kettle finally boiled and afterwards they retreated into Bert's office and drank whisky from small squat glasses and toasted the passing of the man they had loved.

Ned tried not to think back to the funeral which had been lavish and had come from his father's pocket. Strange how his father had disliked and despised his younger brother in life and then been so diligent about the funeral arrangements. Who were they for? Presumably they were for himself and the people who attended the funeral were mostly there because they knew they would be seen by his father and that he would think better of them for being there.

Jasper's friends and workmates had hovered at the back, the men from the printing room, the people who worked in his office. They were afraid for their jobs but not one of them had mentioned it, nobody had been anything other than sorry that day and they had not lingered afterwards, going up to the big house as they called it, Redhills Court, where Ned's father presided.

Ned had been saved by the feel of Jane's warm hand in his grasp. All the way through the service they had stood together, she very close to comfort him. Considering she had never lost anybody near to her he was grateful for her understanding. She was like a small solid wall for him and that was strange because she was slight in stature.

She was the prettiest girl in the world, he felt sure, and they were to be married in a few months' time. It was just a bonus that his father liked her or rather he liked her status. She was the only child of a prominent shipbuilding family on the Tyne, they were wealthy, clever people. Not that it had weighed with him. He would have married her had she been a docker's daughter.

Her parents had whisked her away after the funeral, saying they had to get back to Newcastle. They spoke briefly to his father, said how sorry they were and then left. Ned had gone back to the house only briefly and then had retreated here, to Saddler Street, within sound of the cathedral bells and the best of his childhood memories and he was glad that Bert was there.

When he eventually made his way homeward it was with flagging steps. In going he felt as though he was betraying his uncle somehow, he wanted to put both arms around the building which Jasper had loved so much and he had watched Bert's figure as the older man walked slowly and wearily across Elvet Bridge, beyond the Swan and Three Cygnets pub to disappear gradually into the darkness of Old Elvet. Bert looked weighed down by what had happened and he was not the only one. The chances were that all the men who worked there would lose their jobs, and their jobs, especially the specialist kind, were not easy to find in a small city like this.

Ned's own home was a house so big that he was ashamed to live there and that was strange because he had lived there all his life, anybody would think he would have grown used to it by now but he had never grown used to it and he was almost twenty-one. He would be twenty-one in three days' time and his uncle would not be there to see it. They had planned to have a meal together, to have a toast, for Bert and the men to down a pint at midday in his honour. Now it would not happen.

The house was the biggest in the area and there was no description for it but ugly. It was, apparently, one of the finest Jacobean mansions in the north or even in England. It embarrassed him, there was nothing modest about it. Everywhere you looked it was exaggerated, there were points to the roof and twiddling bits of elaboration and it stretched out to both sides at the front with its many windows and huge gardens and seemingly endless steps at the front. He had to walk up the long winding road from the main road until he reached it and when he did so he wished he was not there.

As he entered it from a side door he could hear one of the maids come through, she had so obviously been listening for him. She looked apologetically at him and said in her soft Scottish voice, 'Your father has been watching for you this hour and more. You're to go in.'

She didn't have to say where his father wanted him because his father always seemed to be in the same place, his library, his study, the one enormous room which did for both. It was the biggest room in the house, it faced south, it got all the sun in the afternoons so that his father complained and had the velvet curtains closed to stop it, it did not seem to occur to him that he could use another room and leave the sunshine for other people to enjoy, instead he would shut out the light and complain.

The walls were lined with books, there were two big marble fireplaces to heat it, and an enormous desk sat in the centre of the room and there his father presided unless he was at the table eating or in his bed sleeping or out doing business at the pits.

His father was a big man, had always seemed huge. It did not occur to Ned at any time that he was now as tall as his father because of his father's keen brain and impatient manner somehow. His father despised people who were intellectually beneath him. He dominated every room he had ever entered, Ned thought of his father owning each room he went into and felt sorry for people who were there because they were afraid of Tranter Fleming's acid words and short temper and because he was a rich and powerful man.

Ned was only glad that the so-called mourners had gone, at least he didn't have that to face. He opened the door and his father roared as he got out of an enormous leather chair by a blazing fire, 'So there you are. Where on earth have you been? Nobody knew where you'd gone. Didn't you know Mr Gibbons was coming and has been waiting for you half the afternoon?'

It occurred to Ned that his father knew very well where he

had been but didn't care to admit it by sending somebody there with a note. The solicitor got to his feet.

'Nobody told me. My apologies, Mr Gibbons, for keeping you waiting.' Ned could hear how soft his voice was against his father's.

Mr Gibbons smiled thinly and only nodded in acknowledgement of his presence.

'Indeed and why should they,' his father said in mitigation, 'but apparently my brother has left you something in his will. I said that we shouldn't wait for you but Mr Gibbons says that protocol must be observed.'

Ned looked at the solicitor with more respect than he had done before. To have stayed his father's hand in such matters, to have insisted on something, was very brave and perhaps not wise.

It seemed strange to Ned that his uncle had left nothing to anyone but his father and himself but then he had nothing to leave. He could not even afford to give Bert or any of the men who had worked so loyally for him a few pounds to see them by and Ned had imagined that his father would get what there was and so he nodded in appreciation of Mr Gibbons' having been so patient and waiting for him and they sat down and then Mr Gibbons went through the formal language and Ned reflected that his uncle had nothing but a small terraced house which was in very bad repair and had not much but basics and a great many books probably of little value, and his business premises with the old machinery and older office furniture.

His father sat and did not move as Mr Gibbons explained the

will. Ned made himself not smile when the solicitor observed gravely that Jasper had left Tranter his books, it was almost an insult, he had done it on purpose and put it first, had probably insisted on that as though the books were important to his only brother.

Ned waited because the language did not seem to include that everything else had been left to Tranter. Could Jasper have made a mistake? But it was worse and better than that. Ned could not believe it. His uncle, loving him as he did, knowing that he could do nothing with it, had left him everything else, the house, the business, the premises.

It was nothing but a gesture and Ned hurt more than he had done when he had found out that his uncle was dead, worse than he had felt throughout the funeral or even standing in the office or drinking tea with Bert. It was a demonstration of his love for his nephew.

Mr Gibbons stopped here, looked up and straight at Ned and murmured, 'The business may continue of course until probate is granted.'

As the solicitor went on his head grew lower so that nobody could see his face but Ned could see even from halfway across the room the mottled purple of his father's cheeks and knew how annoyed he was.

He was not the man to protest or say that it was not so, how could he but he was angrier than Ned had ever seen him. He did not get up when the solicitor was finished, he did not thank him or urge him to stay for sherry or even to wish him good day. Ned did all those things. Mr Gibbons was seen to the door and only then did Ned's father turn and say to him, 'My God, I didn't realize until this moment quite how stupid Jasper was. No, no, I did, I just chose to ignore it. I'm glad he's dead. I'm tired of his petty ideals and his need to be somebody he could never be. I'm tired of how he continually let the family down. I should have expected this or something like, something so absurd.' He got to his feet and there was a weariness about the movement which was new.

'You can have the books, I don't want them. The place is worth nothing, the machinery less, it's all old and his house is a wreck. I can dispose of them for you if you wish, as soon as the law allows, there's nothing else to be done. He was a fool, he was always a fool. As for the business continuing, it won't do it with my money, I don't care what happens to it in the meanwhile.'

Ned didn't say anything, he couldn't think of anything, he was so shocked and his father looked at him and then said grimly into the silence, 'You should have been here to deal with his . . . his friends and you scarcely spent an hour and then disappeared. Do you know how that looks?'

Ned wanted to say that he didn't care how it looked but he had been able to bear no more. He mumbled that he had gone for a walk but he knew that his father was not deceived. He would know exactly where he had gone. Ned could feel the jealousy. His father had always hated how he cared for his uncle as though there was not enough regard to go round and in fact it was true, his father had no affection for him and Ned had none for him, he had tried so often when younger to fit into

34

his father's moods, to try to gain something of his father's love but it seemed that there was nothing left for Tranter to give somehow. He tolerated his son because they were nothing alike and because he knew without anything being said that Ned did not care for business.

His father went and sat down at his desk, sat forward as though he had important work to get on with so Ned went out. Dinner would be another hour or so. His father insisted that he dressed for it. He walked slowly up the stairs and tried to put the idea of Bert's retreating form to the back of his mind.

Three

Annabel sat in front of her mirror and looked at the effect she presented. She was not quite sure and as she saw her mother come into the room she turned and got up with a swish of skirts that almost pleased her. As she did so she was aware of a great longing to please her mother who looked critically at her now and then said, 'It will do.'

She had known that her mother would not approve of the dress because she had chosen it herself in the knowledge that her mother always chose things which would suit her own colouring and Millie's and for so long she had been clad in blue and white and pink while all the time knowing that she suited creams and greens and what people might think of as autumn shades, dull colours her mother would have called them.

This time she had insisted and had looked at herself and been sure and she had the confidence to know that in spite of her mother's lukewarm response she looked as well as she could. Tonight was to be the most important night of her life, it was her engagement party and she was the luckiest girl in the world.

People were already beginning to arrive when they went downstairs. Some people, her mother complained, had no manners and would show up early but she kept the smile on her face and joined her husband to greet them.

Tom and his parents had already arrived. Tonight Annabel would wear her diamond solitaire engagement ring for the first time and try to stop herself from gazing down at her finger the entire evening. She thought she had never been as happy.

When the guests had arrived there was champagne and talk and there was dancing and later there was supper and some- where in between all that Tom had taken her into the quiet of her father's study and kissed her thoroughly there in the peace with nothing but the crackling of the fire around them and she had known a great desire to be married.

'I want you to know that I love you, that I could never love anyone but you and that I'm going to make you happy. This will be our best Christmas ever.'

They were to be married in June and already she could imagine their own house though so far they were to live with his parents. What she really cared for was being alone with him, having things as she wanted them. She wished they could stay closeted like this but they had to go out and pretend to eat – she was too excited to get anything past her lips – and have another glass of champagne and endure more of people's congratulations.

After tonight her mother would begin making preparations for the wedding. She would enjoy the fuss, the dress, the flowers, the guest list, it was to be a huge event, everybody who was anybody was invited and after that she and Tom were to go to Venice and Rome and Florence and Paris and spend three months enjoying one another's company and then they would come home and everything would be perfect.

It was very late indeed when the last guests departed and even then she did not want him to go. A red winter sky was beginning to show itself in the distance over the rooftops. It was almost Christmas and what a Christmas it would be, they had planned parties and visits to the theatre and her father would buy wonderful presents and she hoped it would snow.

There was nothing better than to wake up on Christmas morning and find everything white. She kissed Tom for the last time and saw him from the door. After that her mother sighed with tiredness, her father yawned and they turned towards the stairs and he paused. Her mother looked at him and then he didn't move and her mother said, 'Are you all right, Fergus?' and then he said, 'Yes, it's nothing,' and began to climb the stairs.

They all followed him up the wide sweeping staircase but when he was two steps away from the top he stopped once again and then, as if in slow motion, he swayed backwards and before anyone could do anything, though what they would have done, her father was a large man, tall and weighing eighteen stone, she could not think, he lost his footing and began to tumble down the stairs.

Her mother or Millie, she could never think which after-wards, screamed and the stairs became huge and longer and longer as her father turned and fell like a doll. When he got to the bottom and they had skidded down as best they could in all their finery he was moaning softly. By the time she reached him he was cursing and begging somebody to get him to bed and her mother, who was always telling him not to drink so much and not to eat so much, had already sent a servant for the doctor.

Nobody slept. At first it seemed that everything would be all right, her father was making a lot of noise, which Annabel always thought a good sign, but the doctor was in with him for a long time and when her mother finally came back out on to the landing she was crying.

Annabel hovered in the doorway of her room and Millie who had come in there for support stood well behind her as though if she stepped outside the room dire things would occur. Her mother, hearing them, Annabel thought, cleared her throat and took the handkerchief from her eyes and told them everything would be all right and they should try to get some sleep but Annabel could not rest and later that day when Tom came to call she had to tell him that the doctor had already been back, her father's voice had not been heard beyond the door and her mother was in subdued mood.

'But, surely, if there are no bones broken . . .'

'I think it must be more than that,' Annabel said.

Tom went home before lunch and when they had sat down at the dining table her mother said that it seemed the doctor thought it was his heart, he had had some kind of attack and that was why he had fallen. Annabel begged to be allowed to see him but her mother said he was not well enough to see anyone.

That afternoon the doctor came again and when he had finally gone – Annabel hovered in the hall and on the stairs and on the landing, she seemed to be going round and round, just waiting – her mother said that he was very ill indeed and refused to let them see him until he was feeling better. She didn't like to say, 'What if he doesn't get better?' because it was too awful to consider but she waited through the afternoon until her mother was in the drawing room with friends who had heard he was not well and come to enquire and she went upstairs and slipped into the room.

The curtains were half open but it did not matter, the day was dark and it had begun to sleet beyond the windows. Her father's bed had never seemed so big and her father had never seemed so small. He lay there on his back like an obedient child, the covers neat around him as though that would help. Perhaps her mother thought order would win the day where medicine could do nothing.

Even though the big room was shadowed she could see how ill he was, his face was pale and relaxed and his eyes closed. She was afraid at first that he had died and that she would have to tell everybody and then he seemed to sense her presence and opened his eyes and turned his head and gazed unseeingly at her for so long that she was inclined to remind him who she was and then he said her name and she was so thankful that she went up to his bed and clasped his hand and sat down on the edge of the covers.

His eyes were narrowed and dull.

'I want to talk to you,' he said. 'I may not have another chance to say what I must say, what I've wanted to say for so long and never thought it prudent. It isn't prudent now, of course, it's only the truth and other people know it, at least more than one other person so I cannot die and leave it unsaid.'

She told him that he was not going to die and that whatever it was it could not be so important.

'The thing is that if I do not say it, then after I die the truth will come out anyway, as these things do, and I would rather it was said now and whatever you think of me and whatever you think of my having told you at least you will know that I had sufficient courage to tell you in the end.'

He stopped there and rather than wishing he would not go on because the effort was visibly too much for him she only wished he had not stopped because she could not wait, in horrified fashion, to hear what he was about to say.

'When I was young I was interested in the family business. We had other people to take care of such things and I wasn't meant to become involved but I found myself doing so, wanting to go north and see how things worked.

'We had been married for . . . for several years by then and there was no sign of any child and . . . I was eager to get away because the lack of a child was driving a wedge between us. Your mother was upset and I was frustrated and we quarrelled a good deal. It was hard so I made an excuse and left.

'In some ways I wished afterwards that I had not gone because . . .' He shuddered. 'My father had owned a house up there and we had often gone but it was sold when his health was so bad and we had very little to do with what went on.

41

'I was there for more than a year. In the beginning I didn't want to come back. In the end it was the only thing to do.' He paused again. Annabel stopped breathing for a few moments in case even the sound of it should distract him. 'I met a woman while I was there.'

There had been women over the years, Annabel knew, she even thought her mother might have had another man but nothing had ever been said and since it was never spoken of it was easy to believe it was not happening, that her parents were devoted to one another.

'It was like being very young again. It was nothing but a dalliance, I cared nothing for her. She was poor and I was ashamed but she made me feel as though I could do anything, have anything, and we spent some time together. I shouldn't have done it, it was wrong and I grew tired of her very quickly.

'She told me she was having a child. I was horrified, I pretended it was nothing to do with me, that she had had other men and I wanted nothing more to do with her. I heard that she had had the child, I didn't see her. She had abandoned it in a low house by the river. When I had no excuse to stay any longer I came home and when I got back somehow the time and the distance had improved things between Etta and me because we had a child.'

He stopped again. Annabel was eager to prompt him since the story seemed to be turning out well.

'Me?'

He looked at her and she thought his eyes were clearer.

'No,' he said, 'we had Millie. I brought you back with me.

Your real mother didn't want you, and I thought that a child of mine was better than no child at all. Your mother was horrified but she had been ill and away from the town for some months so the timing was right for me to bring you back and present you to the world as ours.

'It wasn't something she wanted but it looked as if there would be no child and . . . all your mother said was that when Millie was born she would inherit what we had if there were no more children.

'We didn't imagine we would have to face this problem. We thought you would probably be an old maid and it wouldn't matter and that Millie would marry well and you would stay here and be of some comfort to your mother in her old age.'

Annabel was stupefied.

'I wouldn't have told you,' he said, 'if there had been some other way.'

He was exhausted, she could see. He lay back as though he had made his last confession and was spent and felt clean and shriven, like a Catholic, and she went on watching his face and she did not realize she had been watching his face for such a long time before she knew that he was asleep, his breathing was as deep and even as the snow in the wretched Christmas carol.

'What are you doing in here?' her mother said just behind her and she jumped and got off the bed. 'He isn't well enough to talk.'

'I had to see him.' She wished so much now that she had not but then things could not be changed and it must be better to have the truth, or was it?

She was numb. She let her mother usher her out and close the door after her. The doctor came again. All that afternoon Annabel sat over the fire with a book in her lap and did not glance at it. She stared into the flames. He had not told her her mother's name, he had tired before he had told her and beyond her distress for him she longed to have the information though what she could do with it she could not imagine.

That night her father died. The doctor had come back in the afternoon when he grew worse and her mother was closeted up there for hours. She and Millie did not go to bed though her mother urged them to, they sat over the fire and did not talk and did not read and the time passed so slowly and the town settled down into silence. There was a sharp frost which somehow deepened the silence.

She kept listening for the reassuring sound of the doctor's footsteps coming back down the stairs but nothing happened and it was only when the door opened that she realized she had fallen asleep. The fire was out, the gas lamp hissed and Millie was stretched out on the sofa. She too awoke at that moment and when their mother came into the room her face was so grave that there was no mistaking what had happened.

Millie began to cry and their mother – or her mother, Annabel thought with guilt and dismay – came across and comforted her. Annabel stood there numb. She could not believe that only two days before she had been so happy. Now the world had crashed. Her mother was looking clearly at her over Millie's head but she said nothing and Annabel kept waiting for the nightmare to go away, for another day to dawn and everything to be as it had been at her engagement party, her father apparently fit and well and the future sorted out.

Millie went off to her room and over the next few days spent a great deal of time there and although Annabel wanted to comfort her she felt as though the knowledge her father had given her was somehow written upon her countenance and that Millie would know there was something wrong. She did call her name from the other side of the door but there was no answer.

Tom came to the house since it was now Christmas but none of the planned festivities went ahead. Annabel had thought that she would be glad to see him but when she was obliged to greet him in the drawing room alone she realized how everything had changed. He said he was sorry about her father and that he knew the wedding would have to be postponed and how ghastly everything was and she sat like a dummy and nodded and agreed with everything he said.

She thought he accepted that she was shocked and grief-stricken when in fact what she felt for her father was anger and resentment. Why had he not told her these things before? Worse still, why had he told her at all? If he had not said anything she would have gone ahead with the wedding. That brought on new thoughts.

Already formed in her mind was the notion that there would be no wedding. And her father in one important way had been right. Something which was true was bound to come out and how would Tom feel if she married him, left him in ignorance and then he found out later that she was— Here she stopped. Who was she? She didn't know any more. She had always felt so certain, so secure. Now she felt as though her life was on a cliff edge. She was inclined to go ahead and tell him but there was a part of her which was certain that a miracle would occur, that everything would come right if only she kept it to herself for a few more days.

Her mother was always busy now, arranging the funeral. It would be a huge occasion. Her father had been an important man, everybody would be invited and there was the coffin to choose – the very idea made her shudder – and flowers and what hymns they would sing. The thought of singing hymns with her father dead was something which constricted her throat.

She began to wish that Tom would not come every day, it was such a strain and although she did not tell him any lies his presence began to hang as heavily as the recent snow upon the boughs of the tree beyond the drawing-room window. There was a hard frost every night and the snow was crisp beneath her feet during the few times she ventured outside. She found herself longing to get away, not just from the house but from the city itself to . . . she didn't know where, anywhere to escape what had happened.

After the funeral the house was full of people. She could not stop thinking about the way that they had had to leave her father in the snowy cemetery, it seemed so awful to come home to the blazing fires and warm rooms and a virtual feast of cakes and sandwiches. There was soon the sound of teacups on saucers, voices lifted in relief that they were the ones who had come back. Funerals obviously made people hungry. She could eat nothing.

Her only comfort was that Tom had been there in the churchyard, throughout the service and then from the cold church to the colder weather. A few flakes of snow fell as they stood beside the grave. Tom held her hand. If they had not been so public she would have wanted him to put an arm around her, she wished that she could feel his warm lips on hers, she felt as though nothing would be warm ever again and she could not forget what her father had said to her and how she had felt so sick.

The sickness had not passed and in the forefront of her mind, now that the man she had loved so much was put underground and the first dirt beginning to cover his coffin, she felt nothing but anger and she knew that very soon she would have to tell Tom what her father had said to her.

In the meanwhile she had to try to smile at the mourners, listen to the hum of voices, watch the people around her mother telling her what a good man he had been, what a good husband. It made her want to laugh, it made her want to take strong hysterics, wasn't that what they called it? People even came to her and recalled special days they had spent with her father and she had to nod and agree and even seem to be pleased while her heart seemed frozen.

She thought they would never go. The afternoon grew dark

and they lingered because it was so cold outside but finally even the ones who had hogged the fires all afternoon departed. She watched Tom's retreating figure through the library window as he made his way toward his own house in Park Lane and finally peace descended. She had been avoiding the library until now, every time she ventured in there she expected to find her father either seated behind his desk or nodding by the fire.

The solicitor, Mr Browning, was the only person left and her mother was closeted with him in the drawing room for a considerable length of time.

Millie fidgeted by the sewing-room fire and Annabel walked up and down, worrying about she didn't know what, and it seemed to take half the evening before there was the sound of the heavy oak door opening and then voices in the hall and Mr Browning leaving, her mother was showing him out herself.

To Annabel's frustration she did not then come to find them, she went back inside and closed the door and that was the first time that Annabel thought about her, she had just lost the man she had married so long ago.

Millie left the room, Annabel was sure she was going to burst into the drawing room but she didn't, she went on up the long wide sweeping staircase and with the door open, Annabel ventured into the hall and suddenly she could wait no longer. She went swiftly across and opened the door of the drawing room.

She imagined someone sitting weeping by the fire but Etta was not, she was just standing there and the fire had gone so far down – no doubt she had not cared to have it replenished while the solicitor was still there – that it was almost out and the room, being large, was already chilled. A moment or two after Annabel entered the room Etta turned and smiled tightly at her.

'He told you, didn't he?' Annabel didn't answer. 'I can tell by your face that he did.'

Annabel stood like someone turned to stone and she felt cold enough.

'I never wanted you here. It was all his idea. He was so afraid that we would never have a child while all around us other people had two or three children by then and we were so envious. He has other children, of course, he was always a philanderer but nobody thought anything of it. They turned a blind eye and none of them was ever foisted on to me and of course his women were respectable people and married and it didn't matter but you . . .'

'I don't understand why he told me now.'

'Because he didn't want you to think you were going to gain anything financially when he was dead. Millie is our daughter. You . . .' She didn't go on. 'You were like the cuckoo in the nest, only thankfully you didn't get to throw out the only other bird we had, but you were . . . large and awkward and ungainly.'

Annabel's face burned. She was tall, five foot eight inches, and had never been slender while her mother and Millie were small and dainty but she had always been rather pleased to be tall except that when she danced often her partners were shorter than she was, even Tom was an inch or so below her and she regretted that but nothing else.

'I don't want to send you away, there would be talk but of

course if word gets out of how the will was left . . . Tom's family are rich influential people. You cannot marry him.'

And then Annabel asked the question which had burned in her mind since her father had told her. 'What manner of woman was my mother?'

'I know nothing about her other than that presumably she was a pitman's daughter. There's nothing in such a place beyond mines. Could he have sunk any lower?'

'Why did she not keep me?'

'I didn't ask. She didn't matter.' The implication in the silence that followed was that Annabel didn't matter. 'He wanted you here and I had been away for some months in Ireland, my mother was ill and took a long time dying and I wasn't well myself. When we returned to London we had you with us.'

'Nobody need ever have known, surely.' Annabel actually said what had been big in her mind.

'I would have known,' Etta said and then Annabel remembered all the times when she had been jealous of Millie because Millie was always with her mother, was always the favoured daughter. She had told herself it was because she was the younger child, the pet, and Millie was so pretty and so taking but as she thought about it a thousand different incidents came to mind and the explanation was obvious. And then she realized also that Etta was jealous for her second daughter that the first was about to marry brilliantly.

She thought about Tom finding out the truth which he would because people always did and about how when he did he would not want her any more and would not be able to marry her and she left Etta there and went upstairs and put on her outdoor things and she walked the few hundred yards through the slush – the weather had finally given and everything was wet – to Tom's house and there she was ushered in with smiles and into the library where Tom's father rather unfashionably presided over his books.

It was a very small library, only a few hundred volumes, and the strange smell which books had, musty as though the pages were never aired, as though they were never taken off the shelves and perhaps Tom's father only went in there for the sake of peace and to doze over the fire.

He looked as though he did. He preferred the country. They had an estate in Lincolnshire and he loved his horses, rode to hounds, shot and fished and had house parties, she knew, she had been there several times and the last time had pictured herself as one day being mistress of the low Georgian house with the gardens and stables. He was very overweight and red-faced and he smiled at her now though the smile held a hint of sadness, he had been such a dear friend of her father's.

Tom, who had heard her come in, appeared in the doorway and as she turned to greet him she thought that he was different somehow, his smile was not as ready, his manner was uneasy. He drew her away into the little sitting room and she said, 'I have to talk to you.'

'Is it about the wedding, because I know that—'

'It's not about the wedding,' Annabel said and she could barely look at his dear face and she told him in short sentences which she had rehearsed a hundred times what her father had told her. Tom stood there, frowning and not saying anything for so long that she began to worry. She wanted him to say something, she wasn't quite sure what, anything but what he had said so far and then for the first time she understood the huge gap between who she was and who he was. You could have called it stupid, you could have called it many things. The only thing you could not call it was fair. She felt sure now that this was only a word which applied to rich people. To those socially below the salt the word 'fair' was probably not even a concept on any far horizon.

Why had her father not made her legitimate? She felt sure there must be some rule of law which could apply. Then she thought of Etta and she understood. She was the elder child. That must have hurt. She thought of Etta's wounded pride and the humiliation that the child of the man she was married to had come second in birth. That was undoubtedly when she had decided that Millie would come second in no other way. And she had not, Annabel thought sadly. Tom was not looking at her.

'Was he mad?' he said finally and he sounded angry. 'I thought he fell downstairs. Did he hit his head? This is preposterous. I never heard anything like it.'

'It's true. My mother confirmed it and . . . it means that I shall have nothing.'

Tom looked awkward and not at her, his gaze was all over the place, she thought and then he said finally, 'Men are always fathering brats on other women—'

'Not like this.' She was astonished to hear him say such a

thing which nobody spoke of and as though he didn't necessarily disapprove.

'It's part of life,' Tom said.

'She was a pitman's daughter, my mother says.'

Tom stared at her as though this was something he preferred
not to know and then he said awkwardly, 'Yes, well your mother
would say something like that, she's never liked you. I don't
suppose for a second your father went with some common
woman . . .' Here Tom stopped because they both thought
for a second and then realized this was not necessarily true,
some men would tumble a kitchen maid and think nothing
of it but they didn't burden their families with the offspring.
If her father had never brought her home it would have been
something nobody knew about and where on earth would she
have been now and that was the point, Annabel thought. In
some stupid way it made her feel better.

'I never fitted in,' she said.

'Yes, you did,' Tom said bitterly, 'it's just shock, that's all,' but
somehow his words lacked sincerity or conviction and he didn't
look at her. She hadn't known what he would think and society
was a delicate balance.

And the way also that he used the past tense implied to her
that she did not fit any more and once she acknowledged this to
herself it changed everything. She wanted him to say something
foolish like 'Let's run away and get married,' but he didn't and
she knew that he was much too sensible to say such a thing.
When she looked directly at him he no longer looked at her and
suddenly they had nothing to say to one another and she knew

that when he got over the shocking news he would realize that he could not marry her.

'You must have this back,' she said, pulling at the diamond on her finger. He made a protest and then stopped and she drew it off and handed it to him.

'As a matter of fact,' he said, looking ashamed, 'I already knew. You can't keep things like that quiet. The servants all knew and gossip moves quickly. I wanted to come and tell you that but somehow I couldn't.'

He knew there was nothing more to be said, she thought. He was still not looking at her. They could never be married. She couldn't speak or see for tears as she put the ring into his hand and all the things she had dreamed of, all the plans they had made, came crashing down around her.

She wanted to cling to him, for him to reassure her that none of this was happening or for him to say that none of it mattered, he would marry her anyway, but he could not. His parents would never let him marry beneath him even if he wanted to and he did not look as though he did particularly want to as far as she could judge now that the whole world had turned its back on her somehow.

'I must go.'

He didn't say, 'No, please don't,' he saw her to the door and it seemed to her then that he was glad to get rid of her, glad to shut the door so that he would have time to absorb what had happened.

*

She went home and into the drawing room where Etta had just poured out tea and several people were there, all her friends had come to see her, some of them every day. When they had finally gone Etta took something from the drawer in the sideboard which stood against the far wall.

'You should have this now. It was the only thing he left you,' she said and when she held it up it was Fergus's pocket watch.

Annabel thanked her as though it was a welcome gift and afterwards she left the room and went upstairs to her bedroom and it was only when she reached it and got the door shut that she began to cry. She didn't go down for dinner and nobody came near and it was a long night because she didn't sleep, she just lay watching the fire until it died and blackened and the dawn came late in January. It was almost eight o'clock when she got up. She washed and dressed and left the house at nine, not going anywhere near the breakfast room.

She went to Mr Browning's office in the middle of the city and there because she had no appointment she was kept waiting in a draughty room while other people went in and she had been waiting almost two hours before she was shown into his large office. He was, she thought, a prosperous man, he dealt with many people from the top drawer of society.

'Sorry to keep you waiting, Miss Seaton, but you can see how busy I am.'

She sat down and told him what her father had told her and when she had finished telling him he looked at the way that his fingers made a steeple and then he said, 'I do not see what I can do.'

'I have the feeling my father confided many things to you.'

He said nothing and she thought he was not going to help her unless she could press her case home.

'You must understand that I have no right in my father's house any more and . . .' She had been going to say 'my mother' but she didn't. 'I don't think I will be allowed to stay there.'

That brought his gaze up. 'Surely—' he began.

'I have no choice but to go north and try to find my – my mother and any family I might have there.'

'I wouldn't advise it.'

'Why not?'

He didn't say anything.

'Do you have a particular reason for saying that or is it just a general impression that life in places other than London is not worth the living?'

'It's godforsaken, some of it,' he said, 'and not for gently bred women.'

'Do you know where my father went?'

'Of course I do, your father's family had pits in Durham for many years, good profitable pits as well. They were sold. I thought it was a mistake.'

'Specifically?' she said. 'I need a name. I need my mother's family name and I think you have it. Perhaps he sent her money, perhaps . . .' She stopped there, Mr Browning was shaking his head.

'I believe she died,' he said.

Annabel thought that by now she was prepared for anything. She was not however prepared for this. Somewhere in her there had been a last hope, that some woman was waiting for her, that somebody would recognize her, care for her, be glad to see her, welcome her inside. She had a vague image of a door opening and a woman who looked like she did giving a cry of joyful surprise and taking her in. Growing also was the feeling that Mr Browning knew more than he was saying.

'Please tell me what you know.'

He bowed his head again. 'I would much rather you had not come here. I knew this day would come, I always dreaded it. Surely your – your mother will not put you out—'

'She doesn't want me there.'

'Monstrous,' he said, 'how could she not care about you when you have lived there as her child all your life?' Annabel didn't know what to say to that and when he had looked at her for explanation and nothing had happened and he understood he said, 'Then you could stay in London, you must have friends, you could find some employment, some—'

'Please tell me what you know.'

'Knowing things can make it all worse.'

'It couldn't be worse.'

Mr Browning got up and walked about the room which had suddenly become a smaller space than before and when he had taken a couple of turns he came back and sat down at his big oak desk as though the vastness of it somehow shielded him and he said, 'Your mother drowned herself.'

Four

His father had wanted Ned's twenty-first birthday to be a big occasion so that was exactly what it was and in spite of the funeral it followed hard on its heels. He was disgusted. He had wanted it cancelling out of respect for Jasper but his father only said that he had no respect for Jasper, that nobody cared and that the party had been planned a very long time ago and so the party went ahead.

'You're being silly,' Jane Baker, his fiancée, said, kissing him affectionately on the forehead. 'You weren't that close—'

'We were very close until my father kept me busy in his wretched office.'

'Your father is a clever businessman and in spite of what you say he is very much involved there, you just don't see it. You can hardly expect him to care for a brother he had been estranged from most of his adult life and you are important to him. He wants to do this for you, why can't you just let him? He's gone to a lot of trouble, he didn't know that his brother would die so inconveniently.'

She wanted him to laugh, she looked into his face but all Ned knew was that she did not understand how he felt about his uncle, that Jasper had been a bigger part of his childhood than Tranter had ever been.

His father wasn't interested in children, even his only child and a son. He packed Ned off to boarding school when he was six and never visited. Somehow Ned had gained the impression that because his mother wasn't there he was not important and in his worst moments he thought that somehow his father blamed him for it though his mother had died when he was four and as far as he could recollect it had been nothing to do with him.

Ned could remember looking forward so dearly to Jasper's letters and to his visits and when he went home he would spend time at the newspaper office and at Jasper's tiny little house in one of the streets just down from the station. He had tried to explain to the girl he was going to marry how much his uncle meant to him but she was very fond of his father. There was nothing wrong in that, he knew how much his father had counted on the marriage, how much he liked Jane, and she felt obliged to take sides and since Tranter was more important to her than Jasper naturally she saw his point of view.

Ned had fostered a vague hope that his father would give him money for his birthday but nothing of the kind happened. Other young men had their independence, were able to leave home, were in charge of their own affairs but he knew that his father wanted him there, perhaps forever, his father was determined that he should take over the business and he could not think of anything he wanted to do less.

He did not want to be dragged into this tiny world where men were obliged to crawl underground and hew coal to make a living while the owners lived lavishly off their sweat and he had had three years of it now, ever since he had left school, and was desperate to get out. His father had been kinder to him since he had grown older and was proud of Ned's ability, said he was a born pit-owner. His father was to Ned the born pit-owner. Unlike other men he managed his own mines and expected that Ned would follow him.

So Ned was there, greeting people with a forced smile, listening to the musicians striking up in the ballroom, wishing he was anywhere else and that his father's friends had not turned out in force once again because they must or because they admired his business acumen or his money or just because he was famous for his parties. There was champagne, tables laden with whole salmon and turkeys and sides of beef, and each table was decorated differently with huge arrangements of fruit and flowers. The house was alight with candles and through it the dresses of the women sparkled softly and people stood about in groups and talked the better for the champagne.

He had wanted Bert there and the other printers but his father would not allow it. He tried to talk to Jane about this but she said, 'They would feel out of place. You could have a separate party for them.'

'You're right,' he allowed, 'they would have hated it.'

She kissed him. He thought she looked lovely, she was wearing a pale green gown which suited her bright red hair and green eyes and creamy skin. He couldn't stop looking at her and didn't want to give her up to any other man to dance with and she knew that and laughed and teased him by pulling faces at him when she danced. He thought how lucky he was to have her.

Halfway through the evening his father came to him and said, 'Mr Gibbons is here.' He sounded reluctant.

'Whatever for?'

Tranter turned slightly and then he said, 'Your mother left you something when she died, some small token, I gather, to be given to you on your twenty-first birthday and Mr Gibbons says you must be there in person.'

Which was not, Ned thought, what his father would ever want. He always had to be the most important person in any gathering, he spent his life enjoying such things.

'Do you know what it is?'

'No, I don't.' His father spoke shortly and was so obviously annoyed that the woman he had doted on had gone behind his back in any matter and that he had no power to do anything about it. No doubt he had taken legal advice and this was beyond it.

Ned went off into the library and there Mr Gibbons was again for the second time in a week and this time he was smiling.

'Congratulations, young man,' he said.

'Were you my mother's solicitor?'

'No, that was my father. I have inherited the task.' Mr Gibbons coughed. Nobody sat down. Ned didn't invite him to for some reason he couldn't make out and then realized how nervous he felt. It was strange that his mother should make plans for so far ahead, perhaps she had owned something special, perhaps it was something very personal. Mr Gibbons thrust this aside by saying, 'Your mother left you a little money.'

'A little?'

'She hadn't much and your father of course owned everything but this was put aside in a trust which could not be touched, I gather she had inherited it before she married and . . . well—'

'Does he know about it?'

'I think your father selects his memories,' Mr Gibbons said tactfully. 'The money has been invested ever since and although it is still not a large sum it will be helpful to you should you wish to do something with it.'

'Invested? Could it be taken out?'

'It could be but I wouldn't advise it. You should keep it until you need it.'

Ned was beginning to smile. He didn't think he had ever smiled in such a way before. Mr Gibbons went on to the detail and Ned's smile grew wider and by the time Mr Gibbons went he knew that he was positively grinning. He saw the solicitor out and then went back to the party.

Jane was waiting for him, an anxious look on her face. She would be anxious no more, he thought. He could not help smiling again and broadly as he went back into the ballroom. He drew her aside when nobody was looking, led her away from the conversation and the music, into the small sitting room and there he closed the door on the party.

'My mother left me some money that my father didn't know about. I don't think he has any idea.'

'He must have known,' she said. 'Perhaps he obliterated it from his mind. Anything connected with her seems to hurt him. Is it a lot of money?'

'It's enough to get things started.'

'Really? Oh, how wonderful, though what we shall spend it on I have no idea because my father is determined we shall have a beautiful house in Jesmond. He's going to buy one for us as a wedding present. That's your other surprise tonight. I wasn't supposed to tell you yet. Just think, our fathers will be fighting over you and your time but I have confidence in you. I'm sure you'll be able to manage everything.'

Ned found himself frowning. This was not going as it should, as he had thought. He took a deep breath.

'I meant the newspaper,' he said. 'It was left to me.'

'Yes, but you're going to get rid of it, aren't you?'

'I said my father wants to get rid of it. Jane, my biggest dream is to run the newspaper as Jasper did, only – well, with all my own ideas and now I can. I'll be able to buy the very latest machinery and keep on all the staff – I can't wait to tell them. We'll give the *Echo* a real run for its money. I've always wanted to do that.'

'What on earth do you mean?' she said. 'You don't imagine you can help to run the shipyards, the coal mines and a newspaper. It's a ridiculous idea and your father would be terribly hurt. He always disliked his brother. You couldn't do such a thing to him, it would be traitorous, disloyal. The *Echo* is a very successful newspaper, there can only be room for one in this area.'

'Jane, I feel as though this is not a coincidence, that Jasper's newspaper and my mother's money coming together like this was almost meant to be. I couldn't refuse what is so obvious.'

She was staring at him with what until a few moments before had been warm gold within her green eyes. Her eyes were like glass now.

'You mean it, don't you?'

'Don't you see, we could break free from both our fathers and do what we want.'

'What you want.'

'Don't you want to be independent and try something new and different and not what they did?'

'We are both only children, we have a responsibility here, you especially have huge responsibilities to both our families. They have very successful businesses. We couldn't turn our backs on those or any of the benefits we have always enjoyed. It would be worse than ungrateful.'

She was right, he thought. Of course she was and then he thought of how Jasper had struggled on regardless of how he had no money and how Bert and the other men had seemed to him after the funeral and he thought he felt as Jane's grandfather must have felt, who had started with a small boatyard and built an empire. He wanted to laugh at himself. What an ambition. Perhaps he wanted a newspaper empire and why not?

He wanted it as he had never wanted anything in his life. He did feel guilty but his father's and her father's dreams were not his and he did not see why he should not pursue his own course.

Jane did not agree and he found it hard to justify himself under her honest gaze. He presented the case as best he could, told her they could have a pretty house perhaps here by the river in Durham.

64

'But all our concerns are further north-east.'

'They wouldn't be.'

Jane became so still that he could hear the crackling of the big log fire.

'I think it's a completely foolish idea,' she said, 'and I don't want to be a part of it. A great many men would envy you being given such great success—'

'But these things are already a success, at least as much as they can be. I mean to do something different. Newspapers can be hugely influential in all kinds of ways. I want to give the working people a newspaper of their own, something to enjoy, something that is on their side, they that can think of as theirs—'

'And betray everything our fathers stand for?'

'It isn't betrayal, it's just a different way of looking at things,' he said.

'Fine words,' she said and slammed the heavy oak door as best she could on the way out.

He didn't want to but he had to go back to the party. He was convinced that she would understand that he wanted to try something new. He talked to the other guests, he danced half a dozen times with a different girl each time. He could not see Jane. Perhaps he was being unreasonable, he thought. Perhaps there was some middle way. He would talk to her father and his father.

They were not old men, they were happy running their businesses themselves and would not need anybody to take over for the next twenty years, being only in their early forties, and he was not sure that he wanted to play second fiddle to either of them nor why he should at this stage. Later it would be different. Perhaps he could make the newspaper work and he would be satisfied and happy to move on and try to find the enthusiasm and expertise under her father's guidance.

And the miners relied on his father for their very existence. His father was a very fit man and there were other able men to shoulder part of the burden. He was convinced that there was a way.

He saw from the corner of his eye the man who owned the other newspaper, the one his father favoured, talking to his father and several other businessmen in a corner at the far end of the room. Cedric Pattison owned half a dozen newspapers in the county in various of the larger towns. He also owned a great deal of slum property in Durham City and in Newcastle. He stood across the room with a cigar stuck in his podgy scarlet face. His newspaper was opinionated. It championed the owners against the workers and said things which an unbiased newspaper would not have said but was there such a thing as an unbiased newspaper?

Ned, honest with himself, knew that he wasn't trying to do that, he was trying to even the score. Pattison would not like what he did. He had not liked Jasper and Jasper had hated Pattison for the way he treated his tenants, for the bully boys who had put families on to the cold streets in winter and because he would not aid the working man through his influence as he could so easily have done.

He had recently been widowed and had two young children

and every mother in the area was hoping he would turn his attention to her daughter, he was well off, had a fine house just north of the city. Ned had heard that he had been unkind to his wife. It was only whispers but the idea of any man beating his wife made Ned shudder with distaste. Pattison was a bad man.

Jane's father came to him as he stood by the door which led into the hall.

'And just what the blazes do you think you've been saying to my daughter?' he demanded.

Jane had gone straight to him. Ned regretted his clumsiness.

'I'm afraid I didn't put it very well,' he said apologetically.

'Bloody right,' Ernest Baker said, 'my girl has been crying her eyes out for the last hour while you've been dancing with all and sundry as though there was nothing wrong. Just who the hell do you think you are?'

'I'm sorry, Mr Baker, I—'

'You will be,' Ernest said. 'I'm not going to let my only child marry an idiot like you who throws back a perfectly good opportunity for wealth and business. I've already spoken to your father. You can consider the engagement over,' and he turned and walked away before Ned could speak.

Across the hall Ned could see Mrs Baker already with her fur coat on. He couldn't see Jane and he couldn't believe what had happened. Surely Jane wasn't going to turn her back on him like this? As he watched Jane came out of the darkness to join her parents and he called to her but she ignored him, being hurried out of the front door before he could say any more.

He thought it best not to go after them. She would calm down. Whether her father would was another matter.

His father said nothing until the party was over and it was after one o'clock when the last of the merry-makers left. Ned was exhausted. He loved Jane and he was sure she loved him. This could not be the end of the problem.

Tranter came in and demanded to be told what had happened with the solicitor and although Ned would much rather he should not be told there was no real reason why not. His father's face softened at the memory of his wife and then darkened at the mention of the money.

'It's best left where it is,' he said.

'I don't want to leave it where it is,' Ned said, 'I'm going to use it. I'm going to run the newspaper.'

He had known that his father would shout, he had expected it. He had not thought that his father would demand he leave it where it was, that he was so angry that Ned might go against his wishes, but he should have known, he thought with regret afterwards, when had his father ever wanted anything for him but what his father wanted?

'I knew this would happen. I knew something would go wrong,' his father said and he didn't look at Ned, he looked down. 'She did not leave you that money so that you could waste it on some ill-advised adventure—'

'It's not an adventure,' Ned said, losing his temper almost as readily as his father did and realizing they had certain things in common. 'It's what I want to do and I'm entitled to do that, surely.'

'You have nothing other than what I choose to give you and you are too young to know what money can do. Jasper's ventures ruined him. He gave his whole life to stupid ill-judged starts. He could have married, had a child, run a proper business, something which would have been rewarding. Don't throw your money away on this, Ned, wait a little and see what else you wish to do.'

'I think if I had had anything else in mind, if I wanted to be a doctor or a lawyer, I would have known it before now, studied for it. Doesn't it occur to you that I might know my own mind?'

'At your age no one knows his own mind, you should be guided by people who do know.'

'I don't want to come into the business with you, I have no interest in mining. I don't like what it does to the people involved.'

He was afraid that he had said too much, his father looked at him in a way in which he had not done before. 'It keeps thousands of people in work.'

'You call that work? Grubbing in the ground for a pittance while the owners grow rich?'

Now he had definitely said too much and worse still, it was not true and he was ashamed of that, his father was very concerned about his pits and spent most of his time there. Ned wished his temper had not led him into such accusations. His father, head down, said nothing for a few moments and then he said, slowly and softly, 'And is this why Ernest is so upset? He doesn't want his daughter to marry such a fool?'

'He's just angry.'

'Angry?' His father glared at him. 'I think he has every

justification. I thought it was just a quarrel, I couldn't believe that you had thrown back in his face his offer of a house and a place in his office at his main shipyard. I thought all I had to be concerned about was that you wouldn't have enough time to give any attention at all to the mines.'

'I don't want the mines. You run them. I don't think you need my help and Jane's father certainly doesn't. I don't see why I shouldn't spend a few years at least doing what I want. It isn't going to interfere with anything.'

'On the contrary,' his father said grimly, 'it's going to interfere with your marriage.'

'Not if she cares for me.'

His father started to laugh, which seemed strange, he thought. 'I didn't think any son of mine could be so naive. She sees you as my son and I am a well-respected and prosperous businessman. Do you seriously think that a bright, beautiful, clever girl like Jane would put herself into the hands of a feckless man with very little money and a business venture which has already failed spectacularly in his uncle's less than capable care? You're ruined unless you reconsider. You've lost Jane unless you change your mind and quickly. You could never expect her to live in the way that you can afford by yourself. You will never now be able to keep a wife like that, the cream of society. She won't have you any more, can't you get that into your stupid head?'

Ned didn't know what to say.

'If you insist in going on with this idea of taking your uncle's place then you may go and live in his house and follow your way from there. I won't have you doing it here.'

This was a surprise. His father had not been an easy parent but Ned suspected that children were not easy either no matter what their age and for his father to say such things to his only son, his only child, he must be bitterly disappointed. He gave his father the space to reconsider but he knew that his father had never gone back on a decision that he could remember and all Ned could manage from stiff lips was, 'If that's what you want.'

'It isn't what I want. You are an undutiful son,' he said. 'Leave. Go. I don't want you here and don't think you can come back when your ridiculous venture crashes down around your ears like it did with Jasper. If you want to waste your life I shan't stop you. Get out.'

It was not what he had expected and it hurt more than shouting and blustering would have done. Ned left the library as he was so obviously expected to do. In the early morning he gathered together his books and his clothes and asked the housekeeper, Mrs Purvis, if she could send these things over to his uncle's house later in the day and when she, after a hesitation which was full of surprise, said that she would, he left the house and went straight to Mr Gibbons's office which was in Old Elvet not far from the prison. Ned walked slowly up there trying to gather his thoughts but could make nothing from the jumble which besieged his mind.

Mr Gibbons was busy but he had told the man on the desk to give Ned the keys both to his uncle's house and to the newspaper offices. Ned went straight to the offices.

Bert had a key and was already in there and so were the other men, as though they were going on as usual and what else could they do, they had been given no instruction, not told whether they would have their jobs to go back to, but when Ned came through the front door Bert was into the front office very quickly as though somebody might be there somehow to tell them what was happening and he was right.

Ned looked long at him as Bert emerged from the gloom. Bert looked expectantly at him and it was the first time that Ned realized their eyes were on a level. He had always looked up at Bert, literally as well as figuratively, but somehow and all at once they were together.

'Now, lad,' he said, 'how are things?'

'Getting better,' Ned said. 'My uncle left me everything and my mother left me some money.'

Bert spent several seconds taking this in and then a smile grew upon his face like a rose. 'Shall I call the others through?'

'Yes, I think that might be a good idea,' Ned said, trying to get used to it.

Before it grew dark he made his way to his uncle's house, which was within the Redhills area of the city, towards the north and not that far from his father's house but it was a whole world from it in some ways. Jasper had obviously loved the area too much to move far. His house was in Sutton Street across the road from the hospital.

The street itself was well enough built of neat brick among a dozen such streets within the shadow of the huge viaduct which carried the trains to the north and south of the small city.

It had a Durham bay window upstairs which he was somehow pleased about but when he opened the front door with a large key, aware of lace curtains moving in the windows of houses nearby, he began to understand what his father had meant.

There was no order in the house, it was as though Jasper had not been there in months, had not spent time there in years. The furniture, what there was of it, was covered in a thick layer of dust and everything was old and unused and smelled like that. Some of the furniture was good but too big for the house as though Jasper had moved out of Redhills Court, the family home, and taken some of the furniture with him.

Only one room was furnished upstairs and had nothing in it but a bed and a chair. Downstairs were two good rooms and a tiny kitchen on the end. There was no bathroom, something Ned was not used to. There was a back yard with a coalhouse and a lavatory, an earth closet, he thought, grimacing.

In the front room was a desk covered in papers, a bookcase full of books and a dining-room chair as though Jasper had used the place as an extended office. In the back room was a dining-room table and three chairs and it was similarly covered in papers and books. Ned began to feel sorry for his uncle, he had had no comfort anywhere, his father was right. The idea of living there did not appeal. He admitted to himself now that he had no idea what to do, he was used to being waited on, having his clothes put out for him, having his meals arrive upon the table. Well, it was his home now and he must learn to make the best of it.

Five

Annabel stared across the sea of oak desk at Mr Browning and thought that she was going to faint for the first time in her life and the image of the pretty dark woman standing in the doorway blurred and then slowly slid away. It had been her only comfort.

'She was so ashamed of what she had done, her family would not forgive her,' Mr Browning said. 'Your father rescued you.'

'What was their name?' Still in shock but realizing that Mr Browning was vulnerable now as not before she got the question in quickly.

'Reid.'

'And the town?'

He frowned. 'I don't recall.'

'You must.'

'Red Hills,' he said after several anxious seconds. 'It's somewhere in Durham, that's all I know. If I were you I wouldn't go back to such a place. Even your father thought it was godforsaken and he was a braver man than most.'

Annabel walked slowly back to the house. The winter day closed in and it began to snow. She didn't linger downstairs but went up to her room and took down a bag and then considered carefully what to take with her. She would have to carry the bag so she must not take anything heavy like books or anything unnecessary like the silver hairbrushes which had been a Christmas present last year and then she thought she might be able to sell them and realized that they were too heavy and was looking around for anything valuable that she owned that was light, and was regretting that she had no jewellery, when she became aware of Millie standing in the doorway.

'What are you doing?' she asked.

'Hasn't Mother told you?'

Millie came into the room, closing the door.

'Told me what?' Millie's gaze was fixed on the bag.

'That I don't belong here, that we have different mothers, that—'

'What on earth are you talking about?'

So Annabel sat her down and told her and Millie's pretty blue eyes grew bigger and bigger and shinier and shinier and before the tale was half finished the tears had slipped over and run down her cheeks and she stared and long after the tale was finished she sat there, her gaze wide with disbelief.

'It can't be true, he would have said, we would have known. You're my true sister, Bel, I know you are and all of this is nonsense.'

When she thought that Millie had absorbed the shock of what she was saying Annabel began once again with her packing.

'You aren't really leaving,' Millie said.

'I don't see what else I can do. I have no family here now.'

'You've got me,' Millie said, 'and in time – in time I will inherit everything and—'

'Mother got it all presumably with you to follow,' Annabel said and she heard the bitterness in her voice for the first time. 'She doesn't want me here. She had me foisted on her. Can you imagine what that must be like? How she must have hated him.' When Millie didn't answer Annabel glanced swiftly at her and watched the colour drain from her face. Obviously her sister – half-sister, she corrected herself – had not had time to consider such things.

'I suppose they endured one another,' Millie said in a small voice which betrayed that she was close to tears again, and then she said decisively, 'I'm coming with you,' and turned as though she was going to leave the room and go straight and pack a bag of her own and then Annabel regretted her words.

She put down the pretty dress which she really could not take with her and went to her. 'No, you can't,' she said. 'I don't know where I'm going exactly.'

Millie was crying now. 'I'm not staying here on my own with Mother. We can talk to her and you needn't go.'

'I think you'll find that isn't true,' Annabel said and she tried not to say it harshly but the tears went on running down Millie's face.

'What am I to do without you? I've never been without you before, I can't start now. Please don't go.'

'I don't have any choice, really I don't or I wouldn't leave.'

'I wish she would die!' Millie said. 'Then you and I could stay here and be comfortable,' and that made Annabel laugh and Millie realized how silly she had sounded and after that the tension began to ease. 'Will you write to me and let me know where you are and how you are getting on? I shan't rest until you do.'

Annabel assured her that she would. She had by now packed a spare dress, the warmest she had, and two changes of underwear. She was about to put on her coat and boots, hat, gloves and scarf when she thought it was a stupid thing to do. She must wait until the morning, it was going to be bitterly cold with a frost, already the windows were icing up. It would be madness to leave now just as a gesture so she placed the bag inside the biggest of the wardrobes and as though nothing had happened, as though nothing was wrong, she and Millie dressed for dinner. She could not believe it was for the last time.

She ate little. She kept reminding herself that she should eat as much as she could. She was inclined to put everything from the table into the bag upstairs because she was so afraid of the future. Etta chatted about the visitors who had come today and how pleased she had been to see them and how much they had all cared for Fergus and how glad she was of it, it made her feel so much better.

When dinner was over they had tea next door by the fire and it was there that Etta finally said, 'I understand that you're leaving.' You couldn't keep anything quiet in a house where there were servants and it had been impossible to hide from her maid that the dressing table and some of the drawers were decanted into a bag that was out of sight in the wardrobe, she had thought.

'You can't let her go,' Millie said, leaning forward across the fire as she did so, 'you must tell her to stay here with us.'

'She must do what she thinks is right,' Etta said without looking at anybody.

'You don't want her to stay here,' Millie protested.

Her mother did not deny it, she didn't even look up.

Annabel finished her tea and felt she had nothing to stay for and although she could hear Millie pleading and crying when she closed the door after her she did not go back into the room.

Soon afterwards Millie burst into her bedroom and had to be calmed down and told once again that she could not come. Annabel tried to be kind without indulging her. Millie would be no help, she was better off here and Annabel could not help saying, since she thought it was the only thing which would contain her sister, 'If it works out well I will send for you.'

Millie looked at her from wet eyes. 'Promise it.'

'I promise.'

They went to bed, Millie having been persuaded into her own room. Annabel did not sleep and she had made up her mind that it would only distress Millie further so she didn't say goodbye, she didn't want to see Etta again, she could not convince herself that this woman had no affection for her and yet had brought her up, was parenting nothing other than biology and had her father's love for her been on the condition that she was his and nothing else? She swore that she would never do such things and then she put on as many warm clothes as she could and as soon as it got light she left the house.

*

She walked. The bag got heavier very quickly as she had known it would but she had no money and could afford no transport. She stopped in at the first jeweller's she came to. She had debated whether to go to one she didn't know but she felt sure they would cheat her so she went to the one she knew where she and Tom had chosen the diamond ring so recently and once there among the frock-coated gentlemen she asked for the manager, Mr Symonds. He greeted her with polite pleasure she thought, he did not look too closely at the bag she was carrying, nor that she seemed to have half her wardrobe on her back.

'Could I speak to you privately?' she asked, feeling shy and out of place for the first time there.

He hid his curiosity and ushered her into the back room where a fire burned in a small black grate and many ledgers sat in piles here and there as though they had a great deal of rather boring work to do in the back room away from the dance and sparkle of jewellery and watches and clocks and ladies' jewellery cases and black-velvet-lined shelves and comfortable oak chairs for ladies to sit in while they considered their next purchase. It occurred to her for the first time that they were a very high-class jeweller.

'I need your help, Mr Symonds.'

'By all means, Miss Seaton. I was so very sorry to hear of your poor father's passing. Do sit down.'

She didn't. She took the watch from her pocket and held it up in front of him.

'I need to sell this.'

Mr Symonds had been a jeweller far too long to show his feelings good or bad.

'Indeed,' he said.

'I know this is awkward and you will find out in time but . . . you see I have no place here any more and this is the only thing that he left me. I need to go north and find my family. I . . . need the money.'

Mr Symonds didn't speak for some time, she didn't blame him.

'He brought me back with him when he went there when I was a baby. It will all get out and . . .' She stopped there.

Mr Symonds hesitated a moment longer and then he took the watch which was still in her outstretched hand.

'It is of course a very fine piece,' he said, 'but you know, Miss Seaton, there is a price at which the public buys and a price at which the jeweller buys and they bear very little resemblance to one another.'

She couldn't speak. Was he going to cheat her? Was he going to offer the lowest amount of money he could knowing that she had nowhere else to go, nobody else to help and that any other jeweller would do the same?

'Why don't you leave it here and I will give you your train fare and a little more and then when you come home you can pick it up again?'

She stared at him. She was beyond thinking anyone would be kind. 'That wouldn't be right for you.'

'It would be like a pawnbroker, certainly, which is definitely something we are not. I could charge you a little interest and in time you could redeem it.'

'I'm not intending to come back,' she said, 'I have nothing here now.'

'I see.'

Maybe he thought she was mad, Annabel thought, she was certainly beginning to think so herself.

'Will you buy it from me?' she prompted him eventually.

'Certainly.' He took the pocket watch and deposited it in the top drawer of the desk as he went behind it and then he opened a cash box which he extracted from another drawer and he counted out the money. 'Ten guineas,' he said.

It was too much for whatever reason but she was not about to tell him so and she could not meet his gaze, she could only hold out her hand and thank him and turn blindly from him and comfort herself with the idea that when she did not come back he would at least be able to sell it and redeem some of the money.

King's Cross Station. Annabel wasn't quite sure how she had got there, she was like somebody in a dream with only one destination in her mind. Pigeons were strutting about where people and luggage was standing and a sparrow flew, confused, up in the roof. She felt like panicking. She had nobody and each foot of space around her seemed to reinforce the feeling. Other people were in pairs or in families, with small children or in groups standing casually about talking and there was the excitement of the idea of moving on, going somewhere else, perhaps somewhere new or to visit friends and maybe some of these people were going home.

Was that how she felt about it? The very idea made her breath shorten. It wasn't home, this was home, her own part of London almost like a village where she knew the people, the houses, the way that the sun slanted across the grass in summer and who walked their dogs out at what time of day.

It was home no more, she thought, trying to be brave. She would not come back here. The idea of not being able to turn and run, to pretend that things had not altered so much that she could not go back made the panic rise once more and then people began to move towards the train which she knew was hers. She had paid for her ticket, she could not go back now.

She hoisted her bag off the floor, it seemed so heavy and yet most of her belongings she had had to leave behind. She carried it on to the platform where the train, getting ready to leave, began to roar into life. She could see the man shovelling coal into the furnace as she hesitated, not sure which carriage to get into, and then she took a deep breath and got on, found a carriage which had other women in it, put down her bag with relief and sat down.

Other people took off their coats, disposed of their luggage, chatted, settled themselves and as she waited more people arrived and sat down and then the doors were slammed shut, the guard blew his whistle and the train began to move, slowly at first as it trudged out of the station into the winter sunlight.

It was some minutes before the outskirts of the city were left behind and it was like a last letting-go. As the little fields and villages and more isolated houses rushed past – even a church at one point, seemingly in the middle of nowhere – she had a momentary panic again at how fast they were disappearing, as if her life was doing the same thing. Then she grew used to the rhythm of the train and sat back and thought if only she didn't have to reach her destination, if she could just stay on the train forever, that would be easy.

She had thought there was some kind of physical north–south divide but she didn't see it as the train reached Doncaster – a beautiful church of some kind there, was it a cathedral, and then York – she could see nothing from the train other than a few houses and it was misty and the city lost and she had sat well back in her seat by then thinking that it was not that much further. She was really in the north now.

It wasn't until the train steamed beyond Darlington station and she saw row upon row of rather poor-looking terraced houses that she felt how different this place was. From there she knew it was not far to her destination and the wings of panic started up again. The minutes passed and she could see the little villages, smaller versions of Darlington, and she noticed for the first time, the washing hung in the back lanes, blowing there with a stiff breeze behind it, it being the first fine day of the week.

It was cold here too she could see, the roofs were white but it was a bright sunny day so why wouldn't the housewives hang out their washing to dry? She liked the different colours, it all looked so normal and she had thought that nothing in her life would be normal any more.

She thought back to how the washing would be going on in her house, Tilly and Mrs Evans who came especially to do it would be labouring in the wash house outside the back kitchen door, steam everywhere and the warm smell of wet clothes and they would be mangling the water out of the clothes and the front of their long white pinafores would be wet.

She had always like the smell and how on fine days they would go out into the big back yard and put up the lines and methodically hang the different clothes together as though it mattered. Mrs Evans was particular that way.

Annabel was prevented from thinking longingly even of wash day at home by the fact that she was sitting on the right side of the train and she had a view of the city such as she had never seen before in any place. The train came in on a big viaduct way up above the town and from her window she could see an enormous church and a castle. As she drew in her breath at the wonder of it the woman sitting next to her sat further forward, the better to observe it, and she said, 'Grand, isn't it? It's the best view in the world,' and somebody else said, 'Aye, but only until you get to Newcastle,' and everybody laughed.

Annabel was pleased that her introduction to the place was accompanied by laughter. She hoped that was a good omen.

The road from the station was down a long winding hill which plunged into the town. Opposite was a pub, the Bridge Inn, below the viaduct, brightly lit and as she walked the viaduct towered above her. The first thing to do was find somewhere to stay. She could not go into the pub, it was full of men, she could see them through the windows and it was not like somewhere which looked as though it had rooms for people to stay in, it was not that big.

She began to walk up the hill away from the town. She was not quite sure why, but the town itself looked intimidating and she was not used to being out on her own in a strange place. The hill wound like a snake, on one side was a high wall with iron railings and lots of trees, it must be some kind of park, she thought, and on the other side were big terraced houses with gardens going down steeply to the road and stopping short several feet above the pavement.

Her bag became heavier and heavier because it was not an easy climb. The park gave way to a churchyard and then to a tall spired church and finally she saw a building on the right-hand side which had a sign outside saying that it had rooms. The building sat well back from the pavement and she liked the look of it, it was welcoming and it said The Garden House Hotel which was a nice idea and it seemed friendly.

She hovered outside. She could see people in there so in a way it was just as intimidating as the other pub had been but it was very cold now, a heavy frost was twinkling on the pavements and on the trees and she knew that she must find shelter soon so she made herself go inside.

The hot air, the smoky fire, the sound of male voices and the smell of warm beer hit her as she moved inside but she was thankful to be away from the weather. Nobody took any notice of her. There were rooms either side of the hall but the doors were closed. She made her way to the back of the building where there was a tiny reception desk. It was deserted. She rang the bell, it sounded so loud to her ears but nothing happened and she waited and rang it again and still nothing happened so in the end there was nothing to do but go into the bar, ignore the looks she got from the men and how they stood aside and let her through and say to the fat red-faced woman behind it, 'Good evening. I need a room.'

'Hang on a minute, love, I'll just serve these and then I'll be with you.'

Pint after pint of foaming golden beer was placed on the bar, Annabel had never seen anything like it, lined up was a dozen, another half-dozen. Ready hands grasped the glasses and they were all, from what she could see, local working men, they wore shabby suits and cloth caps and she could see at one man's knees a very thin long-legged dog, it looked like a greyhound. The dog seemed quite happy there among all the men's legs, as though it was at home, as though it was used to standing around, the air blue with cigarette smoke and fuggy with beer fumes and the noise coming from the crowded bar was deafening. She had never been in such a place before and was mesmerized and then finally the woman indicated they should go out into the hall and she said, 'Now then, my love, what can I do for you?'

'I'd like a room, please.' Annabel wanted to enquire how much it would be but she was afraid to go back out into the night again so it didn't matter, she would have to pay for it and surely she could afford several nights' lodging.

The fat woman looked her up and down and then she said, 'Are you on your own?'

Annabel was inclined to reply caustically and she said, 'Does it matter?'

'Well, it isn't every day you get a lass on her own in a place like this.'

Annabel decided to be frank. 'I'm from London, I've come here to find my family.'

'Have you now?'

'Please let me have a room. I have money and I don't know where else to go. I don't know anybody and it seemed sensible not to be further into town. You do have rooms, it says so outside?'

'It does, my love, yes, it's just that in my experience lasses on their own only mean one thing and that's trouble but you look very respectable to me. Mind you, if you make trouble you'll have to go and if there are any men involved—'

'I don't know anybody, really I don't, I've just got off the train. Please help me.'

'All right, then. Come through.'

In the hall at the small reception desk was a book so that she could write her name. The woman pushed the book towards her so that she could sign and asked how many nights she wanted the room for and when she said two nobody said anything until she had signed and she signed it, automatically somehow, 'Annabel Reid'.

'Joe!' the woman shouted and a small skinny middle-aged man came out of the bar and he picked up Annabel's bag and carried it upstairs for her and the woman followed along a dark narrow hall, the woman holding up a lamp all the way so that the shadows lit. Annabel was not used to dark halls. The man went back downstairs after he had gone in and put her bag down. The woman went into the room and Annabel followed. The room was freezing cold, the air hit her.

'Oh, it's perishing in here,' the woman said.

She lit the lamp on an octagonal table and also the fire. It was a very small room but neat, tidy and clean, it had in it a single bed, a wardrobe, a dressing table and a little table and chair over by the window. There was a rug in the middle of the floor. She was about to pick up the other lamp and leave. Annabel gathered her courage.

'I'd like something to eat.' She wasn't hungry but hadn't had anything since she had left London.

'Come back downstairs when you're finished up here. The dining room is at the other side. Go in there and I'll find you something decent to eat. You look like a good meal would knock you sideways. I'm Mrs Hatty,' the woman said and gave her the key to the door, which Annabel locked behind her.

Six

Nobody else was in the tiny dining room and there was no fire. She could see her breath. Mrs Hatty brought in a plate of something she did not recognize and she could not help but think back to the elegant meals she had had in her father's dining room, two dozen people, the women's jewellery glittering in the candlelight, the servants standing behind the chairs, the white-linen tablecloths, the blue shimmer of Waterford crystal, the decorations of fruit and flowers and the best food lovingly prepared by her father's French chef.

'It's panackelty,' Mrs Hatty said, seeing her stare. 'Eat it up, you'll enjoy it,' and she disappeared into the bar. For a few moments when the door was opened Annabel heard the sound of conversation, raucous laughter, clinking tankards and glasses and then she was alone again and the noise was muffled.

Steam rose from her plate and with it the smell of bacon, onions and potatoes. She began to eat. It was a poor man's meal and since she was poor and had had nothing all day she enjoyed it, drank gratefully the tea she had been given and poured out two more cups from the big brown teapot which she thought was friendly and after that thought of her room at home, the high fire, the comfortable bed. She thought also of the tiny freezing room upstairs but there was no fire here so she was losing nothing by going upstairs.

She took the candle which Mrs Hatty had left with her to light her way and trudged slowly up the barely carpeted stairs. She unlocked her door and the first sight that met her gaze was the fire. Someone had been in and built it up with lots of coal so that it was giving off a proper warmth now which hit her as soon as she closed the door and moved into the cosiness and when she undressed hastily she found that Mrs Hatty had put a hot-water bottle in her bed. She was so grateful that she could have cried.

She undressed and got into bed and the sheets were rough and warm to the touch and the fire was still giving off heat. She had built it up once again with a shovel of coal before she got into bed but put up the fireguard in case the coal should fall out. She thought that it was all too strange and that she would not sleep but she spent only a few seconds being afraid of what would happen next and, listening to the fire crackling comfortingly, she went to sleep.

When she awoke the fire was out but the room retained a semblance of heat and she remembered almost instantly where she was and wished that she could go back to sleep. A sliver of light was making its way past the almost closed curtains so she got out of bed and pushed them back even further. It was a typically dreary winter's day, wet and still almost dark.

She heard a knock on the door and Mrs Hatty came in when

she opened the door and she had a jug of hot water in her hands. There was a thin towel.

'Breakfast is in ten minutes,' she said, putting down the jug and leaving the room.

Hastily Annabel washed and dressed and went downstairs. Once again she was the only person in the dining room but at least the fire blazed up as though other people were expected and as she sat there an elderly couple came in and sat down and two business men on their own at separate tables.

Without her saying anything a great plateful of bacon and eggs and toast was put in front of her. She ate hungrily. The eggs had deep golden yolks almost orange and better than anything she thought she had tasted before and the bacon was crisp. She drank her tea and then made herself eat another slice of toast since there was raspberry jam and because she was paying for it and did not think she could afford lunch. When Mrs Hatty came in to clear Annabel said, 'Do you know of a town called Red Hills?'

Mrs Hatty looked curiously at her.

'Red Hills isn't a town, it's a part of Durham, just down the hill from here. Why?'

'My family used to live there. Do you know of anybody called Reid?'

'It's a common name hereabouts, I should think there are a good many of them, but the only people I've heard of have a house in Waddington Street beyond the viaduct. I don't know anything more about them. You could always try there.'

'Do you know what number it is?'

'I don't,' Mrs Hatty said and she picked up the tray where she had put the dirty dishes and left the room.

Later when the rain had cleared Annabel put on her outdoor things and ventured outside. She made her way back in towards the town and under the huge viaduct which dominated that area and from there she turned right into a clutch of terraced streets where she found the one she wanted and knocked on the door of the first house. Nobody answered so she went on to the next and then the next until finally a large woman in a flowered pinafore with iron-grey hair opened the door.

She frowned as Annabel explained she was looking for some people called Reid and she told her they were towards the other end, two doors from the last, so she continued down the street and then needed a big breath before she banged on this door. It was shabby, there must have been paint on it at one time but it was so long ago all that was left was the bare wood. She was not hopeful. There was a long silence. She was just about to go away when the door finally opened and a woman appeared, short, fat and dressed in clothes so shabby that any colour they had once had was gone.

'I'm sorry to bother you but I'm looking for some people called Reid. I think we may be related and I'm looking for my family.'

The woman blinked from eyes that looked like raisins and then she looked suspiciously at her. 'What?'

'I'm just trying to find them. I have no family of my own, you see.'

Reluctantly the woman ushered her inside. Annabel peered

through the long dark passage and looked at the woman and then thought she might as well go in. This person could be her only link with the past and she had come a very long way but as she plunged into the narrow gloom the smell which assailed her nostrils was not a pleasant one.

It was dirt. She was surprised to understand it because she had not met its like before. It was grit under feet and dust in the air and greyness upon the walls. The house seemed as full of it as though it was smoke. Into a room then, not the first she came to but the second, she thought, a back room with a range in it, a range which would in any other kitchen have been shining brightly but it was dull, neglected and only the smallest of fires burned there.

A window which she could barely see through overlooked a tiny yard with coalhouse and lavatory. Inside she had never seen anything as poor, a table bare, a couple of rickety chairs. Her heart plummeted. Had she come more than two hundred miles for this?

'You aren't from here, then?' the woman guessed, urging her to sit down.

'I'm from London.'

'And you came all the way up here to find some folk you don't know?'

It was not an easy thing to explain and Annabel's face burned worse and worse as she told it. It was just as shameful for the other people involved she realized and as her tale wore on the woman looked more and more keenly at her.

'Aye,' she said, 'your mother was my late husband's sister and you have the right of it. She drowned a very long time ago, before I knew him.'

'Is there anyone else?'

'Just the other sister, Bessie.'

Annabel was about to enquire about the sister when the back door opened and a young man entered the house. He was so big that it was difficult to see around him, not just tall but wide and he was unmistakably related to the woman, Annabel could see even in the gloom.

'This is my son, Billy. Billy, come in and meet your cousin, Annabel, she's come up from London especially to find us.'

Billy's eyes were lost in his huge round face but he smiled in a way which made Annabel feel grubby.

'She must come and stay here with us,' his mother said.

'Oh, no, thank you, that's very kind but I couldn't.'

'It's no problem. You're staying at the Garden House, you said? I'll get our Billy to go and fetch your things.'

'No, really,' Annabel said, 'I can't stay. I've said I'll be there for at least two nights.'

'You just got here, lass, and we're the only family you've got. You must.'

'I have other enquiries to make.' Annabel was determined to leave now but Billy somehow was standing in her way.

'Go and get her things,' his mother said.

'I should go with him.'

'He can manage, can't you, Billy?'

The boy looked at her, he was about the same age as she was, she guessed.

'Have you got any money?' he said.

'Only enough for my room.'

'Oh, I dare say she has some and maybe pretty things,' the woman said.

'Give it to me,' Billy said. He didn't threaten but he did look straight at her and for the first time since she had reached Durham she was afraid and gave him the small amount which was in her purse.

He went off and locked the door behind him. Annabel, venturing into the back, tried the door there but it was locked too. Mrs Reid did not even follow her through into there.

'Have a cup of tea until Billy comes back. He won't be but a little while.'

There was nothing to do but agree. The tea smelled so musty that she could not drink it and when Billy came back he had her bag and was carrying it like it weighed nothing.

'I told the woman at the hotel you were staying with us and I paid what you owed,' he said.

Mrs Reid opened the bag and began to drag Annabel's belongings out, sighing over the pretty nightdress, the delicate underwear and the lace petticoat.

'Eh, what lovely things. You must be rich.'

'She doesn't have any money,' Billy said despondently, 'there was just enough for the room she was staying in, like she said.'

'I thought you might have had nice jewellery,' Mrs Reid said.

'No, I told you, I have nothing.'

Mrs Reid folded everything up, sighed, said, 'Nowt here that would fit a woman with any meat on her bones,' and placed

Annabel's clothes carefully back inside the bag. 'It could be sold of course and might bring something decent.'

The two books Annabel had brought with her, her favourites, by Jane Austen, were missing. She thought that perhaps Billy had managed to sell them, perhaps there was a second-hand bookshop in the place but then he wouldn't have had sufficient time to do so, maybe he had not seen the books or maybe Mrs Hatty had not given them to him.

'I must go. Please give me my bag.'

'I thought you didn't know anybody.' Mrs Reid held the bag away from her in a way that made Annabel's heart flutter with panic.

At that moment there was a banging on the back door and when Mrs Reid went to open it Annabel could hear a man's voice and even having not heard it she knew it for deliverance.

'Miss Annabel is staying with us. She said two nights and she's only had one. Where is she?'

As nobody spoke, Mr Hatty, small and thin though he was, somehow pushed his way inside and spied her immediately.

'There you are, lass. My missus says she needs to hear from you that you don't want to stay another night.'

Annabel thought she had never been so glad to see any-body, nor so grateful for anyone's good sense. If they had not thought of her she had the feeling she would have been trapped here.

'Yes, I am staying another night with you.'

'I thought so,' he said and, glaring at Mrs Reid and Billy, he picked up Annabel's bag, said, 'Are you sure you haven't forgotten anything?' and when she assured him that she hadn't he ushered her out of the back door in front of him.

She had never been so glad to get outside. Mr Hatty walked quickly in spite of the bag back up North Road. Annabel kept up with him and thanked him.

'Not nice people, even if they are your relatives,' he said. 'My dad used to say "our friends we can choose, our relatives are thrust upon us." My missus wasn't happy when that lad came in, wanting to know what you owed. I hope you didn't give them any money.'

She didn't like to tell him but her money was fastened with a safety pin inside her clothes, attached to her underwear.

When they reached the hotel Mrs Hatty came straight into the hall.

'Didn't I tell you, Joe, that that lad was odd?' she said. 'Are you all right, lass?'

'Oh, Mrs Hatty, I've never been so glad to see anybody as I was to see Mr Hatty. Thank you so much,' Annabel said and Mrs Hatty shook her head as Joe went off once again up the stairs with Annabel's belongings and she said, 'You're going to have to be a lot more careful until you know your way around. You've no more about you than a bairn. You shouldn't be junketing about on your own.'

'The woman told me she had a sister, Bessie, have you heard of her?' Annabel said, though now loath to go anywhere.

'That's Bessie Hardcastle. She married the Methodist minister over Heath Houses way. It's a pit village just outside of the place.'

'What are they like?'

'Very respectable, not like that lot. They'd take the clothes off your back by the sounds of things but Bessie's religious of course and thinking she's a cut above the rest.'

That afternoon when Mrs Hatty had given her a sandwich, a cup of tea and strict instructions to be careful and that if she was not back by teatime Joe would be over there looking for her, Annabel, following directions, walked through the small city, around by the outside of the public school which was the oldest in the country and had lovely buildings, she thought, past big detached houses with fields around them and on to where there were no houses, just fields and then the now-familiar sight of the pit workings, the big wheel and the rows of terraced cottages which made up the small place. There were shops, the miners' institute, a church and further along the big square stone building which was the Methodist chapel and next to it and adjoined was a house.

Annabel was nervous. She knew she ought to have accepted what the first woman said but it was the only lead she had and she had not come all the way to Durham to give in now.

She banged on an unknown door for the umpteenth time in a day and nothing happened. She was just about to bang again when she noticed people going into the chapel next door so she followed them. When she got inside it was not the chapel, it was another big room on the end and to her amazement there were tables the full length of the floor at either side and heaped on the tables were clothes, and women, badly dressed, were fighting to get to them. At one table the clothes were being thrown up into the air and coming back down again as people sorted through them.

The woman who seemed to be in charge, stout and middle-aged in dull black clothes, was hovering nearby and Annabel could not help asking, 'What is it?'

The woman looked at her as though she had lost her mind. 'It's a jumble sale.'

'Are you Mrs Hardcastle?'

Again the woman looked at her strangely. 'I'm Bessie Hardcastle, yes. Who are you?'

'Annabel Reid. I think we might be related,' Annabel said. 'I would like to talk to you.'

Mrs Hardcastle stared and quite obviously didn't believe her. 'I'm sorry,' she said, 'I'm busy,' and she walked away, the full length of the room. Annabel followed her.

'Please. It would only take a few minutes. I came especially from London—'

Mrs Hardcastle relented. 'All right,' she said, 'but you will have to stay until the end. If you go into the kitchen Mrs Chesters will make you a cup of tea.'

Annabel went gratefully and found the tiny kitchen and the woman there and said Mrs Hardcastle had sent her and Mrs Chesters sat her down on a stool and gave her tea and sponge cake.

About an hour later, the jumble sale was over and to Annabel's surprise when she went through after the crowd had dispersed the tables were completely empty and two men had arrived and were moving them.

Mrs Hardcastle took Annabel into the house next door and into a small study where there were lots of books and there she sat her down and asked how she could help so Annabel told the story again. Mrs Hardcastle said nothing to this but Annabel could not help noticing that she grew pale as the story went on. When the tale was finished Annabel waited for some response but nothing happened except that eventually Mrs Hardcastle let go of her breath quite suddenly and then she said, 'I'm sorry you met up with that woman first. My brother passed away some years ago. As for the rest – our sins always come back to haunt us. I'm sorry that you have experienced such heartache but you see it was a very long time ago.'

'And you know nothing about it?' Annabel said.

'On the contrary, I know everything about it. If you are indeed who you say you are then my sister Sarah was your mother. She drowned herself in the river.'

Annabel had not thought that this could get any harder but it seemed that she was mistaken. To think that a woman had had her and it had been so awful that she had killed herself.

'She was, until then, as good as any other girl. I think he turned her head. He owned the mines you see, he was rich. She did not say anything about it, she just left. We never saw her again, we just heard that she was pulled out of the river, dead.'

'It must have been a terrible shock.'

'My parents were so upset. We were always so good, you see, hard-working people and clean-living, she had let her family down. I'm so sorry for you, my dear, especially being told like that when your father died.'

A man opened the door of the study and then hesitated. 'I didn't realize we had company.'

'Come in,' she invited him. 'This is my poor sister Sarah's daughter, Annabel. Annabel, my husband, Jacob.'

He looked shocked and Annabel was not surprised but she remembered to be polite and so did he. It reminded her of how much she had lost. She got up and said she must go but Mr Hardcastle protested. 'Do you have somewhere to stay?'

Annabel hesitated only for a moment. Mr and Mrs Hatty had proved that they could be kind and she had said she would stay there for two nights whereas she did not know these people.

'I'm staying at the Garden House Hotel. They are very nice people.'

'A woman alone should not stay in a place where the men drink beer downstairs. When men are drunk they may do anything.'

'I feel quite safe with Mr and Mrs Hatty.'

'I'm sure they know of us too and unless you have a great deal of money you won't want to waste it in board and lodging,' Mr Hardcastle said. 'You are welcome to stay with us.'

Annabel went back to the hotel and only when Mrs Hatty was satisfied that she really was going to stay with the minister and his wife was she happy to let her go the following morning. 'If it doesn't work out you must come back here.'

'I can't afford it.'

'We'll find you some kind of job, don't you worry. If you don't like it you come back, do you hear me?'

Annabel was inclined to hug Mrs Hatty but she had realized people there didn't go hugging one another unless there was a good reason, they were strange like that she thought but it didn't stop them being kind to her so she thanked them both before she left.

When she got back a young man of about her own age was standing in the hall.

'Cousin Annabel,' he said, 'I'm John.'

He was slight, skinny, white-faced and she didn't think he was very attractive, his eyes looked like coal and were impenetrable. Mrs Hardcastle came through, hearing her.

'There you are,' she said, 'this is our son. He is going to be a minister like his father and has been at Bristol, studying. He wants to be a missionary. We're very proud of him.'

Annabel made what she hoped were all the right noises.

'Where will you go?' she said.

'Wherever I'm sent but I'm not sufficiently experienced yet. My mother says you come from London. You must tell me all about it.'

The evening meal was served by a diminutive maid in the small dining room at the back of the house and was boiled beef, dumplings and vegetables. There was a rice pudding to follow and Annabel thought that their maid, who appeared to do everything in the house, was a very bad cook. The beef was leather, the vegetables were limp and the rice pudding was gritty.

John asked her about London but seemed more intent on telling her what his life had been like in Bristol and how many friends he had left there and she thought that if he were honest he would say that he had not wanted to come back here and help his father in the little village just outside the city.

She was shown into a bedroom at the back of the house. It looked out over the yard on to the road and across the street so it was a dark little room and tiny. It had a fireplace but no fire. It looked, she thought regretfully, as though no fire had ever been lit there. The bed was old and creaked when she sat down on it and there was a chair on which to place things, a bedside table with a half-used candle and a wardrobe which was so rickety it moved when she touched it.

She lay awake for hours, aware of the cold in the room and in the bed, her feet were freezing long after the rest of her had warmed up and when she finally slept she was awoken by the shouts of people outside. At first she thought they were inside the house and then realized they were beyond her window and some way down the street and she even ventured out of bed though the room was now so cold that she shivered and drew the curtain slightly aside but as she did so the men concerned disappeared away around the corner and she could not hear anything further.

In the morning at breakfast Mrs Hardcastle said she was not to worry, it was just the pit lads, they got too much beer and were always fighting on the streets. She and Mr Hardcastle and John worked diligently to show the people the error of their ways and many had given up the drink but there was always an element who would not do so and the village had many such men.

'Some of them have wives and children who starve because of it,' she said.

Her husband said, 'It's a hard place to live is this, the work is savage and the men drink because they cannot stand it and everybody suffers. We have a great deal of work to do here. You can be a good help to us, Annabel,' and Mr Hardcastle smiled at her.

He was eating a big plateful of bacon and eggs but all Annabel got was a piece of bread buttered and a cup of tea which had been left to stew for a very long time.

'Weren't any of your family miners?' she asked and Mrs Hardcastle looked scandalized.

'Our family was always of respectable middle-class stock,' she said, 'and you should think better than to say that we were ever common. The Reids were always God-fearing people, proud, farmers and millers from the top end of the dale where the air is pure and the people likewise,' she said.

Seven

Annabel had been with the Hardcastles for two weeks. She was unhappy. They led the kind of dull life which was the exact opposite of the life she had led in London and she could not help daily comparing the two. There was no comfort in their house; they seemed not to care. The house was always cold even though, she thought in despair, there were pits both in and outside the village.

They ate badly and John and his father were given the majority of the food, the women of the house ate the leftovers as far as she could judge. God only knew what the poor maid, Edna, was given. She was half grown and skinny so Annabel tried not to think too much about it.

There was chapel every day and three times on Sunday if you included Sunday school which Mrs Hardcastle had got her to help with. Annabel thought the children at the Sunday school would have been a lot better for a good meal instead of so many Bible stories, they were badly dressed and not very clean, and spoke a language which she found unintelligible. There were Bible classes for the older children and for adults and she was expected to be at those too.

The everyday life of the little village went on, the pitmen

went to work, the housewives struggled with their houses and children, there was not even a book to read except for the Bible, Mr and Mrs Hardcastle did not approve of fiction, and most of all she missed music.

There was no music of any kind here except on Sundays and she found herself standing outside the village hall and listening when the brass band were practising. They made a great many mistakes and kept starting the same piece over and over again but she stayed out there in the cold, listening until the rehearsal was over, and when Mrs Hardcastle asked her where she had been she told her what the problem was.

'We sing hymns.'

Annabel was glad of it, and lifted up her voice even when she didn't know the words but it was not enough, she longed for a concert of some kind and went into Durham that week to see if she could find anything to go to. She didn't think the Hardcastles would approve so didn't tell them but when she came past the Victoria pub in Hallgarth Street a man coming out backed into her and when he turned around to her surprise it was John.

'I've just been in to see what it was like, my parents urge us to tell people what they are doing wrong but it was too difficult in such circumstances and I was cowardly and came back out again.'

They fell into step and he asked her what she was doing in the city as though it was some den of iniquity and she was obliged to lie and say that she had just felt like a walk and she could no longer pretend that she had further to go and found herself walking back from the town with him.

'You led a very decadent life in London, my mother thinks,' he said.

'Decadent?'

'Your family was rich?'

'Yes, we had everything we wanted and wore beautiful clothes and went to lots of parties and drank champagne.'

'You liked that?' His face was shocked as though she could never have cared for such things.

'I was engaged to a young man. We were going to be married.'

'And true to form he gave you up when he found you weren't really of his kind?'

'I gave him up, there seemed nothing else to do,' she said but she felt uncomfortable, remembering how Tom had taken back the diamond engagement ring almost readily. 'I have come here to find what happened to my mother but I haven't made much progress.'

'I thought she drowned herself because of her shame.'

'I don't know yet.'

'That's because you find it difficult to understand but we must accept the things God sends us. You won't be able to make any progress with your life until you do.'

'I don't see why I should accept something I'm not sure is true.'

'And if you were never to find anything else about her?'

'I don't think that should stop me from trying. I'll know when to stop.'

'You're a very headstrong young woman,' he said.

Annabel wasn't sure she was happy about the way he spoke to her, like he was older than her or she was less important.

'Headstrong young women make good wives of missionaries. There is such a lot of work to do and it's very important and in difficult circumstances,' and he smiled at her. They walked back in silence but she wasn't sure that she enjoyed the smiles he kept sending her way.

That evening she excused herself and went early to her bed to read. She had brought with her *Pride and Prejudice* and *Sense and Sensibility* and hid them in her room for fear that Mrs Hardcastle would find them and throw them out. She remembered that she had been reading *Sense and Sensibility* when she was meant to be polishing the brasses that morning and had hidden it at the bottom of a pile of religious books on the little table in the hall.

She left the lamp on by the bed and made her way downstairs in the darkness, only to stop short in the freezing draught of the hall because voices came through the parlour door, slightly raised. She stood there in the shadows because what was being said stopped her from going any further.

'You couldn't possibly marry her.' It was Mrs Hardcastle's voice lifted in protest.

'Because she's my cousin?' said John.

'We don't know that she's anything of the sort. She certainly doesn't look like Sarah. We've nothing for it but her word.'

'You took her in,' John said.

'I felt obliged but I'm more and more convinced that she's nothing to do with us. Sarah was small and dainty, pretty, and what's more she had red hair and blue eyes. Do you think this girl looks anything like her?'

'She could take after her father.'

'She has not our ways,' Mr Hardcastle was saying. 'There is a levity in her which I cannot like. She would never be the right woman for you and I think she has led the kind of life which is against everything we stand for.'

'Just the other day she told me how much she misses music. And dancing, I expect,' said Mrs Hardcastle in strained tones.

Annabel crept back up the stairs, taking *Sense and Sensibility* with her, and tried to read even though she got into bed with socks on and her coat but she could not concentrate, she was not sure whether it was the cold or the conversation she had overheard. She could not keep it from repeating over and over in her head even when she put down the book and tried to sleep.

The next day she was more conscious than ever of John's gaze following her everywhere she went, when she helped in the kitchen, when she cleaned the chapel in the afternoon. He kept popping in to see her and at meals he would gaze at her and eat little so that his mother complained he was wasting food. Also her tone was sharper towards Annabel now that she could see he was thinking of her as a possible wife.

Annabel tried to remember how grateful she was to them for taking her in but things were changing. Mrs Hardcastle contrived to keep her busy and out of John's way and he kept trying to speak to her alone though she was glad that at least he didn't touch her. Finally Mrs Hardcastle took her aside and said that she was not to look at John in that heathen way, he was an upright, God-fearing young man and she should think herself lucky that they had taken her in and keep her eyes to herself.

Annabel said nothing. It seemed wiser. She couldn't think of anything that would ease the situation. Mrs Hardcastle, like most mothers of her experience, thought nobody could resist her son whereas Annabel knew that nothing would have induced her to marry him and denying that she had looked at him in such a way would have been fruitless.

The first day that she could get away by herself was almost a fortnight later and that was only because Mrs Hardcastle had asked John to go into the city with several messages to be delivered and Mr Hardcastle said that he could not spare him. When she offered, John said eagerly, 'We could both go. Father, I'm sure you could manage without me for an hour or two and I wanted to show Cousin Annabel Wharton Park.'

His mother insisted that his father needed him and therefore was obliged, since someone must go, to let Annabel go off by herself.

Setting off rather joyfully she felt like she was escaping from prison. It was a fine day, bright like spring. When she went past the churchyard of St Oswald's in Church Street the snowdrops were making a fine show and there were swathes of golden and yellow crocuses and then she was walking up Saddler Street on the way to the cathedral when she stopped short in front of a newspaper office.

It looked rundown, not as though it was doing well, but it stated in bold letters *The Durham County Chronicle*. It occurred to her that she had stopped with a purpose and she did not realize her intent until she had been standing there for several seconds and then she went inside.

It was gloomy and in the semi-darkness she could see a desk and a young man seated behind it and she went over and said to him, 'Excuse me. Do you keep the back newspapers, I mean a long way back?'

He looked at her. He was about her age, tall and dark, wearing a black suit and a white shirt and he didn't have his jacket on and he got to his feet and then he said in a slight northern voice, which surprised her because she had by now got used to the thick northern accents and he didn't have it, 'As far back as we go. What were you thinking of?'

'Twenty years.'

'Yes, of course. Was it something in particular?'

She glanced around her but nobody else was about and there was a door which obviously led into the back rooms and it was shut and she told him the exact year and when it would have been and then he said, as he saw her further into the bowels of the place, 'A particular incident?'

She hesitated and he said, in a friendly manner, 'I don't mean to pry. I thought I might help.'

'It was a drowning. You would report those?'

'I suppose. It depends.'

'On what?'

'On whether we knew about it, who it was and how it happened, and whether any special circumstances were attached to it.'

He took the appropriate newspapers from wherever he had them at the back and there seemed to be a good many of them even though it was only a weekly newspaper and they sat down together, she quite enjoyed the way that he assumed she wanted his help, and they began to scan the inky columns.

It was not an easy task. For one thing the smaller events that had taken place were scattered through the newspapers and he told her that if it was nobody important it might be just a paragraph or nothing at all but eventually, when her neck ached and her eyes were beginning to see double, he jammed his finger down on a couple of paragraphs which had made page two and there it was, the report of the drowning. She read and as she did so she went very cold.

'It doesn't say who she was.'

He came over and looked over her shoulder. 'If she'd been in the water a long time then they wouldn't know and that's why it didn't make big news, because she wasn't or couldn't be identified.'

She knew nothing about drowning. She didn't like to say anything. She read the piece several times but all it said was that a young woman had been taken from the river, no detail about how and that nobody knew who she was. Annabel could not believe it, she couldn't speak and she couldn't move.

He closed the newspapers and put them away, leaving the

one she was still staring at until last and then he took it slowly from her and he offered to make some tea, and Annabel, who could not have moved further than the nearest chair if somebody had offered her five pounds, accepted and she watched him put the kettle over the fire and they sat there in silence until it boiled and she was glad of the time and the quiet. She could hear people's footsteps on the pavement beyond and it had begun to snow beyond the window and for some reason she wanted to sit and cry.

When the kettle finally boiled he got the teapot and made tea and she waited until he provided biscuits and poured out the tea and added milk from a bottle and sugar from a bag and stirred it and then she accepted the tea and ate a biscuit. He put the top of the biscuit into his tea, she thought it was a strange habit, and began putting it back in and eating it soggy and then he started drinking his tea and he said, 'Do you want to tell me about it?'

'I don't know.'

'You don't have to. It's none of my business and I'm not so much of a reporter that I would do anything about it whatever it was.'

This aspect had not occurred to Annabel but he had been nothing but kind so she told him what had happened and what Mrs Hardcastle had said and how she had assumed it was her mother.

'Mrs Hardcastle said that they got her out but she had just drowned and that was so obviously not the case that . . .'

'That you think it might have been somebody else and she

could still be alive,' he finished and it was exactly what she would have said if she could have got the words out and it was such a relief to have somebody else say them. She looked at him in a different light, he was so understanding, he had fine blue eyes and blue-black hair, he was, she decided, very good to look at, rather Scottish-looking, she thought, and she liked the way that his hair was so straight and neat and shiny and inclined to fall forwards at either side when he looked down and sitting there with him was somehow quite comfortable as it should not have been. She nodded.

'On the other hand,' he said, frowning as he thought, 'people drowning in the Wear isn't an everyday event.'

'But if they didn't recognize her she could have been in the water for a long time. What if she is still alive?'

He shrugged and strangely not as though it was not important but only as if he would say something when he had something helpful to contribute. As they sat there a tall older man came through from the back, nodded at her in acknowledgement of her presence and then asked, 'Didn't Fred come in at all today, then?'

'I had a note from his mother and his dad's insisting he goes down the pit so he won't be back any more.'

The older man pulled a face and Annabel found that she liked him as he had warm eyes and wore an ancient suit.

'We need to get somebody else to help. Shouldn't we put an advert in the window?'

'Yes, I suppose,' and then the young man seemed to remember her and he said, 'I'm sorry, I don't know your name.'

'Annabel Seaton, at least I was. I'm Annabel Reid, which is the name I'm going under, my mother's name.' She didn't understand why she felt like explaining everything to him just that he had sympathetic eyes full of understanding, that she had the feeling of wishing to unburden herself and leave her problems on his shoulders. She suspected it was stupidly because he was tall and looked so capable of sorting things out.

'I'm Ned Fleming and this is our chief sub-editor and master printer, Bert Brown.'

Mr Brown nodded at her and disappeared once again into the back of the building. Annabel thought she ought to leave as they were clearly busy and he had spent so much time with her and then a thought occurred to her. As she was leaving she took all of her courage and she said, 'What does Fred do?'

He looked surprised at the question and she was embarrassed and her cheeks flushed because she knew how rude it was to say such things and couldn't think what had compelled her to do so.

'All kinds really, he goes round to the various shops and businesses getting them to place advertising with us, he collects reports from various organizations and goes to see people when they have special occasions or something newsworthy happens, he keeps the shop when I have to go out—'

'Mr Fleming—' She stopped, amazed at herself, and then couldn't help going on. 'I'm looking for some work. Do you think I might be able to do it?'

He thought. 'I don't know. I've never considered employing a woman.'

'Does it matter?'

'I suppose you could try. We could give you a week and see if you're any good at it. Have you done work like this before?'

'I've never done any work before but it sounds quite interesting and I am well read and . . . I was good at English grammar when I was at school.'

The afternoon grew dark and it was a long walk back so she told Mr Fleming that she lived at Heath Houses and he insisted on seeing her all the way home.

'It's too far, it'll be dark by the time we get there,' she said but in fact she was rather glad that he had offered to walk her home, she liked him, she hadn't had any conversation with a man her own age who she liked since she had left home. She didn't really want to go back there. She had begun to doubt what her aunt had said about her mother and there was something about it which frightened her, she wasn't sure what. She had not found out anything which should alarm her other than that her aunt seemed to think her mother had been pulled from the river after she had taken her last breath rather than weeks later.

Surely it was a mistake anyone might make or perhaps her aunt did know and was not willing to admit either that it might not be her sister or that her sister could end up in such a way. It must have been an awful shock however it had happened.

Mr Fleming paused as she stopped outside the chapel.

'You live here?'

'Yes, I'm staying with my mother's family. Why don't you come in and—'

'No, I had better get back before it's too late, there are still things to do.'

'Shall I come in the morning?'

'As soon as you can, considering how far it is,' he said and wished her good evening and turned around and walked away.

She somehow needed to take a deep breath before she went back into the house and her aunt came down the passageway to the hall, hearing the door and she said, 'Oh, I was worried about you, you've been gone such a long time. Did you do everything I asked?'

Annabel had almost forgotten her original purpose for going into the city but was able to say that she had, thankfully before she had reached the newspaper office because she had done nothing in that way since.

'I did and I've got a job,' Annabel said and explained, 'Working for the local newspaper.'

Her aunt's face darkened. 'What on earth made you do such a thing?' she said.

Annabel, stupidly, she realized now, had thought that her aunt would have been pleased at her try for independence, at her using her initiative.

'Well, I've trespassed on your hospitality for long enough.'

'You've taken it?'

'I have.'

'Without asking me?'

'They had just lost the person who helped and no doubt

there are lots of people looking for work and it seemed like an interesting thing to do and they are very nice people.'

'Which newspaper?'

She hadn't realized there was more than one. 'The *Chronicle*.'

Her aunt shook her head. 'That's not suitable for you.'

'Why not?'

'Because it's run by Edward Fleming. He's a disgraceful young man. He left his home and his family and runs that dreadful paper. It's not fit for people to read. There is a perfectly good newspaper, the *Durham Echo*, which has proper news and is not full of scandal and . . . advertisements for public houses. You don't need to go out to work,' her aunt said, 'there is plenty to be done here.'

That made her feel guilty. She knew that what her aunt and uncle did was good work and that it ought to make her feel useful and wanted and they had been generous by taking her in but somehow there was a rosy glow around the newspaper office, the atmosphere was exciting, she didn't know why.

'I want to do it and I've accepted the post.'

Her uncle came in then and his face darkened when her aunt told him what she had done.

'You can't live here and work there, it's too far,' he said.

'I shall manage.'

'Not at this time of year when it's only light for a few hours a day.'

'It'll be spring soon and the nights will get lighter.'

'We need your help in the chapel and with the various events we have here. Surely you want to assist?'

Annabel felt even worse but she did not want to give up the only piece of independence that she had ever had. She was not sure whether Mr Fleming had meant what he had said when she was so inexperienced and if she insisted on doing this then she could be taking on problems she knew nothing about.

'May I not try?' she appealed.

'You cannot live here and work in the city, it isn't practical and I thought you were a sensible girl. We took you in and this is the way that you show your gratitude. You will stay here, we don't give you our permission to do such a thing,' her uncle said and as though that settled the matter he walked out.

Her aunt watched him go. 'He's disappointed in you,' she said, 'we had high hopes.'

The meal that evening was a silent affair and Annabel was obliged to finish what was on her plate as always because food was expensive her aunt would say but she had trouble getting the food down, she felt sick with apprehension and the idea of responsibility and all that night she lay sweating and worrying that she had made the wrong decision.

John had followed her out into the hall after dinner and said, 'Is this right, you wanted to go out to work?'

'I am, yes.'

'That's not right for someone like you.'

'I have very little choice in the matter.'

'If we got married you wouldn't need to work.' He clutched at her hand. Annabel tried to draw it back without making any fuss.

'Thank you, John, I'm deeply honoured that you should ask me but you must know that I was recently engaged. You wouldn't think much of me if I could change my sentiments so quickly,' and she pulled away and hurried up the stairs in the knowledge that he would not dare follow her to her bedroom.

Eight

She had an almost sleepless night wondering if Ned Fleming really was as awful as her aunt and uncle thought and that she might be digging a deep pit for herself instead of moving on to what she thought could be better.

The following morning however she remembered how dull the life was here and she went off without breakfast since she could not face her uncle and aunt and went into town, arriving at the newspaper office early.

When she went in Mr Fleming was already hard at work and his office smelled wonderful, of paper and ink, and the fire was already lit in there so it was cosy and he told her to sit down and tell him what the problem was and she told him that her uncle and aunt thought it was too far for her to come into the city to work and walk back in the darkness each day.

'Yes, I can see their point,' he said.

'They are against my working. They are particularly against my working for you.'

'Are they?' He sat back in his chair. 'Why?'

'My aunt says you are not a suitable person for me to work for, that you are a disgraceful young man and gave up your home and family when you inherited the newspaper.'

He didn't look at her for a second, as though he might say the wrong thing and was reconsidering. 'My father was angry when I wanted to run the newspaper as it was left to me by my uncle and has been doing very badly and when I wouldn't give up the project he told me to leave. My mother died when I was small and when I was twenty-one I came into my inheritance so he couldn't stop me though he tried.'

'Don't you like him?'

'He doesn't like me. I don't think he ever liked anybody except my mother and he blamed me for being there somehow. I can't help it, I had to do what I wanted and we disagreed.'

'My aunt says the newspaper is full of scandal and advertisements for public houses.'

'I thought your aunt would have been pleased at the idea of a newspaper for working people with things to interest them though of course she would object to anything to do with beer.'

'Is that what it's for?'

'The *Echo* goes on about Parliament and lots of things which don't occur here and while that's important I think people like to read about what's happening in their own area and about the shows that are put on and the various clubs they go to and they like to read about their own activities. I don't think there's anything wrong with that.'

Annabel didn't either, it was just serving a different need and surely there was room for both. She spent the rest of the day happily being instructed as to various tasks and put her aunt and uncle from her mind until the late afternoon when once again he walked her home.

Over the evening meal she told her uncle and aunt that she would lodge in Durham and take the job. John kept his gaze on his plate. Her aunt said stiffly that she must do as she chose, her uncle said nothing. The meal was brief and both of them had meetings afterwards, Mr Hardcastle telling John quite sharply that he would need his help. She packed and spent the rest of the evening feeling as though she had thrown their hospitality back at them but the following morning when her aunt said as she left early, 'You're as bad as your mother was, but I think the best place for you is probably away from my son so that he recovers his senses,' she was glad to leave.

The bar at the Garden House was crowded and full of men but she only peeped in at the door to see if Mrs Hatty was there and she was not so she went in through the hall, calling politely and Mrs Hatty came out of the back and then she smiled.

'Hello, lass, how are you?'

'I'm not staying with my uncle and aunt any longer, I've got a job at the newspaper office, the *Chronicle*.'

'I can't give you that room, it's too dear and I have somebody in it. There's a little room at the back. It's not as nice but I would think it might do for you.'

Ned had carried her bag to the Garden House at the end of the day. She had enjoyed her day, she knew that she had made the right decision though it was difficult to discover that having found what family she had they were not the kind of people she wanted to be with.

She had come all that way for nothing and then she thought, no, it was not for nothing. Ned and Bert and the other men who worked in the back were good people and she had enjoyed being at the office.

Ned had sent her off to various addresses for reports from the organizations within the city, the Townswomen's Guild and the local flower-arranging group and the people who wrote up about the various sports which went on round about had to be contacted.

Ned loved football and went to the football matches himself but there were darts leagues in the pubs and painting and poetry groups and there were lots of events, like dinner dances and sales of work at the churches and events which would go on in the town the week that the newspaper came out, so that people would know what was happening.

She was eager to see how the printing worked and Bert showed her to the back of the building where the paper was printed. She loved the look of the big rolls of paper and the smell of the ink and the work which had to be done setting the type, it was noisy and interesting and exciting.

They ate at six because they very often went out in the evenings to cover different events and there was a concert on that evening. Ned asked her if she would go with him as he was going to write a review. The following night there was a play on at the theatre and the night after that they would work late because it was what was called 'putting the paper to bed'.

It was printed after Monday's news and came out on Thursday so they had to work well ahead and at first she had to keep reminding herself of what not to include because it would already have happened and what was vital and what was less important. If something important happened over the weekend or on a Monday it would take precedence over everything else, it might even turn out to be the front-page lead. Ned prayed for events that happened on a Monday so that he would have something fresh and new to give the readers.

Annabel tried to put from her mind that her mother was dead but although she put it to the back of her mind for now because she didn't see what she could do about it, it was always there and when she went to bed at night she thought about it and remembered and although she tried to convince herself that her mother was dead and had been pulled out of the river there was a small voice which was not convinced, something which hoped she would find her but didn't see how it was to be accomplished and she did not want to waste the rest of her life on it.

Late at night on the Sunday when Ned had stayed at the Garden House for something to eat and they were sitting over the fire in the lounge he asked her about it. She pretended she wasn't thinking about it.

'I know you're distracted,' he said. 'We can find out whether the woman was recorded as your mother. Births, marriages and deaths. We would only get whether it was supposed to be, though, nothing conclusive. It might help, you never know. We'll go to the Town Hall and ask.'

She was so grateful to him, it was at least something, so that she slept that night as she had not slept since leaving home and when they had a free hour – Ned was not averse to taking time off since they very often worked weekends and Saturdays too so nobody said anything when they went out of the office – they went off and looked it up and sure enough when they found the right year and then the date which they got from the newspaper the woman was not recorded under the name of Reid, it was Ann McGilivray and she was almost thirty years old which Annabel thought was possibly too old for her mother to be somehow.

'Why didn't my aunt and uncle know this?'

'Possibly it was easier for them to think it was her.'

'It might have been.'

'It could have been easier to explain it away and there was obviously more than one woman missing. Maybe your mother moved away.'

'Would she have left her child?'

'If she panicked.'

They didn't talk any more but he took her to the Silver Street cafe and they had ham and eggs for lunch and big pots of tea and Annabel worried far less when her stomach was full and her thirst quenched.

After they had eaten he said, 'Do you write to your family in London?'

'No.'

'Don't you think you should let them know where you are?'

'My mother – my supposed mother – doesn't care.'

'And your sister?'

Yes, she would care very much and would be worried, Annabel knew but she didn't want to write, she didn't want to give herself away, she didn't quite know why. She only wanted to write when she had found some kind of satisfactory family and that obviously wasn't going to happen overnight.

She must write to Millie, just to let her know where she was, and so she agreed that she would and when she got back and had half an hour free before dinner and sat down to write she found that she had good things to tell her sister, so much better than she would have thought a week or two ago.

It wasn't until she had finished the letter that she read it and thought what a positive thing it was and how it would relieve Millie's mind, she would not worry any more when she knew that Annabel had a job and somewhere to stay among such good people.

She felt better when she posted it the following day and then gave it no more thought. Ned was teaching her about advertising, about how to get people to put advertisements in the papers about births, marriages, deaths, anniversaries and she found that she was good at going around the different shops and businesses and telling them how much more they would sell if they announced their products to the world through the *Chronicle*.

Saturday was always a busy day at the newspaper and Annabel had been to an afternoon production of *The Tempest* given by the university and was just coming back into the office to write her review when she thought she saw someone familiar as she made her way from the Bailey up by the cathedral down Saddler Street to where the newspaper offices lay. She stopped.

It was snowing, not hard, just lightly, but the street was cold and older people and those who cared for such matters as weather had stayed at home so she observed the young woman standing just beyond and somewhat precariously in the middle of the road with awe.

She was too well dressed for anybody who lived locally. Even the wives of the university professors and the matrons of the rich businessmen did not come anywhere near this vision in furs and a neat fur-trimmed hat and tiny black boots and a sable muff. It was the kind of dress which only very rich people wore and Annabel had never seen anybody look so out of place. Her heart lifted.

'Millie!' she shrieked, forgetting she was in the middle of the street and people turned and looked and the young woman stood there with a huge smile on her face and as she ran, regardless of the cobbles and her boots, Annabel held out her arms and within seconds Annabel was stifled in the warmth and earthy smell of her sister's sable coat. 'Oh, Millie,' she went on saying to assure herself that her sister really was there and to put off the moment of saying to her, which she soon did, 'What on earth are you doing here?'

They stood back slightly from one another and Millie said, 'I can't think what made you imagine I could spend a second longer than I had to with that dreadful woman.'

Annabel was taken aback. Millie had never said such things so vehemently before but then Millie now knew how her parents had treated Annabel.

'She's your mother.'

'Yes, well,' Millie said, looking older than she was for a few seconds, 'you should think yourself more than lucky that she wasn't yours. Ever since you left she has treated me like a prisoner. It was awful. I had to come away. I was so glad when I got your letter.'

'Oh, Millie, I'm so glad you came and you shouldn't have.'

'Indeed I should and if you had only let me know sooner I would have been here well before now. You can't think how bored and lonely I've been without you. That house makes a morgue look cosy now that you aren't there any more.' Her face worked as though she was going to burst into tears. 'It's been awful, Bel, she treats the servants so badly that most of them have left and we have strangers in the house. Father's friends have completely stopped coming to us and she wants me to marry some dreadful man who's old enough to be my grandpa!'

'What man?'

'He's a lord or something, I don't know, and she was so taken with the idea of my being married to a man with a title that she encouraged him when there were other young charming men about. Not that I care for any of them. He is very kind and once or twice I even entertained the idea just to get me out of there but he must be fifty if he's a day so I did the only sensible thing I could, I ran away.'

Annabel was beginning to think she would say nothing but

'Oh, Millie' for the rest of her life and tried not to do it again and admired her own practicality by saying starkly, 'Have you got any money?'

'Not a bloody penny,' Millie said with vulgar spirit and Annabel was once more taken aback. Everything had changed since their father had died. Millie was no longer the obedient daughter, her father would have been horrified. Annabel couldn't help being rather pleased. 'She stopped giving me any the moment you left. I had to borrow my train fare and I've walked from the wretched station and it's such a long way.'

It made Annabel want to smile, the idea of her sister trudging all the way down the hill from the station, down the long length of North Road, under the viaduct and across Framwellgate Bridge, up the twisting cobbles of Silver Street and through the Market Place to here in her finery.

'I would give away my furs for a cup of tea.'

A dozen questions came into Annabel's mind but she saved them for later, guiding Millie the last few yards to the newspaper office.

Ned had been at a football match and he was standing with his back to her, making tea in the big brown teapot and didn't turn around, only glimpsing the two women as they came in and then he paused with his back turned and that was when he wheeled all the way around and stared.

Annabel was not very surprised. Her sister was a great beauty and here against the shabbiness of the brown walls, the old furniture and the papers strewn everywhere she stood out like a candle in a dark room. Her blonde hair shone even though most of it was hidden under her hat, the blue eyes danced because she had found Annabel, her fair complexion was perfect, she was discarding her gloves from her slender white hands and everything about her was as neat as wax. She was, it had to be said, looking at Ned with some dismay, because he was obviously not a gentleman.

He was in his shirtsleeves and he was unkempt, it was one of the things Annabel liked about him, so involved in what he was doing that he didn't notice anything around him. His hair would fall forward, his hands were grubby from news-print and he wore the kind of suit which at home would have long since been given to the gardener. He was distracted at the moment too because he had just invested every penny he had in new machinery and was worried that it would not work or he would regret the expense because they would not sell any more newspapers.

'Millie, this is Ned Fleming who owns the newspaper. Ned, my sister, Millicent Seaton.'

'How do you do?' Millie said with frosty manners.

Ned stared. 'Oh,' he said. 'Hello.'

'She is dying for some tea.' Annabel tried to cover the gap in Ned's manners and she pushed a pile of papers off an old-green painted kitchen chair and set it for Millie who stared at it rather as Ned had stared at her and didn't move.

Bert came through from the back at that point with some of her copy in his hand. He had obviously heard her voice and he was always showing her where she went wrong and trying to improve her grammar but he too stood as though turned to marble while

Annabel introduced them. He had more presence of mind than Ned and actually said, 'How do you do?' before coming forward, waving the paper and putting Annabel in mind of her spelling mistakes but he went through into the back again, muttering, 'I wish they'd made them like that when I was young.'

Annabel poured the tea. Millie sat down on the chair she was offered for a moment and then got up and went to the window and Ned said softly, 'What is your sister doing here?'

'I'll explain later.'

The biscuits were broken and there were very few of them but Annabel found a cracked plate to put them on and was able to give her sister a cup and saucer. Millie looked down at it.

'Milk?' she said.

'We've run out,' Ned offered. 'There is sugar.'

'Too kind,' Millie said but the sarcasm was lost on him as he offered her two pieces of what had been fingers of shortbread. She drank her tea in spite of its blackness and Annabel poured her another cup. Ned went through into the back to talk to Bert and it was then that Millie looked despairingly at her.

'What are you doing among these workmen?' she said.

'I have no money either,' Annabel pointed out.

'It's hideous,' Millie said, shuddering. 'Haven't we somewhere else to go, somewhere with a fire and a decent chair at least?'

Annabel excused herself and went into the back.

'My sister's luggage is at the station and I have to see Mrs Hatty so that she has somewhere to stay,' she said. 'I'll write up *The Tempest* later.'

Saturday and Monday were their busiest days.

'She's staying?' he said.

'Of course she's staying. What did you think? That she'd come all the way from London on a whim?'

'I have no idea,' he said shortly.

'Will you send for her luggage?'

'I have nothing else to do,' he said with fine scorn.

Annabel was not going to argue with him. She collected Millie from the front office and they set off.

'We have to go all the way back to the station?' she objected as they made their way across Framwellgate Bridge once again.

'It's further than that.'

'My feet ache.'

They ached even more by the time Annabel got her to the Garden House but she could see by then that Millie was too weary to care about the way that the men were doing their Saturday afternoon drinking. She didn't seem to notice the whippet which sniffed at her furs or the noise, fumes and talk from the bar or the way that Annabel called Mrs Hatty out of there – Mr Hatty was there too, so Mrs Hatty was able to leave the pints on the bar – but Mrs Hatty merely looked at the vision in sable before her and said, 'Now what's afoot?'

'This is my sister, Millicent, Mrs Hatty. Could she move into my room?'

'There's only one bed in your room,' Mrs Hatty said, 'there isn't much space for more.'

'Please. We could manage. It would only be for a short time.'

Mrs Hatty looked offended. 'You're taking advantage of my good nature, Miss Annabel.'

'I will pay for her, of course.'

'She looks well able to pay for a room at the County,' Mrs Hatty said, regarding the expensively dressed young woman before her.

'Well, she can't,' Annabel said starkly. 'She doesn't have a penny.'

'Why is that no surprise to me? All right, then, I'll put up the foldaway bed in there but you won't have space to move.'

Millie was in tears by the time they got to Annabel's room and sat down on the single bed there.

'Sorry, Bel, to cause you all this trouble but it's all so horrible. This room . . . the maids at home have better.'

Annabel sat down on the bed and hugged her. 'It will be all right,' she said.

'I don't think it will. I don't think it ever will be all right again,' said Millie.

Annabel gave her sister her bed and she slept on the tiny folding-out bed and it was indeed as uncomfortable as she had suspected. Millie was too tired not to sleep and Annabel lay awake, listening to her sister breathing and wondering how things had ever got as bad as this. The room had been small enough with only her in it. Now there was hardly any room at all so she had nowhere to retreat to but she was glad that Millie was there. Whatever would Etta think now that her true daughter had fled also? How could she have been so unkind to Millie? Did she not think what might happen or did she imagine that Millie's sense of loyalty would carry them through?

The following morning, however, Millie, dressed as plainly as she knew how in a dress so pretty that the other people in the dining room stared, looked at the bacon and egg on her plate and asked if she could have some plain bread and jam.

'Eat it,' Annabel advised, 'you'll offend Mrs Hatty and then how will we manage? And besides I'm paying for it. We won't be having anything other than a sandwich for lunch, I have work to do.'

'It's a horrid place, I don't understand what anyone says and I'm not used to eating so early.'

'Well, get used to it. I have to be at the office in half an hour.'

'But it's Sunday. Aren't we going to church?'

'Ned wants us there. They're trying the new machines today to see how they work.'

'And what am I meant to do?'

In the end she took Millie with her though she wasn't quite sure what Millie would do there all day.

The noise from the new machinery at the back was comforting. Ned went through into the print shop and soon returned and put before them the new front page which he and Bert had been devising. It looked quite different.

'We've been working on it for a while, headlines over two columns, more space between the lines of type so that it's easier to read, adverts which don't rule the page, more news on the front. What do you think?'

'I think it looks wonderful,' Annabel said, studying it carefully, 'very professional.'

'We have the new Linotype machines. The other paper doesn't,' he said with some pride.

'Will it mean people buy more copies of our newspaper, then?'

'I don't know. I think there's room for both, there's nothing wrong with competition, giving people a choice but I want to be ahead with what I can.'

Annabel thought for a few moments and then she said, 'Do you think we should do other things too?'

'What do you mean?'

'Well, you've got nothing in the paper to interest women in particular and nothing for children either. If you had part of a page for children and articles which were especially about women's concerns—'

'That's brilliant.' Ned beamed at her.

'I can think of all kinds. We could have cookery—'

'You've never cooked,' Millie pointed out.

'I could ask Mrs Hatty. She does lots of cooking and must have no end of tips for people cooking for big families and we could have gardening too and connect them up so that people would know what to do with a glut of tomatoes or potatoes or such.'

'Lots of the pitmen have allotments,' Ned said.

'The children's space could have jokes and puzzles and even stories.'

That afternoon Annabel and Millie went back to the Garden House because she knew Mrs Hatty was least busy in the afternoons at about five o'clock and she seemed taken with the idea of Cookery Corner as Annabel had decided they should call it and they sat around in the kitchen by the fire and drank tea and made notes and Mrs Hatty got very enthusiastic and thought they should have articles about knitting and embroidery and cushion-making and flower-arranging and Mrs Hatty knew recipes for treacle tart, carrot soup and black pudding.

When Mrs Hatty went off to open the bar for the evening Millie said, 'You seem to have got very caught up in things here.'

'It isn't that, it's just that I need to keep myself.' She didn't add 'and you too now'. 'I was lucky to get the job at the newspaper.'

'I thought you would discover what had happened to your mother and then come back to London.'

'How can I ever come back?'

Millie didn't answer that.

'And besides, I haven't managed to discover very much at all. I don't know what happened to her. It seems unlikely that she drowned but the family that she had think that she did and know nothing about her.'

'I don't see where it would get you if you did know. I don't understand what you're doing here living among working people. You have nothing in common with them and Ned Fleming is unmannerly, uncouth. How can you stand it?'

It was just because he had not admired her, Annabel thought, and was about to defend Ned, saying that his father was rich and owned pits like they did and then realized that it was not the same. Ned was not really a gentleman, he lived in some little terraced house near the hospital and worked in his grubby office every day.

That night when they got back it was late. She had had to write up the review of *The Tempest* and a good many other things and Millie had been bored and had wandered about the room sighing all the evening which made things even more difficult and Annabel could hardly bear the thought of the put-up bed and another night listening to Millie's soft breathing but she had only just got back and they were in the dining room thinking about dinner when Mrs Hatty came in and said, 'There's a man wanting to see you, Miss Annabel.'

Annabel gazed at her. 'What kind of a man?'

'How should I know? He asked for you special in the bar.'

'Can't he come back after we eat?' asked Millie, who was hungry, but Annabel had already got up and gone through into the hall. It was dimly lit in there and noisy since the doors to the bar and the snug which was the other little room where men tended to take their lady friends or sit if they wanted to have private conversation were both open and at the far end of the hall stood a tall medium-set man. She recognized something about him in the gloom but she was not sure what. He was wearing a shabby suit and holding his hat in his hands. When she got nearer she realized that it was Bert.

She stopped and then he opened the outside door and since she knew they could not hear one another inside she followed him out into the cool air which was not as cold as it had been recently.

'Is there something the matter?' Suddenly she was assailed by the idea that something had happened to Ned and her heart beat hard.

'No, no,' he said, 'at least not like you mean. I just wanted to have a word with you, quiet like, you know.'

She didn't know but she didn't like to say. Bert hovered. That was the only word for it, he didn't speak for a long time and he looked up the road and down the road and then he said, 'They used to have public hangings here.'

She looked past him up at St Leonards which was what the area around there was called. She shuddered.

'I knew your mother,' he said when she had begun to think he was not going to say anything at all.

She was amazed. She had not realized she had spoken about her mother in front of him. Perhaps Ned had told him, perhaps he had thought that Bert might be able to help.

'Sarah.' He looked down as though getting to here had taken a lot of doing. 'I thought she was going to marry me but when your father came along she changed her mind.'

Nobody spoke and the cool silence seemed to go on and on.

'I didn't want to say anything, I didn't see that I could help but . . . you look exactly like her.'

'I always thought I looked like my father.'

'Sarah was bonny like you though different colouring and . . . and wilful. It hurts me to see you and yet I want to be reminded of her.'

'Tell me about it.'

Bert hesitated and looked down the road before he began speaking.

'We'd been going together for a while. Her father wasn't very keen because I'm not chapel, you see, and they were very religious that way but I think he liked that I was steady. I had a good job, I worked for the *Echo* then. But when she met Fergus Seaton it was like she became another person and she didn't want anything more to do with me. She thought he could give her everything. He did in a way.' Bert laughed harshly. 'I wanted to kill him but it was no use. I could see how she felt about him.'

'Do you know what happened to her?'

'No.'

'The woman they pulled out the river wasn't her?'

'Not as far as I know.'

'Did you know about me?'

'Yes.' Bert turned away almost completely. 'That's what I'm doing here. I wanted to tell you but I was too ashamed. I knew she was expecting, I knew where she'd gone and I was so angry. I could have helped, I could have married her then and everything would have been all right but my pride wouldn't let me. I was a very proud lad then. Well, I've regretted it since every day. I let her go.

'When her parents wouldn't have her in the house because of her wild ways I didn't stop her from going down to Paradise Lane. I knew she was there, I knew she had no money and that she was having a bairn and I was too . . .' Bert stopped and took several deep breaths. 'I was too hard.

'When I saw you I couldn't believe it, I thought she'd been born again. I could have been your dad, I could have brought you up as mine and had her to wife and everything would have been all right. She disappeared, she went from me and he took you away. I married and it wasn't a good marriage. I was married all these years to a lass I didn't care for and because I didn't care for her she learned to hate me and there was no bairn. I was glad when she died last year, I really was. I thought I had my freedom at last but that isn't freedom, it's just another form of hell and then I saw you.' He stopped again and she waited but this time it was for good and there were harsh sobs coming from him, his hand up to his face.

Annabel was so astonished that she couldn't think of anything to say and was left to go to Bert and put her arms around him. That made the storm worse before it subsided.

'You won't tell anybody,' he said, 'I don't want them to know what kind of a man I am.'

'You're a lovely man,' she said and she tried to persuade him to come into the hotel but Bert wouldn't. He moved away from her embrace as gently as he could and strode off down the pavement back toward the town like someone trying to shake off the past.

Nine

She wished that she could have told Millie because having to come back and make explanations was difficult. She said that it had been Bert, she said that it was about work and Millie had to be content with that but she could soon see that Millie was unhappy. She had not been happy at home and had thought that coming here would help but Annabel could tell that it was just as bad though in a different way. She was not used to a life like this and Annabel did not think that she would grow used to it but it seemed impossible for her to go back home.

Annabel could not put Bert from her mind and could not help thinking of what it would have been like being brought up here with parents who loved her and she understood that Bert realized he could have saved her mother from whatever fate had befallen her and it seemed to her when she spent a second sleepless night that he was right, he could have had a relatively happy life, but would he have been happy with a woman who was in love with another man?

She could not imagine any woman in love with the kind of man her father was but he must have been handsome when he was young, tall and slender and dark a bit like Ned, only a gentleman, well born and rich with every possible benefit that he could have and somewhere in that upbringing he had been taught to disrespect women and he had caused the breakdown of whatever feeling there was between Bert and her mother but perhaps the feeling was not so strong on her mother's side.

It could not have been if her mother had been so eager to spend time with her father and then she tried to see it from her mother's point of view, a man educated, rich, good looking, powerful. What woman from a poor background would not have been flattered by his attention and foolish enough to believe that he was honest in his dealings with her? Annabel hated her father now, she looked back and saw him falling down the stairs and was glad and then she was horrified that she could harbour such feelings for anyone.

The following day she left Millie sleeping and went in early and into the back because Ned had not yet arrived and in the back she found Bert alone. No doubt he too had had a sleepless night. He must have heard her but he didn't turn around. She went up behind him and then to the side of him and she stood on tiptoe and kissed his cheek. The cheek immediately flushed and he turned a haggard face to her. She found that she was smiling.

'I'm so glad I found you,' she said, 'it was worth coming all this way for that.'

Bert shook his head.

'Oh, don't let's do that what might have been thing. I think you're a lovely man, Bert, and I'm going to have you for my dad now.'

Bert looked down.

'Don't you see, you're my first real root here.'

And that was when he laughed. 'I've been called a lot of things in my time but "root" isn't one of them,' he said.

'It's a lovely word,' she said and he said:

'You'll make a fine reporter in time.'

She went into the front again just as Ned arrived. It was one of those spring days which starts out misty and when the mist lifts as it was doing now the sky is blue and the sunshine bathes the streets.

'What have you done with Little Miss London?'

Annabel was stung at the term. 'Don't you like my sister? Most men think she's beautiful.'

'She's very beautiful,' he said.

'I'm surprised you noticed.' And then she realized he hadn't answered the question.

He went into the back ostensibly to see Bert but really to get out of the way.

Millie turned up within the hour and said nothing about being left or that she had had to breakfast alone. She was wearing a very plain dress in grey in faded material which Annabel didn't recognize.

'Where did you get that?'

'Mrs Hatty gave it to me. She said I couldn't keep coming here looking like a fashion plate.' Millie pulled a face. 'Isn't it hideous?'

'It's awful,' Annabel said and they laughed.

*

That afternoon Ned was so busy he didn't speak and he was looking for a front-page lead and didn't have one and it was vital that he should have an important story to carry the paper forward so he was just in the middle of deciding which story should make the lead and trying not to wish disaster on the world so that he could report it when they heard a shrill noise outside. Annabel had no idea what it was but it was obviously important because Ned immediately looked up and the men came in from the back and as she looked uncomprehendingly at him he told her.

'It's the pit siren.'

He ran outside but all he could see was that various people were hurrying past and he came back in for his jacket and Annabel said, 'Do you want me to come with you?'

He looked at her. 'Would you?'

She snatched up her coat and they made their way down across Elvet Bridge and up towards the pit which lay on the edge of the town. Annabel had not been anywhere near until then. Her uncle and aunt had kept her well away when she had lived at Heath Houses. She was astonished at the size of the pit wheel high in the sky, the crowd which gathered and most of all how the men in general came across to Ned and asked him, 'Where's your father?'

'Is the old man coming down, then?'

'Is Mr Fleming here yet?' and that was when she realized that this pit was one which his father owned. She hadn't known, she hadn't thought about it.

And Ned, probably unlike any other newspaper reporter,

went into professional pit mode, asking curtly whether they knew what had happened and whether the agent was there and they said, no he was at the Ruby Pit at Heath Houses that morning and while she watched, numb, he turned and said to her, 'Take notes.'

'What? Why, where are you going?'

'I'm going down to see what can be done. The roof's fallen in. Men are trapped down there.'

Off he went with several others to do she wasn't sure what and didn't like to ask. She stood there and the sentence went round and round in her head. He hadn't said 'they have men trapped' or even 'we have men trapped' but as though it was his total responsibility. The spring sunshine which was warming the whole scene suddenly seemed like an insult somehow and the women who stood about waiting, she realized, had a husband, a brother or a father beneath the surface.

It seemed so rude to record it but no, she thought, this was what mattered to the mining community, of course it was, it was their first concern, their whole lives and so she went back a little to the edge of the crowd, where nobody might feel offended, and there she wrote swiftly about the day and the noise of the siren and how the sunshiny afternoon had turned into potential disaster.

There was eventually an arrival of some kind, she could see by the way the women turned and a tall well-dressed middle-aged man was among them and she could hear his reassuring words in what to her when she had arrived in Durham was almost incomprehensible language. She had learned to understand it and she could tell that it was to him like her a second language and when she saw him she understood.

This was Ned's father, the man who had turned him from his home, and he was nothing like she had thought. He didn't look like any kind of monster and she, like all the other people there, looked to him and he did as Ned had done, he went down the mine immediately with another man she heard spoken of as 'doctor' and she felt better for him being there, she thought, this man knows what he's doing.

The afternoon gave way to a cold sharp evening but nobody went home. The most stupid part of all was that for the first time she understood why her father had wanted to be here. She could understand what he had been doing here, she knew that however much he cared for the frivolities of life perhaps he had seen something here of importance and for the first time she could see how anybody would want to stay.

One young woman about the same age as she was stood there with a baby cradled in her arms for the whole time, a closed expression on her face, and people came out of the nearby houses with sandwiches and tea though Annabel could not eat for the growing frustration she felt as nothing happened and then there was sudden movement beyond the crowd and three men came up, and there was a cheer and women went forward to claim them.

She looked in vain for Ned. The men were unhurt and she was pleased and there were a few minutes of thankfulness but she knew from general comments in the crowd that there were more men down there and that the rescue party were busy trying to move the roof fall and that it might take more time to clear it.

'Davy?'

Ned had lost all sense of time. The roof fall was not as bad as some had been and there were several men stuck behind it but they could be heard, they were shouting, they did not seem hurt. It took some time to shift it, that kind of thing always took longer than you thought it would because you were so impatient, he thought, wanting to get them out before the roof should come in any more, wanting to get them clear and up to the surface so that the waiting families would not have to suffer any longer than necessary and so he was relieved when finally they had broken through and after that things seemed to move faster and then there was sufficient space for the men to crawl through to safety.

He was glad to hear their relieved tones, only to be told that there was another fall beyond it, not a big one but they feared for two unaccounted men, one was Davy Smith, his childhood friend, and the other was an older man called Matthew Simpson so they had to begin again, firstly more rock had to be cleared and then they had to burrow still further.

It seemed to take forever and he was so afraid and he knew that the men helping were afraid. His father's voice was still encouraging now but it held a note of tiredness and the doctor who had been dispatched to the surface to see that the rescued men did not need to go to hospital but their wounds tended on the spot, came back down and the time went on and on and he was afraid and they went on in silence, each of them fearful of what they would find.

Being amongst the slenderest of them Ned crawled through the hole they had made and there he found the older man when he had the light. There was rock over him, he was pinned but he was not dead, and when the rock was removed and he was freed Ned did not think he was even badly hurt and his heart leapt. He was in pain, Ned thought, he could have broken his leg and his arm, the doctor crawled through as the hole was made bigger but as Ned went on he could see the other man by lamplight and he was afraid because this man was not moving. He got down and as he did so the other rescuers came through, and they moved the heavy rocks away from the young man's body.

It was as he had feared, it was Davy Smith. He had been pretending to himself all this while that it would not be, that it could not be, which was nonsense because Davy was the only man not found and then Ned got down even nearer and said his name. 'Davy?'

The young man looked up at him, the features tortured with pain by the dim light. He closed his eyes in acknowledgement of it and then opened them again and he focused and recognized Ned.

'Is this what it teks to get thoo down here?' he asked in a hoarse, forced voice. Then there was a moment or two before he said, 'Hold us, man.'

'I don't want to hurt you.'

'Ah, Ned, man, we both know I'm not going no place except to me maker. Hold us, I don't want to die on me own.'

The other men lifted him as carefully as they could. The pain made him close his eyes again. In Ned's arms Davy's face was brought close to his own so that hopefully Davy could see him. All Davy could manage was, 'Tell her I love her and the bairns. Tell her there was never nobody else.'

Ned tried to save his anger for later but it was hard. How could Davy die down there when there were dozens of hard-drinking, hard-living lads who had betrayed every woman they had ever met, and even married ones who left the wife and bairns at home and went drinking until they were seatless every night and there was nothing left with which to feed their families because it was all too hard.

Ned knew the very second that Davy died but he went on holding him and then gradually became conscious of his father saying very gently, 'He's gone, Ned, let go of him,' but somehow he couldn't, he had forgotten how as though his holding on would bring Davy back.

'Ned,' his father prompted and he knew what his father did not say. They needed to get out in case the roof came in further. In the days to come it would be investigated but now they had to get clear.

When they got back to the surface his father looked him over for damage.

'You're hurt, boy,' he said.

'No, I'm not.'

The doctor took him aside and into the pit office.

'It's just cuts and bruises,' Ned insisted.

'I think you're right but you should come to the hospital to be looked at.'

Ned refused. The doctor scanned him carefully. 'If it turns out to be more you come straight to me, do you hear? And take it slowly for a day or two.'

Early evening and still people waited and a sharp frost had descended. Millie arrived and her face was white. Annabel was so glad to see her that she wanted to cry. Millie wore a fur coat, it was the only coat she had any more and Annabel didn't think anybody noticed how she stood out from the crowd or cared. Annabel hugged her. The coat smelled of Millie's perfume and somehow when she closed her eyes they were back in London and everything was all right, only, she thought now, nothing had ever been all right, her father had never cared for her and neither had Etta so in a way she was more right here than she had been there and it was a strange discovery that here in the midst of possible disaster she felt at home as she had never done before and Millie had been practical and brought food and she might look out of place but her face was grave and composed.

A little while longer and then the cage came up again and they carried someone out and her heart sank all the way to the cold hard ground beneath her feet and she heard a pitiful cry and then sobbing. The ambulance which was standing by came and took away two men, one hurt and one not moving, and

Annabel couldn't see what was happening and her hand, when she tried to write, was shaking and then the crowd began to disperse and when it finally cleared she could see Ned and his father standing together at the front.

They looked so alike and were talking rapidly in low voices. There were other men with them and it was so very subdued that she wished she wasn't there and as the crowd melted there was nobody left but herself and Millie and the little huddle of men. She waited and finally they broke away from one another.

They went off in different directions, Ned's father too and there was a moment when Ned stood there by himself and then he turned wearily and came towards her. He was filthy, covered in coal dust. What had been a good though old suit was torn at his knees and there was blood and his hands were bleeding too and his cheek where she could see only his dark and guarded eyes.

He didn't say anything, they just walked, his tiredness showed in his gait. They went back to the office. She wanted to say that he should go home but she couldn't suggest it, she could see. When they got back to the office all he said was, 'Will you write your piece?'

'What?'

'It has to be something personal and good because the dailies were there and they will have the immediate story so it has to be something which the people can see from their point of view, something sympathetic,' and then he sat down and began writing swiftly.

She couldn't do anything for several minutes and then she

began to write and the words flowed because what she put down was what she had felt, and what she had seen as a newcomer to such things and the detail was rich. She didn't need the notes she had made, she remembered it all so clearly and it was the woman's point of view.

Bert took Millie back to Mrs Hatty's but Annabel stayed on until she thought she had finished and until Ned looked up and then she gave the copy to him and he read it.

'It's really good,' he said. 'I don't think such a thing has ever been in any newspaper before.'

Annabel was astonished and pleased at how straightforwardly he said it. Finally he said that he thought they ought to go home.

'Would you like me to come with you?' she offered.

He tried to smile but he shook his head. 'It isn't fitting,' he said.

'Maybe you should go home to your father.'

'I cannot. He doesn't want me there.'

'After today—'

'No.'

'Then I'm coming with you,' she said with new authority and she could see that he was too tired to argue.

She didn't know that part of the city, all she knew was that it was called Red Hills and was the area her family came from. Her only direct experience of it had been when she had gone on the first day to try and find her family and discovered the dirty little house where Billy and Mrs Reid lived. She had passed by on her way to the Garden House Hotel every day but never looked over, not even glanced beyond the huge viaduct which dominated the area.

The viaduct split the area with the neat terrace of Waddington Street and the Presbyterian chapel on one side and Sutton Street and others across the road and next to the viaduct. A very steep hill cut up through the centre towards Crossgate at the top and further over the road twisted and went out into woodland beyond the town.

He led the way to halfway down Sutton Street and opened the door. It was so much the same as Mrs Reid's had been and yet it was quite different. It was clean for one thing and orderly and she thought that she should not have been surprised because that was what Ned was like and what made him such a good newspaperman, he liked order, it was a way of life to him.

The rooms were neat and there was good furniture in them, not the kind of place anybody would sit comfortably she thought in slight affection, there was an oak desk in the sitting room what they called here the front room and as he went in and lit the lamp she could see neat piles of papers, a lot of books and boxes. The house was cold but he put a match to the fire which was laid ready to be lit and it instantly took as though the paper and sticks were dry and the coal was good which it would be, his own coal. The little fireplace was small and tiled and had a tiny tiled hearth and a white surround and the room was instantly pulled into life. There were two chairs which you could sit on as well as a chair at the desk and there was a rug which covered most of the floor.

'Can I go and find you something to eat?' she said.

'I'm not hungry.'

'I can go if you want to be by yourself,' and that was when he got hold of her and pulled her into his arms.

She was amazed. Nobody had done such a thing before. Her closeness with Tom had been gentle and always with the idea of kissing in mind but this was nothing like that, it was the sort of thing you would do to family, he pulled her so close that she could hardly breathe and then he put his face into her shoulder.

She knew that she should have drawn back but she also knew that if she did so he would never reach for her again and that he wanted her there for comfort because the day had been too hard. She wrapped both arms around him so that he could feel he was being squeezed against her and then he seemed to realize what he was doing and he said, in embarrassed tones, 'God, I'm sorry,' and tried to pull away and she hung on to him, which was what he really wanted her to do she thought and she said.

'You knew the man who died?'

'We were friends. I know them all. I worked there, on and off from being a boy. He was not much older than me and he had a wife and two little boys. There are better places for men to die,' and he choked. 'I should have been there.'

'You were doing what you were supposed to be doing,' she said. 'Your father runs the pits, that's what you said, that he was perfectly capable. You're the newspaper man, remember?'

He drew away, nodded. 'They think the other man might be all right. Do you want some tea?'

'I'll do it.'

He didn't argue. She went through and could not help exploring the little house when it was lit and she liked it. There was a back room, the dining room and it too had a lovely little fireplace which she wished she could light, it was cold in there, and then the kitchen and a black range and this she lit too and put the kettle above it.

There was a big white sink and various cupboards and she thought of these things as she never had before in a domestic way, what it would be like to come back there and make a meal, and how you could sit in armchairs around the fire and listen to the sounds of the little city, people's footsteps going by and maybe in summer children playing in the street and the ever-present noise that the trains made overhead. Ned was probably right, there were better places to die than down a pit but she was beginning to think that there might not be better places to live than here.

When there was hot water she made tea and when the tea was drunk and he was more calm she poured water for him to wash, to bathe away the coal dust, the blood and the cares of the day and at his request she went upstairs to find clean clothes for him. She lingered up there, she was unused to people undressing and washing anywhere near her and wanted to leave him to it. In such a small house, she thought, you would have to get used to such things but she was not ready for that.

He wasn't thinking, he was in shock because the young pitman had died, but she must try to maintain some decorum so she went into the bedroom which was being used and where there was a wardrobe and a dressing table and a chest of drawers. It was so very personal that she was quite embarrassed even here because it could not have been anybody else's room.

He had books on the bedside tables and even on the floor and was using the dressing table as a desk and she wanted to smile. Did he have to make even his bedroom look like the office? She found a great pile of shirts on the bed, and then she heard him call and went back downstairs.

'Did you find one?'

'You obviously have dozens of shirts. Will it do?' This to hide her discomfort. She was not used to half-clad men but she was only uncomfortable for a few seconds. His young smooth body was covered in cuts and bruises.

'What's this?' she said, scanning him.

'Some of it fell on me.'

'You didn't say.'

'It's nothing to worry about. I'm all right.' He took the shirt from her and put it on and began to button it and he looked closely at what he was doing and he said, 'I'm sorry, I know this is bad form and not what you're used to but I needed somebody here just for a little while and I needed help. I do hope you don't mind.'

'You should have let me—'

'No.' He smiled a little. 'I'm already way beyond decent manners here—'

'But if you're hurt—'

'I'm not. Really I'm not. The doctor took a look at me at the scene and he said I could go home, it's just that I had nobody to go home to and I wanted company and somebody to talk to. I'll find a jacket and take you back to the hotel.'

'I don't think you should.'

'It's not a bad night now and the walk and the fresh air will help.'

He was right, she thought when they got halfway up the long hill which led up to the Garden House, it was a cold night even though it was spring, the sky was full of stars and there were lights on in the houses; there was something about it which was a sort of going-on of things and then she remembered the young miner and his family.

'Who will take care of the widow and her children?'

'My father and the union.'

'Is that usual?

'In some places it is. In some places the blame would be placed on him and his family would get little or as little as the owner could give, perhaps nothing so the union would have to pay it all, especially if nothing could be proved.'

'And was it his fault?'

'I don't know. I shouldn't think so, he was a very good miner. A roof fall can be caused by a number of things.'

'Will your father look into it?'

'Yes, but only to determine whether there was weakness in the pit props or in the roof itself or for some other cause like that.'

'He isn't a monster, then?'

'It depends how you look at it. He's seen as a fair master yet he lives in luxury and the miners toil and risk their lives. He's better than most, but that isn't saying much.'

'Would you be better?'

'I don't know. Possibly not. Sometimes accidents are just that, there isn't always somebody to blame.'

When they reached the outside of the hotel Annabel suddenly realized how tired she was. 'I feel as if I ought to walk you back now,' she said and that made him smile.

'Thanks for everything you did. Don't come in early in the morning, there's no need,' and he wished her goodnight.

She watched him walk away down the long winding hill, back towards his house and she thought of the little house and his lean bruised and cut body and of how the widow would be sitting over the fire without her husband or perhaps trying to get her children to sleep. Annabel hoped somebody was there with her, a mother or a sister.

She thought of her own sister then and was glad to see, when she went into the hall, that Millie had been watching for her and Mrs Hatty came through and fussed and sat her down to a big bowl of broth and ham and pease-pudding sandwiches and a large cup of tea. After that Annabel was thankful to climb into the put-up bed. It no longer felt lumpy, it felt like bliss just to lie down and let the day get away from her.

Ten

It was a long time since Ned had been down among the pit rows beyond St Oswald's Church in the part of the town where the pit was. He had not noticed them the day before after the pit siren had gone and he and Annabel had hurried there. He thought that a sadness sat among these long lines of houses which his grandfather had had built many years ago. They were not bad houses, owners had built much worse and got away with it, these were solid and in squares with great big greens in the middle of them so that there was space for the children to play and the washing to be hung out if anybody so desired and even for the occasional goat to be tethered.

He remembered each house, each occupant. He remembered being a child and playing football here in the holidays even after his father had sent him away to school. He had wanted to maintain his friendships and the other lads accepted him, maybe at first because they had to but after that because he was essentially one of them such as his father had not been. And maybe because his father had not been he encouraged Ned.

He walked up to the third gate in a particular row and up the back yard. The door was open. Most back doors were kept open because the fire was on in the kitchen winter and summer alike for hot water and cooking so when the weather was at all good the little houses would be stifling if the doors were kept shut.

There was silence from inside. He did not knock. He was not even sure whether he should be here and then he saw Hannah standing alone in the kitchen. He had not expected that, hadn't been sure what he would say if her mother was there or her sister. The house was silent as though no children lived there. She looked small, beaten. And then she sensed his presence and looked at where he stood in the entrance and he felt obliged to say, 'The door was ajar.'

'Aye,' she said, 'even for the likes of you,' and she almost smiled and then she began to cry.

He went over and got hold of her and she came into his arms and hid her face against his shoulder. He wanted to say to her his friend's last words but he found it impossible and he didn't think he had to say it, she knew. He didn't want to distress her any further. Maybe in the future she would need to hear it but not now.

'What was it? What did it?'

'I don't know.'

'It wasn't neglect, your dad's not like that, for all he's a bastard.' She stood back blocking the tears with her fingers.

He had always liked her profane mouth. Her mother had brought her up strict Presbyterian so it was somehow inevitable she should swear so well.

'If he doesn't—'

'He's already been over. He always liked Davy.'

It was true. His father had wanted Davy to go to the grammar school, would have paid for the uniform, encouraged him to read and try to do well at school but Davy wasn't like that. He came from a proud family, pitmen through and through. He wanted to work with his dad and his uncle and his cousins, he wanted the routine, to be a part of the village pit life and everything which made it what it was. Ned didn't blame him for that. Grammar-school boys moved away and never really belonged anywhere, they had pit accents and working-class parents but they were no longer accepted in the village. He knew what that was like, how hard it was to make yourself as other people were, to fit anywhere. To fit nowhere was the hardest thing of all.

He could remember the halcyon days, playing football with Davy and the other lads when he was little and he could remember how Hannah had always loved Davy. What would she do now? He had his answer when the footsteps sounded in the yard and her mother and sister stepped into the house, each with a child in her arms. They said nothing to him and he felt awkward. He nodded and left.

The pit accident changed things, Annabel knew. She saw Ned differently now. Before he had been an ambitious young man with an ability to make the newspaper work, at least she thought he did, she had had faith in him but she had not seen him in connection with the whole town. He was a part of things here and in some ways she envied that and wanted it for herself and then she found Bert coming in and talking to her and he began to look happy as he had not before and sometimes when Ned was not there they would sit over a cup of tea and he would tell her things about her mother, what she liked to do, what she had liked to eat, simple things which mattered more and more. She felt near to her mother now as she had not previously done.

The week of the pit accident the newspaper sold out and Ned was half pleased and half upset, she thought, but people stopped her in the street in the days that followed and told her what a clever lass she was and how her view of things had changed the way that they looked at it and how she had brought the awful scene home to them such as had not happened before and even some of the pitmen stopped her and told her that the woman's touch made the whole thing seem quite different and that such things should be given an importance and she had done that and she had made the whole thing come home to them. Those were one man's exact words, that the whole thing had come home to him, and in spite of the horrors of that day she was glad of his words and she was beginning to feel that coming here had been worthwhile and that she might make the kind of reporter that she was beginning to want to be.

Ned had thanked her for her report and told her how good it was but she was hungry to hear praise and Bert did that for her. He knew so much about these things and he had said many good things to her about her report and she was glad of that.

Ned was very quiet in the days which followed and seemed to get no pleasure from anything. She wished he would go and see his father, she thought it might help but she didn't dare to suggest it since his closed face did not encourage frankness.

The spring was here properly now and at night in the small city if she lay with the windows open she could hear the young lambs crying in the fields. The days were bright and cold with the odd snow flurry and there were celandines and daisies and primroses everywhere and some of the bank sides were blue with forget-me-nots.

Millie came with her to work and though she would not make a reporter she was very good when people came in to place advertisements. She would chat in her polite London voice. It was quite funny, Annabel thought, that the advertising had increased and it was almost solely because Millie was the person at the front desk now and the men seemed to love her pretty face and strange accent.

She sometimes found them difficult to understand, she said to Annabel, but she was learning and fast and in the late evenings when they were lying in bed she would imitate one or another of them with comic effect and tell funny stories and she and Annabel would giggle.

The women approved of her too and when they came in with the Mothers' Union or other group reports or to let the world know that they had a grandchild they would tell her that they admired her manners and Annabel realized that the people liked to see how she and her sister had gone to work here and made what they could of their circumstances.

It very soon got sociable in the front office which Annabel was not sure it usually did in such places because people began to use it as a meeting place and it was not long before there were a couple of tables and some chairs and Millie would make tea. It should have interrupted business but somehow it did not and the whole place began to thrive and buzz and she kept her ears open for gossip and learned a good many things before anybody else.

Bert was given to reading their rival newspaper, the *Echo*, and one day in late spring he was sitting in the back, the newspaper having just arrived, and he was having tea. For once it was quiet because it was late afternoon and most people had gone home for their tea. Annabel was alone in the front office, Millie having gone out to see about an advertisement for a new shop which was opening at the bottom end of Gilesgate. She heard Bert let go of his breath and swear, not once but several times before he realized where he was and silenced himself.

Bert never did such things. She left the report she had been writing of a production by a local amateur-dramatic club and went through. He sat there in the gloom with the newspaper in front of him and a barely touched cup of tea beside him.

'What is it?' she said.

'Nothing,' Bert said roughly and he folded the newspaper.

'But it must be. You don't get upset over nothing.'

'I'm not upset. I'm just ... well ... surprised and ... we've had enough upset and he won't like it.'

Ned was always 'he' to Bert, like other people had God, Bert had Ned.

'What won't he like?'

Bert hesitated and then he opened the paper again and let her look. She couldn't see anything other than a badly written report of a recent break-in at the carpet factory.

'The facts aren't right,' she said.

The only other story of any significance if it had was that the proprietor Mr Pattison was apparently getting married.

'I thought he was married.'

'His wife died. He has a couple of kiddies,' Bert said. 'It's not that. It's who he's marrying.'

'Miss Jane Baker,' Annabel read. 'Who is she?'

'She's the only child of Ernest Baker, who is a prosperous shipyard owner and until he took over this place he was going to marry her.'

It took a few moments for Annabel to understand what he meant. Ned was going to marry this woman?

'Oh, you should see her. Pretty as a picture. They were engaged, wedding was all planned and then she threw him over because he wanted to make this right. She thought he was going to be like her father and build ships but he wouldn't have it.'

The words 'pretty as a picture' echoed and went on echoing in Annabel's mind. It was not just that Ned had been going to get married that she had not expected. After all he was quite young but then Tom was not much older. But also that she knew nothing about this.

Why should she have known? How could you feel left out about something which had happened before you knew the person concerned? But she did. She felt empty about the whole thing which was strange somehow as though she didn't know who Ned was, like there were aspects of his life which were not as she had thought.

She felt shocked, she could not get used to the idea, and yet

Bert was sitting there looking at her and he should not be able to read what she was thinking so she stuttered into language to hide her from her thoughts and his ideas.

'No, he's very stubborn. So he lost her as well as his home and his father's affection?' she managed as though mildly interested and nothing else.

'That's right.' Bert sighed. 'There's no hoping he isn't going to see it. He reads every word to make sure they've got nothing we should have had.'

She went back to her desk and in trying to accustom herself to seeing Ned as she had not thought of him before she found that she was not working and no matter how hard she tried to concentrate she couldn't put anything down on paper which would have been suitable for print. Bert would have had a fit if he had seen what she was producing.

Millie went back to the hotel in the early evening but Annabel stayed, making an excuse that she would come along later. She watched for signs that Ned had read the *Echo* and she thought about him differently. She did not realize that Ned was like she was, that he had lost the person he wanted to marry, the person he had thought he would spend the rest of his life with.

When she could think of nothing else that it was absolutely necessary she did and she was tired, she went into the back and the newspaper was folded on his desk and he was working.

'What are you doing tonight?' Often he stayed and worked or went out to various functions to make reports.

'Nothing much.'

'Why don't you come up to the hotel and have a meal with us?'

'Thanks, but I'm busy.'

He didn't even notice that he had just said he wasn't doing anything much, she thought patiently.

'I could come back with you and make you something to eat.'

He looked up at that. 'You, cook?'

'I might.'

'When did you ever?'

'Well, never actually but . . .'

'What is it?' he said and he looked straight at her so she thought she might as well say.

'Bert told me about Jane Baker.'

'Oh.' He didn't look at her and she was not accustomed to seeing him like this, as though he had just lost something precious. Had he loved this girl very much? He must have done, he would hardly have been marrying her otherwise.

'I do understand.' She hadn't meant to say that, people were always saying such things when they didn't but for once she did, she knew exactly what he was going through and he saw the truth in her words because she looked directly at him as she spoke and he looked hopefully back at her.

'How?'

She hesitated and then she plunged. She must tell him, having gone that far, what she had experienced. Whether it would help him she didn't know. It might help her in time to know that he had been through what appeared to be the same thing.

'I was going to be married and when he found out that I wasn't who I had thought I was it all fell through.'

There was silence. There was never silence in their offices, always the sound of machinery or the noise of people talking and working and moving around and the cries from the street of other people's business but there was nothing here.

'He gave you up for that?' Ned said eventually.

'It wouldn't have worked. His family were terribly important. They owned half of Gloucestershire.'

For some reason that made him smile. 'Gloucestershire?'

'Well, it could have been Lincolnshire,' she said on purpose so that he would smile again. 'They had lots of money and a huge house and all the right connections.'

'Did your family have all the right connections too?'

'They certainly did.'

'Only you weren't one of them?'

'Half of me was. Unfortunately even that half wasn't legitimate and you know how important such things are. He bought me the world's biggest diamond for my finger and . . .' She knew that she was babbling but going on was easier than stopping somehow because she had the feeling that once she shut up she would burst into tears. 'And I had to give it back to him.'

'Shame,' Ned said.

'Yes, it was. It was a . . .' and then she couldn't manage any more and searched furiously through her head to think of something else to say so that she wouldn't cry here and disgrace herself but nothing came and she ran out of the office and into the front, breathing heavily to control the sobs. She hadn't thought of Tom in days.

She stood there until her breathing came under control again and then Ned was coming into the room, putting on his jacket and saying, 'I think you should come back to my house and cook. It should be a very interesting experience.'

'You have no idea,' she said.

In the end she didn't cook, they didn't get that far. They were going past the fish and chip shop and it was dark and cool and the smell was so good that they stopped there and got the fish and chips just as they were with salt and vinegar so that they could eat them going down the road but they still went to his house and he lit the fire in the sitting room. There were big boxes at the back of the room.

'What's all that stuff?'

'It's just papers and such. I meant to go through it and throw most of it out. It belonged to my uncle but I haven't had time to take a look at it, I'm not here long enough and I can't throw it out as it is just in case anything important is stuck in there.'

Somehow without anybody speaking again, they sat down by the fire and began going through the boxes. Most of it was papers to do with the house, receipts for furniture bought or private letters which she did not like to go through and so from the bottom of the box she opened what looked like a diary and closed it again and handed it to him and Ned stopped what he was doing and took it and opened it and he said, 'It's in his handwriting. It's some kind of journal. You'd think the last thing he would want was to write when he wasn't at the newspaper.' He flicked through the pages. 'It's all very dull, day-to-day stuff about the weather. You wouldn't think he was a newspaper man,' and then he stilled because he was holding up the book and a flower fell out and the book opened where there were two pieces of blotting paper as though Jasper had meant to dry it and then remove them and perhaps had forgotten.

It was a yellow flower. She thought it might have been a buttercup or a celandine, a common wayside wild flower not something anybody might have as a keepsake like a rose or an orchid or something special. Odd. And then Ned took the blotting paper from the pages and began to read.

'What is it?' she said, becoming impatient when he didn't say anything.

He didn't answer her for so long that she almost prompted him again and then he looked up from the page, only so far as though he didn't want to stop reading or didn't want to lift his eyes from what was obviously so fascinating.

'It's about her.'

'Who?'

'Sarah.'

For a second or two she still didn't understand.

'Sarah Reid.'

She was no further forward because her brain, not expecting it, did not take it in.

'What? But how can it be? You must have made a mistake,

Ned, it's impossible. It . . .' and then he began to read and she stopped.

She didn't hear the words and his voice trembled so she should not have been able to get past them to the images beyond but she did. Her mother had not drowned, that was the first thing. She had not died down there in the Wear.

And the next thing that came to mind was that she would not have to avert her eyes from the water any more because it had not taken away the person she should have been able to think of and see in a more positive light. Jasper had found her, Jasper had seen her and he had gone in after her and swum and rescued her and brought her out and he had thought she was half dead.

In the night, so dark, so long, he had carried the girl home. She had come here to this house, Annabel thought, shuddering. How did she not know, how could she not feel that her mother had been here? It felt as though it was meant to be, as though all this time she was meant to come here because her mother had been there and that somehow it was a connection between them. He had brought Sarah here and given her brandy and stripped off her wet things and wrapped her in a blanket and sat her by the fire and she had revived in the warmth but would not tell him anything.

She did not speak and he did not know who she was and when she finally told him what she had done he ran down to the little house in Paradise Lane to find the baby but the child had gone. Annabel tried to think of him attempting rescue and what a wonderful man he must have been to save her mother and then do his best to do the same for her but she had gone. Fergus had collected her, had found her somehow, and he had taken her to London. If he had been later she might never have had to leave.

He had had to look further but he had had to come back and tell her that the baby she had been so swift to leave behind had gone.

Ned stopped. Annabel stared and then glared at him.

'Go on.'

'There isn't any more.'

'That's ridiculous.' She snatched the book out of his hands and saw how the writing left off and that the blank pages went on. Nothing had been torn from the book but there was no more information. 'There must be more. Search in the other boxes. It can't stop there.'

They spent the next two hours going through box after box and when they had done it twice and nothing more was to be found he stopped her from starting again.

'There's nothing more to find,' he said. He said it again before she accepted it. 'I've gone through everything. These are all the papers. I've thrown nothing out and there are no private papers at the newspaper office so there's no point in you insisting on going back there and taking that apart or in the morning either.'

'It's awful.'

'It's better than thinking she drowned.'

'But what happened?'

'Take the diary. Perhaps there's a clue. Come on, it's very late and you should go back to the hotel. Millie will worry.'

There was nothing for her to do but agree. All the way up the long road towards the hotel she clutched the diary to her as though it had something more to give.

'I can't just leave it like this but I don't know what to do next.'

'We're both tired. We'll think of something more in the morning.'

'But what?'

'I don't know,' he said gently and she let go of her breath in a rush. He had had a bad day before they got to this.

'I'm sorry to go on about it,' she said.

'It's frustrating for you but we'll work it out.'

He turned to go and she called his name so that he turned back towards her.

'I'm sorry about Jane too.'

'Thinking back now it was never right. If she couldn't accept me as I really was and only as her father's lackey then it wouldn't have been a good marriage.'

She nodded and then they parted and she walked slowly into the hotel. Ned couldn't see that Jane's father had no son and had been counting on Ned taking over eventually. Perhaps he didn't want to see it or had he not cared sufficiently about Jane to give up his personal ambitions for her?

Millie had gone to bed but not to sleep and when Annabel got upstairs they lit the lamp and she sat down on Millie's bed and told her about the diary and they lay awake trying to think what they could possibly do next and when they couldn't think about it any more she told Millie about Ned and Jane. There was a short silence and then Millie said, 'Do you still think about Tom?'

. 'I hadn't thought about him in days until I heard about what had happened to Ned.'

'I can't imagine any woman marrying somebody like Ned,' Millie said, snuggling down in the darkness. 'He has no money and no real prospects. No wonder she gave him up. She could hardly disoblige her parents to that extent.'

'But she's marrying a man twenty years older than she is with two children.' Annabel shivered at the idea even though she was nicely warm in bed with plenty of blankets.

'He sounds repulsive. Old and fat. Imagine kissing somebody like that. Ugh.'

'What do you know about kissing?'

'Nothing but I'd rather die unkissed than marry an old man,' Millie said.

Silence settled but Annabel was glad that she had put the diary under her pillow, she could feel it there now, it felt so reassuring and stupid though it was it made her feel closer to her mother than she had felt before and now she had time to think the whole thing through without anybody around she was relieved and pleased that her mother had not drowned. She saw the woman in a whole new light. Yes, she had tried to end her life, because she was not acceptable as an unmarried woman and she would have left her baby because she could not see any way beyond her own foolishness or live with it. Jasper Fleming had rescued her.

That made Annabel feel closer to Ned and she realized that she did not think of him as her sister did. She thought he was enterprising and intelligent and he was also kind, he had been kind to her and to Millie for no reason. It was not as though he had, like many young men, fallen in love with her beautiful sister and he regarded her as a co-worker and she was glad of that, many men in a similar position would never have given her a job and she was learning to be good at it, she knew.

She lay there for a long time, listening to Millie breathing and glad they had found the diary. Her mother had not died in such a horrible way. She could not get used to the positive thought. If her mother had not died then she might have lived a long time. And then Annabel thought what had seemed impossible before then. Her mother could still be alive.

She tried not to get excited by the idea. If she had been alive then surely she would have got in touch years ago, tried to take her baby back. Annabel tried to think why she might not have done and could not. She would not have wanted Fergus to take the baby, not want her child brought up by people she didn't know, headed by a man who had treated her badly. Perhaps she even thought he might have not wanted the baby and given it away but then he would not have taken the child in the first place. Her head began to spin, her thoughts to make no sense.

As she fell asleep, very confused and worn out by the doings of the day, she could still feel the edges of the book beneath her pillows. It was in a way a bit like the story of the princess and the pea, the book was reassuringly there and although she was not a princess, sufficient had happened that day for her to be positive that something good would come now and she would believe that in the end she would find her mother and all would be well. There was a niggling thought in the back of her mind about why her mother had not come for her if she was a good person but it dissolved into sleep and all she was left with was the contentment of having got this far.

Ned didn't want to go home, he wanted to find companionship in some pub and get drunk. He had said things about Jane which he did not think. He did not really think they would have had a bad marriage. He wished he could brush off the feelings like that but he did not want Annabel to be concerned with such matters, she had enough to think about.

He still thought about Jane such a lot and whenever he thought of her he had to remind himself that they were not going to be married and it was still a shock. He could not see his life without her yet it was so. He was telling himself at night that he would see her again the next day but it was not so and now she had gone and said she would marry that awful old man.

He could not bear to think of Cedric Pattison putting his hands on her and worse. He tried not to think about them in bed together, it made him want to go to the Bridge Hotel just at the end of the road beyond the viaduct and drink until he couldn't think any more. It was a stupid way to go on, he knew, if he drank too much now he would never get up and work in the morning and that would not only be setting a bad example but they would all know why he had done it, because Bert would no doubt tell them or might already have told them.

Ned thought they had been glad he was going to marry Jane,

sorry when it didn't work out but glad he had chosen the newspaper and them over her. He was sure that was what it looked like to them whereas in fact it had been nothing more than bad judgement on his part, he had thought he could have both, he had gambled and lost Jane and now there was no way back, he could not retrieve his mistake. He would never see her again except as another man's wife. The thought was unbearable. He made himself walk all the way to the bottom of the hill and under the great black shadow of the viaduct and to his house without looking in the windows of the pub where he could see from the corner of his eye the shadows of the men and the fire and the bar.

The warmth hit him when he walked in. The fire had died down but he went and sat in front of it until it was black. He thought of how disappointed his father had been with him and how much he actually missed his father. Sometimes, like when the accident had happened at the Oswald, he ached to go home and he did now but he couldn't because he had made a mess of things and Jane was marrying Pattison. His father would be livid at the idea and even more so with him.

There was no way back and he didn't want a way back, he wanted his newspaper, he wanted it to be successful, he wanted to see people reading it on the street corners, folding it up as they left the newsagent, taking it home for their families to see, he wanted children laughing at the jokes and women perusing the recipes and for people to be pleased at all the information and most of all for them to be glad that his newspaper was for them and of them.

He was glad too to think that Jasper had been the person who rescued Annabel's mother. It was somehow in his mind so fitting. He had always admired his uncle so much and he knew that when Annabel had time to think about it she would be glad too. It was in its own way wonderful. He only wished he knew where they were to go from here. He had no idea.

Eleven

Annabel read the journal so often that she began to remember passages from it and always, rather like a favourite novel, she imagined that the ending would surprise her. She hoped that it would go on to some kind of conclusion and she would think, 'Oh, so that was what happened to her next,' and yet if she was somehow given to think that Sarah had left Jasper's house Annabel would have been disappointed.

She wanted her mother to have remained there for a considerable time, she daydreamed that Jasper and Sarah had got married and been happy. There was no evidence of it but, she argued with herself, there was no evidence to say that Sarah had left either. Annabel found herself wanting to go to Ned's house since it appeared to be the only thing linking her with her mother.

She managed to contain her impatience for several days but once she could get nothing more out of the journal she tried to think of an excuse for going to Ned's house and somehow without him there so that she could mooch about and dream and even poke around in the different rooms. On the Wednesday he was doing an interview in the evening and she could not work at all that afternoon. Finally he noticed and mid-afternoon he came across to her and put a key down on her desk.

'There's a stone by the wall. Just put it under there when you leave.'

She was so grateful for his comprehension that her heart leapt.

'May I take Millie with me?' She was feeling guilty at having left Millie by herself at the hotel for several evenings by this time.

'If she wishes to go.'

Millie had to be talked into it but she was so concerned at the idea of Annabel being there by herself that she agreed to go with her. It was not that the evenings were dark but even so Millie looked carefully around her as they made their way up North Road from the middle of the town and when they got inside the house she whispered, as though someone might hear, 'Oh, Bel, it's a horrid little place. It's tiny.'

Annabel felt the opposite. Knowing that her mother had been there, the place fascinated her and she wandered from room to room while the light held and imagined Jasper and her mother sitting by the fire, talking in the kitchen. Finally she went back to where Millie was hovering by the sitting-room window.

'Are you wanting to go?' Annabel asked.

Millie turned. 'Of course not,' she lied, Annabel knew, 'we can stay for as long as you like.'

'Do you miss London?'

Millie sighed. 'No. At least – there are many things that I miss.'

'Did you write to Mother?'

'Yes. Not that I imagined her hurtling up here to rescue me.' She paused and then she said, 'Everything is so poor here. I can't remember good food, parties or pretty dresses.'

'You can go back.'

'Not to marry someone I don't care for.'

'You might find someone you could care for.'

'And leave you here? I don't think the future is going to treat you very kindly. There's nobody here you could possibly marry and the thought of you writing about amateur theatrical productions for the rest of your life makes me want to shudder.'

Annabel was so engrossed in the past that she couldn't even consider the future. She was proud of her ability to write and she liked having a byline on her work. It had been the proudest moment of her life when she saw her name against the piece she had written about the accident and had enjoyed people coming in to say they were appreciative of her writing in such a good way about something so awful and the man's widow had written to thank her. She had not known that work could be so exciting and so satisfying and also, though she would not have said so to Millie, she didn't think she could live now in a place where Bert was not. She had become so fond of him.

She felt frustrated, thinking of Jasper. If only she had met him before he died, he might have been able – certainly would have been able to know when her mother had left and where she had gone and what their life had been like for however long they had known one another but then if she had died he would also tell her that and her real hope resided in the faint inkling that Sarah was alive and that somehow they would be united.

The trouble was that she had confessed this to Bert and he had shaken his head when she finished telling him about the diary and the little house and he said, 'Sometimes it's best not to know.'

'What do you mean?'

He tried to shuffle into the back with the excuse of work left undone but she would not have it so finally he looked into her eyes and said, 'If you discover she's dead you'll be disappointed and if you know she's alive you will wonder why she never sought you so either way it won't be good. A mystery is a better thing because it's inconclusive and you can have the ending any way you want without heartbreak but reality is always cruel.'

He got up then and she didn't stop him but later she could not resist going to his office where there was very little natural light in the heart of the building and saying to him, 'Did you not know about Jasper?'

'I would have said so when you were first looking.'

'Did he conceal it then?'

'I don't know. In those days men kept such things to themselves. We never talked about Sarah as mine and I didn't know what had happened to her and he obviously thought better of telling me what he had done.'

'Are you glad then to think she was rescued?'

'Like you I'm in two minds about the whole thing. She can't have thought much of me whichever way you see it and I don't like to think about that. I'd rather have been left with my illusions.'

Annabel had never thought of herself as selfish before but

now she did and she wished she had not told Bert about it, that she had thought more and said less and she tried to heed what he had said but it was so difficult.

She didn't know what to do and for several days did nothing and she did not like to mention it to Ned but in the end on a Saturday afternoon when she was trying to think about the piece she had been writing he came to her.

'You didn't get any further thinking about your mother, did you?'

'Bert rather put me off,' and she told him what Bert had said and then she watched him standing considering.

'I've been thinking about it too,' he said, 'and it seems to me that she couldn't possibly have lived there with him for any length of time unless they were married and I think we must assume that they weren't so she must have left almost immediately otherwise people would have talked, it would have been a scandal and my father would surely have got to know about it and he never could keep anything to himself. It would have been known within the family.'

'You really think I should pursue it?'

'Didn't you intend to?'

She hesitated.

'It was what you came here for,' he said.

'Yes, but – what if she's dead, what if she's the sort of person I don't want her to be—'

'People are seldom what you want them to be.'

'If she didn't want to find me then maybe Bert's right.'

'She would assume that your father had taken you to London.

Maybe she thought you were better off there than with an unmarried mother in a place like this where it's such a disgrace.'

'It's a disgrace everywhere,' Annabel said.

'She couldn't have stayed here, her family would have known about her so we're safe to assume that she didn't.'

'And?'

Ned sat down opposite to her across the desk. 'I don't know. That's as far as I've got.'

Annabel glanced towards the back though it was evening and everybody had long since gone home.

'I do want to find her despite everything. I want to belong somewhere.' She heard her voice wobble and was ashamed.

'Don't you feel as though you belong here? You've made a place for yourself,' he said and she thought it was a very kind thing to say. 'Maybe it's because you have that you feel safe to go on looking for your mother.'

'I just wish I knew where to look.'

'You met other members of your family. Did they never talk about where they came from or about any relatives in other places?'

She tried to think. 'Not that I can remember.' And then she did. 'I'm wrong, my aunt said when she was angry with me that the family came from the dales, the top end where they were millers and farmers. Perhaps my mother went there.'

'Weardale is a big place and there are lots of families there.'

'But someone might remember if she was an incomer. They probably don't have many of those.' Annabel was beginning to feel excited now, right from the pit of her stomach.

'You can't remember anything more that might narrow the search?'

'Nothing at all and I don't want to go back and ask her, I don't want to go back for anything.'

'Surely they looked for her.' Ned was frowning.

'Not if they thought she had drowned. Now I'm scared.'

'Why?'

'In case I find her. A few moments ago I didn't know whether I wanted to. Before that I was afraid I wouldn't and that I would never know her. It seems there's no pleasing me.' Ned didn't speak and then she turned to him earnestly. 'What if we go up to Weardale and look and look and never find her? What if I spend my whole life looking for her?'

'You won't.'

'No? What if she's – left and gone somewhere else and—'

He came over to her and got down beside her chair, something no one, not even Tom, had done, and he looked at her and he said, 'There's nothing to be afraid of.'

'There's everything—'

'Whatever you find you will bear it.'

'Bert doesn't think so.'

'Bert can't accept that he lost her. He married a woman he didn't love, they were very unhappy. He thinks that if he had married Sarah he would not have been. It's always easier to imagine we might have been happier with someone else but it wasn't within his power. You haven't married the wrong person.'

'Or even the right one,' she said with an unsteady little laugh.

'Was he right?'

'It seemed so.'

There was a little pause during which Ned got to his feet but as he did so he said, 'Do you want to go to Weardale? We could take the train.'

'You would come with me?'

'If you like. Or maybe you would prefer Millie to go?'

'I'd rather you came with me. She would feel strange in such a place and you must know it, at least some of it.'

'It might take some time. I have friends in Stanhope which is halfway up the dale. We could stay for a couple of days, I'm sure they wouldn't mind.'

'Could you leave the paper for that long?'

'On a Tuesday and Wednesday I could and so could you but ask Millie first.'

When she got back to the hotel that night she couldn't have any private conversation with her sister, Mrs Hatty kept coming into the dining room to talk so it was not until they finally went to bed that they were by themselves. It was a fine evening and Millie opened the window wide and looked out across the fields.

'I like the way the city is so small and that within even a few minutes' walk you can be from the centre to the country,' she said. Annabel didn't know what to say and Millie sensed her mood and turned around. 'You've been nervous all evening. Is there something wrong?' and she told her about the conversation with Ned.

Millie looked serious as the story ended.

'I don't think I want to go. After all it's nothing to do with me and I'm not very good in out of the way places. You go. Ned's good at things like that, I think, he would be better than me. I'll be fine here with Mr and Mrs Hatty and I can go into the office and help Bert while you're away.'

'You aren't worried about what I'll find.'

'I don't think you'll find anything but I understand that you must go and look. I know I would want to,' Millie said.

Stanhope was much smaller than Annabel had imagined. She didn't know why she had thought it would be a much bigger town, it was nothing much more than one long main street on which there were a number of shops, the parish church on one side in the middle, the vicarage on the other, several public houses, a castle which had recently been rebuilt or refurbished and streets of houses which led away down to the river or up the hillsides to the moors but she was so impressed by Weardale by then that she didn't mind the size of the place.

It was a narrow valley through which the river ran twisting mostly over low flat stones in the bottom and the villages were clustered around the road and the little farms and houses were of grey stone. There were lots of trees and the sky was clear and the air was good and there were sheep in the fields, cream dots everywhere as the train ran past.

Ned's friends met them with a pony and trap and they did not live in Stanhope itself but owned a house not far outside, up a very steep hill which twisted and turned until they got almost to the top which was quite a long way and their house had a view all around of the rest of the dale. It was a substantial place, they seemed to have plenty of money from what Annabel could make out.

They were recently married, Charles was a solicitor and Annabel could not help envying them because he and his wife, Barbara, were so obviously in love and she almost smiled at how at one time she would have considered these people poor because they had no help other than a cook and a housemaid, whereas now she thought them rich and it was not really their lovely house with its warm rooms, the smell of good cooking and the new well-polished furniture, it was the atmosphere they created because they were so happy.

When the maid had gone off with the last of the dishes they sat by the fire with their coffee and Ned explained though tactfully that Annabel was searching for her family and nobody asked embarrassing questions but gave what information they could, that Reid was a local name, that there had at one time been Reids living nearby, that they did not know if any of them was called Sarah but Charles was enthusiastic and said he would do everything he could to help.

Barbara showed Annabel to a comfortable bedroom, the biggest bedroom Annabel had seen since leaving her home in London. The windows were open to the warmth of the night and she could see the same view as she had glimpsed as they came up the road.

'It's beautiful here, you're so very lucky,' she said.

'I understand you lived in London.'

'I spent all my life there until very recently.'

'I'm from Newcastle. You can probably tell I don't have the same accent as people in these parts. I miss the town though I expect I will get used to it.'

'How long have you been married?'

'Only a few months.'

It made Annabel think of Tom and that made her uncomfortable so she asked about Stanhope and Weardale in general and whether they ever went to Durham.

'We thought Ned would be married by now,' Barbara said. 'I think he was very upset. I never liked her. You're much nicer.'

'Oh, it isn't like that,' Annabel hastened to tell her. 'I work for him and he offered to help right from the beginning. That's all.'

'I didn't mean to jump to conclusions,' Barbara said.

It was strange sleeping in the country, much more noisy than the town, she could hear an owl hooting from time to time in the garden, and far away some sheep was making a deep throaty noise and the air was still. In the morning a cock crowed early and the birds awoke her with their twittering. She lay for a while, worrying that she would find something she didn't like, anxious that she might find nothing at all.

Ned dropped Charles off at his office in Stanhope and then had the horse and trap and they went to Frosterley which was the next village down the dale because Charles said there were some people by the name of Reid living on the front street there, quite prosperous people, by the look of the place, a big stone square house with gardens around it. She held the reins and Ned got down and went to the front door. A middle-aged woman opened the door and for a few seconds she thought the woman was the right age to be her mother and she waited for Ned to beckon to her or to say something but he merely stood for a few minutes talking while she fretted and then the woman closed the door and he came back.

He took the reins from her.

'No?' she prompted when he didn't say anything immediately.

'They don't have family in Durham and she doesn't know anybody who might.' He looked at her downcast face. 'It's quite a common name in these parts. This is only the beginning, you cannot expect to find anything yet. Don't worry.'

They went down the dale to Wolsingham which had a pretty market square with shops all around it and here they found they could sit outside of a small public house and keep the horse and trap in view and eat sandwiches and drink beer. Annabel had never done such a thing before and thought it charming.

The whole conversation revolved around work and she could have laughed to think that people who had known her in London would ever have thought she could talk about such a thing with interest but she found that she could have gone on all afternoon because she came up with several good ideas for the newspaper and discovered that Ned was apt to say, 'What a good notion,' or, 'Yes, splendid,' or, 'I wish I had thought of that,' as though she was the cleverest person in the world, and they talked about the people they worked with and whether Millie would be happy to stay on and about the people who came in and how Millie gave them tea and coffee and biscuits and how business had increased since she had been there and about past events and future theatre productions and the miners' gala which would be in July.

She knew nothing about that and he was eager to tell her all about the banners and the bands and the noise and the singing and the drunkenness and the politicians and it was fascinating so she was not surprised when it was halfway through the afternoon before they began again and Ned enquired at the various shops and having found no one they thought to go to the parish records which she said they should have thought of first and he agreed. It didn't help. There were no Reids other than the ones they had visited that morning. So much for it being a common name, she thought.

She was therefore rather downcast as they made their way back to Stanhope for tea. She felt as though the first day had given them nothing other than an enjoyable time on a fine day in a beautiful place and when she had thought about it it seemed like a lot.

That evening Charles would take Ned to meet several of his friends in the public house at the bottom of the hill and she was rather resentful at being left with Barbara. Her hostess was very kind but they drank rather a lot of tea and there was no other company and she could not help thinking back to what a good time she had had with Ned in Wolsingham that day and wishing he had not gone out.

It was late when the men came back and she was not inclined to say much but when they went to bed he caught her on the landing and said, 'Sorry, I didn't intend that. Were you horribly bored?'

She laughed behind her hand. 'She's very nice.'

'They're both very nice but I would much rather have spent the evening just you and me,' he said.

She was pleased at this, she had felt so envious of the men in the pub enjoying his conversation and it was awful to think she was glad he had thought his evening dull too or was it just that he had interpreted her mood as he sometimes did and hadn't wanted her to feel left out?

'They are kind to have us to stay and to give us the pony and trap.'

'Tomorrow we are going to the villages just further up.'

'And no tea,' she said.

'What?' he said but she had already wished him goodnight and gone off into her room.

There she hugged to her the things he had said and that was when she realized that it was the time spent with him she had so much enjoyed. She hadn't known that before, she had thought it was only work, and because they worked together she had confused the two.

After that she couldn't sleep. Did Ned matter to her? She hadn't thought he did. And he loved another woman. She was not confused about that. She had seen the look on his face when he spoke of Jane. He was not the man who would go from one to another without thought. And she still loved Tom. She thought she would always love him.

Each night she brought his face to the front of her mind before she went to sleep. It was the little bit of London that she retained. It had been her only joy but when she went to sleep that night she could not help thinking of sitting outside the Black Bull in Wolsingham and eating beef sandwiches and drinking rich dark ale and talking about the concerns of the newspaper, how they would expand it, what they would do and how animated his face had looked in the sunlight.

The second day was to be the last day of the search because Ned would want to be back in Durham and at the office when the newspaper was printed there that night to make sure nothing went wrong with the printing process. Annabel was convinced that Bert could manage. In fact Bert was always saying that Ned was 'nowt but a bloody nuisance' with his fussing and no help whatsoever during the printing process but since Ned had been kind enough to try to help her she could hardly ask for another day.

She lay in bed, panicking, trying to convince herself that if she did not gain any more knowledge of her mother she could come back and spend more time here but she had the feeling that she could not, that if there were no more leads she would be too afraid to come back or would give up and spend the rest of her life not knowing what had happened to her mother.

When she went down to breakfast Charles said that he thought he might have more information. A man who had heard what they were doing was coming into the office that day early so they breakfasted at speed and went down to his office and there a man of about sixty, a countryman with red cheeks, old clothes and a singsong Weardale accent, said that he thought he had heard of some Reids who lived up at Rookhope in a house a mile or two beyond.

He had not been beyond Stanhope for years so he knew nothing more about it but he remembered 'a lass with red hair' just like Annabel's.

'It's brown,' she protested but she was sitting in the sun which was pouring in at the office window and the old man pointed at the red lights which changed its colour. She pressed him for details but he kept on shaking his head, saying that all he knew was the location, the colour of the woman's hair, it had been such a long time ago, he had seen her only at a distance, he could be certain of nothing.

'And the name of the place?' Ned asked when the old man had furnished direction. He frowned and then his brow cleared. 'Paradise Fields.'

It was further than she had thought though Ned said it could be no more than seven or eight miles but it was a hard distance up through the narrow winding country roads and through the little village of Eastgate, past the public house and right at the crossroads. It was a pretty village with a church, and a few houses. Once out of Eastgate the land rose steeply and twisted up and along into the village of Rookhope which was much more interesting than she had imagined, it had not just been a little rural backwater, it was here that silver, lead and fluorspar had been mined for many years, he told her.

Beyond Rookhope was the stream at the bottom of the valley, the Bolts Burn, which went on and on and there amidst the hills and quite a long way away from anywhere or anything was what looked like a house on the horizon high above the valley. Annabel's heart began to pound as they got nearer and the road turned this way and that as it reached the top of the valley where there were sheep on the moorland and nothing much else but the odd tree. Finally the building came into view around the corner and to where she would have been able to see the roof but there was no roof. There were walls and some semblance of what had been windows, a door and fireplaces and there was a sign which said 'Paradise'.

The sign was broken off so it didn't say 'House' or 'Hall' or as the old man had imagined 'Fields', nothing but the old white roughly painted letters on a piece of wood which was barely held up by two nails.

It seemed so cruel to her. She got out of the trap and gazed at the place. Stones which had been part of the house lay scattered. She walked about for a while hoping to find something, anything in the long grass which might give some kind of clue. And then Ned enticed her back into the trap and they drove to the village.

They called in at the pubs and shops and several of the houses but all anyone remembered was that the house had been inhabited years ago and it was almost in ruins then. There was nobody left here of that name that anyone in the village could think of and nobody was buried in the little cemetery who bore that name and there was nothing to be found in the church records.

By then it was late afternoon. They had to leave. They thanked Barbara and collected their belongings and Charles drove them the short distance to the station. All the way back Annabel thought what a waste of time it had been. If her mother had ever been there it was some kind of fleeting visit and she had left nothing beyond the memory of her name and the colour of her hair, if indeed it had been her at all.

Annabel didn't like to ask Ned what he thought she might do next. He had been very patient. They didn't talk. He went to the office but when she made as if to go with him he stopped her.

'There's nothing more to be gained today,' he said. 'Go up to Mrs Hatty's and see Millie and rest. You must be exhausted.'

She thanked him for what he had done and he said it was nothing and he would come by later with her bag and drop it off but it would be very late by then and he would see her the next day. Thursday being publication day was always busy for them. It would be enough to keep her mind occupied and to try to get used to the idea that her mother had eluded her once again.

Twelve

Never had Millie looked so glad to see her, Annabel thought when she was safely inside the hotel. She had been so glad to reach the sanctuary of Mr and Mrs Hatty's. It was like coming home and Mrs Hatty's face was anxious as she took Annabel's coat and said, 'It didn't go well, then, I can see.'

'It didn't,' Annabel admitted.

'I'm so sorry, my dear. Come in, I've kept a meal for you. You'll feel a whole lot better when you've eaten and Miss Millie has a surprise for you which I'm sure will make you feel different again.'

How mysterious, Annabel thought, and as Mrs Hatty disappeared into the kitchen in search of food for her she went into the dining room where she imagined Millie sitting alone by the window which led out into what was almost a garden – a few flowers amongst the long grass and a path of sorts to the far end where a gate led off to the country.

Millie, having finished her meal, was there but she was not alone. There was a man with her, a man so well dressed that he accentuated the plainness of Millie's faded summer frock and made the carpet, the curtains and Mrs Hatty's sturdy though much-used furniture look twice as old as it was. Annabel stepped just inside the room and let go of the door so that it slammed in the warm evening breeze.

The man stood up. It was Tom. She could not have moved had the ceiling fallen down. He did not look pleased to see her and Millie was looking anything but happy.

'Why, Tom,' Annabel managed and she knew as she said it how stupid it sounded, 'what are you doing here?'

'Exactly what I was going to say to you.'

He sounded so southern, so polished, his clothes were rich and elegant and had of course been made to fit him perfectly. She thought of Ned, how rough he would sound with his northern accent even though it was not thick, how shabby he was now because he was always at work and had nobody to look after him and how in Stanhope she had noticed his frayed cuffs and felt almost ashamed as though he was something to do with her which as she had pointed out to Barbara was not the case.

'How could you stay in such a place and how could you subject Millie to it?'

'She isn't subjecting me to anything,' Millie said, getting up and going pink in the face with unaccustomed anger and Annabel could not help but think how much Millie had changed.

She sat there in her grey washed-out dress and was far more beautiful than she had been when she lived in the confines of London. It was the way that she asserted herself, looking straight at him with fire in her eyes. And Tom was astonished, Annabel could see.

'Neither of you should be staying in such a place,' Tom said.

Mrs Hatty came in then and Annabel was embarrassed to think that she might have heard Tom's deprecating remarks when she had been so kind to them both. Mrs Hatty said nothing but she didn't look at anybody and then she said, 'You sit down here, Miss Annabel, and have your dinner. Your stomach must think your throat is slit,' and she went out.

'How could you be so rude and insensitive?' she said to Tom and then was astonished at herself. She had spent weeks thinking that if he ever did come north she would be so glad to see him and she was not, but then she was tired and she felt defeated. The last two days had been harder than she could ever have imagined and Tom saw it straight away, she could see, and he hung his head a little and then looked straight at her in the way she had always liked and said, 'Please eat whatever concoction it is before it gets cold.'

She wanted to reprove him again but had not the energy. She was about to say that she was not hungry but she knew that Mrs Hatty would be offended if she did not eat. It was sausage, black pudding, potatoes and various vegetables and if she didn't enjoy it at least she was grateful for it. Who could eat in comfort with Tom standing about in disapproval?

'Do sit down, Tom, you're making my neck ache,' Millie said. And then she added mischievously, 'We had the same. I don't think Tom was completely approving of the black pudding.'

When Annabel had finished her meal and Mrs Hatty had collected it and brought in some tea and gone again he said, 'Your mother is worried about you.'

The two girls looked at one another.

'Is this why she has come here so speedily?' Millie said and Annabel said, 'She's not my mother,' and Millie looked at her as though to enquire if anything had happened while she was away with regard to her real mother and she shook her head, hoping that Tom wouldn't notice.

'She does care for you. She knows that you shouldn't have been allowed to come here. She was so upset about your father that she didn't know what she was doing,' Tom said. 'She told me to tell you that she wants you both to come back to London and how much she misses you and that she will do everything to help once you get home.'

Annabel was not convinced, she had the idea that Tom was speaking only in respect of Millie but hadn't the nerve to say so.

'She hasn't bothered to write once,' Millie said.

'Don't you understand how difficult it has been for her, losing her husband like that?'

'Oh, Tom, don't be naive,' Annabel said, 'my mother wasn't the only woman in my father's life and I don't think he was the only man in Etta's.'

Tom stared at her. 'You shouldn't say such things.'

'Why not, if they're true?'

'I don't believe anything mattered beyond their own family.'

'So my mother was just a dalliance and is to be put from everybody's mind?'

'I think we ought to talk about this tomorrow when you aren't so tired. I understand you have been out of the city for a day or two.' His words held a question but she didn't feel inclined to answer it and she was about to give him another hot reply when she thought that it was possible he was right at least to some extent.

'I for one am going to bed.'

Millie preceded her from the room but Tom stopped Annabel, caught hold of her arm.

'My apologies. I'm sorry, I just didn't think it was as bad as this and then I got here and you had gone and I was so disappointed. I've longed to see you. Don't let us quarrel. I'll come back in the morning—'

'I have to go to work in the morning.'

He paused at that. 'Surely that isn't necessary.'

'Didn't Millie tell you that we have jobs?'

'She hasn't told me anything. She made me wait here all the day before she would see me. I've been kicking my heels around this wretched little place for hours.'

'Well, then, I suggest you go back to your hotel now and you can come and see me here tomorrow evening—'

'That's a long time.'

'I know and I'm sorry but Thursday is the most important day of the week to us and it's unlikely I'll be home before nine. Take it or leave it. You'll have to excuse me now. If I don't get some sleep I shall drop.'

'What were you doing?'

'I'll tell you about it tomorrow,' she said, 'goodnight, Tom,' and she followed her sister from the room.

Mrs Hatty was in the hall. She looked anxious. 'Are you all right, my love?' she said and for some reason it made Annabel want to cry.

'You're very kind, Mrs Hatty.'

'Don't you worry, I shall send that young gentleman packing, I've dealt with many bigger, harder men than he is. He can see you when you're less pulled around,' Mrs Hatty said and she pressed her lips firmly together and went off into the dining room.

Annabel went wearily to bed, only to find Millie crying at the open window.

'Why did he have to come here and spoil everything?' Millie said.

It was not what Annabel was expecting.

'I was getting used to being here and how things are,' Millie said, drying her eyes with her sleeve as she would never have done in London. 'He makes me remember all the things I'm missing.'

Annabel soothed her and then they went to bed but she thought that was the trouble, that was why she was angry. She should have been married to Tom by now, they should have had a pretty house, perhaps she would even have been pregnant with their first child. In some ways he was right, this was no place for them but they had had no choice in the matter.

The life which she had wanted was gone and with it all her dreams. Millie was right, they had learned to live with the reality of their situation and it was hard to be reminded of all the things they had had to give up. She could smell and see London on Tom, from his expensive tailored clothes to the smell of Havana cigars. She was angry with him for not being the man she had wanted him to be and for coming here and seemingly making things worse.

They undressed and it was only when they were in bed that Millie said, 'Nothing came of your search, then? I could see by your face when you came in,' so Annabel described what had happened.

'Ned was very good,' Annabel said. 'I don't think though that he will suggest anything further. He can't spare the time and there are no leads, there's nothing I can think of to explain what happened to her.'

'You won't be happy until you find out.'

'Then maybe I shall never be happy.'

There was so long a pause that she thought Millie had gone to sleep and then. Millie said into the silence, 'You will in time. I'm glad it's Thursday tomorrow. I like Thursdays best,' and she thought that Millie was right, there was an excitement about the place on the day that the newspaper was published. She loved the smell of the paper and the fresh ink and the way that she saw people in the streets with the newspaper under their arms, the people who called in to buy a copy and those who came in to get extra ones to show their friends and families because their names were mentioned or there were special stories they cared about.

She was too tired to be upset about Tom or about the way that she felt she was no nearer to finding her mother than she had been at the beginning. She fell asleep almost instantly and was glad that the last sounds she heard were from the bar below.

She was so used to the men's conversation that it soothed her, she felt safe there and somehow she had never needed to feel safe like that before. She was glad to be back at the Garden House with Millie breathing so softly beside her and the gentle hum of talk from below where Mr Hatty was filling pints of ale for thirsty men and nothing but the clack of dominoes broke the rhythm of it all.

Thirteen

Round about five o'clock the following afternoon when the rush had died down and the streets were emptying Ned came and leaned against her desk and folded his arms and when she looked up he said, 'What about a piece in next week's paper on your search for your mother?'

Annabel stared at him. All that day she had not been able to erase from her mind their failure to find anything positive in Weardale and her low feeling that there was nowhere else to look. She felt boxed in.

Her first feeling was that it was a good idea, her second defensive because she would be going public with the search.

'We could be delicate about it,' he said, unfolding his arms and leaning back slightly further. 'People around here know you and everybody loves a quest.'

'A quest?' She hadn't thought of it like that. It sounded lighter and it made her spirits lift.

'We could just say that you've been living in London for a long time and lost touch and that you would be grateful for any help that anybody could give.'

The outside door opened and Ned turned around and she looked. It was most unusual for anybody to turn up when they were officially closed though the door was still unlocked.

Tom stood in the doorway.

'I thought you might like to come back to the Royal County Hotel where I'm staying and have tea with me.'

She got up. 'Tom, this is Ned Fleming. Ned, this is Tom Grant, a friend from London.'

Annabel had never seen a fight or a boxing match but she could see how such things might begin between men for no obvious reason. There was such a feeling in the room of instant dislike. Ned seemed slightly amused and then looked Tom up and down as though he couldn't believe anybody could have a reason to be so well turned out at that hour. Tom looked through him as though he was a servant, something Annabel had never liked but she had always blamed Tom's upbringing. Nobody spoke and Annabel felt compelled to fill the huge gap which threatened the room.

'I've not finished my work,' she managed. 'I dare say Millie will go. She's at Mrs Hatty's so you could go there and ask her. I could join you in an hour or so.'

She waited for Ned to be polite, to say that she must go of course, the work could wait but he didn't. His other acceptable behaviour would be to speak, to shake Tom's hand, though it wasn't offered in truth, and then to leave them alone but he didn't move, he just stood there, leaning back slightly against her desk, so obviously owning the room and Tom didn't come further into it, as though he knew it was another man's territory like a garden or a stable would be and he turned without a word and walked out.

Ned stood up straight, still eyeing the door, and then he went into his office. Annabel let go of her breath. She wanted to go after him and shout at him or to go after Tom but she didn't. She got on with what she wanted to finish and it was about an hour and a half before she ventured into Ned's office. He was sitting at his desk, looking through some papers.

'I think it's a good idea,' she said, 'will you write it?'

He stopped what he was doing and looked up.

'We might get a lot of false leads,' he said, 'but sometimes—'

'I couldn't have left it like this,' she said and then wasn't totally surprised when he said.

'Who was that?'

Irritated at his attitude she said shortly, 'We were engaged to be married—'

'To him?' She was almost amused by the scornful tone, as though Tom was somebody she had met on the street. 'And then he found out about you?'

'Yes.'

'And now?'

'I don't know what he's doing here.'

'Does he have accomplishments other than his tailoring?'

She looked at him. 'That isn't fair,' she said, and she went out.

It was strange walking into the County Hotel by herself. It was nothing like Mrs Hatty's. It was the best hotel in town, by the river in Old Elvet, following the road down from the office and over the bridge and then across the road, only a few minutes' walk away.

The moment she went in she was aware of her own clothes, the fact that she was unaccompanied and how people stared. It was a warm evening and people were sitting about with iced drinks, the women in pretty dresses and the men in cool pale colours. The dining room was full and she glanced in as she went past but she wasn't hungry and she knew that Mrs Hatty would have something for her when she got home, was used to her being late.

She found Tom and Millie outside on the terrace, drinking gin and tonic. Tom looked her up and down, offered her a seat and, unable to see a waiter, he went to procure a drink for her.

Millie said, 'I wouldn't have changed if I'd known you'd have to come like that.'

'Do I look awful?'

'Like you've come in to clean the stairs,' Millie said, pulling a face and then they looked at one another and laughed.

Annabel didn't feel like laughing, she only did it to make Millie feel better, she felt mis-stitched, that was the word for it, everything was in chaos again somehow.

Tom came back and was followed by a harassed waiter who had brought the drinks on a tray.

'Couldn't your friend give us his company?' Tom said, taking a huge mouthful of gin and tonic.

'You were very rude.'

'He's a boor. It just shows how long you've been in a place like this, that you should have to work for such as that. The fellow's nothing but a jumped-up workman and quite over-familiar.'

'He owns the newspaper,' she said and then wished she hadn't defended Ned, she doubted he needed it.

'Precisely,' Tom said.

Annabel took a sip of her gin and tonic and regarded the river with interest. It was a perfect evening, still and warm. Some energetic souls were rowing. The gin and tonic was cold and bittersweet and tasted as good as anything she had ever drunk before. They were soon called in to dinner.

'I told Mrs Hatty we wouldn't be in,' Millie said so Annabel was obliged to go into the dining room in her crumpled clothes. She had never felt so out of place.

The conversation was general but she knew by his face that Tom wanted to talk to her. He insisted on seeing them all the way back to their hotel but as they went in he took hold of her arm and said, 'Am I never to have five minutes alone with you?'

Millie went on and Annabel could hear her speaking to Mrs Hatty so she paused in the relative darkness of the hall.

'Not here,' he said impatiently, 'the place stinks of beer.'

, She called as Millie shut the door, 'Tell Mrs Hatty I won't be long,' and stepped back into the street with him.

She glanced down the long length of North Road where the leaves were thick on the tall trees at either side and where the road wound away into the city.

'I've come over two hundred miles to see you,' he said. 'It wasn't just because your mother is so worried about you—'

'I wish you would stop calling her my mother. She is

undoubtedly worried about Millie, I don't think she ever cared for me.'

'That can't be true.'

'Oh, but it is.'

'I want you to stop this ridiculous charade and come back to London with me and make it up with her. She's completely alone.'

'Nasty selfish people generally are,' Annabel said.

He looked at her and it was not an approving look. 'You used to be fond of saying what you thought, regardless of other people's feelings. Now it seems to have become a complete way of life with you.'

'It isn't a charade,' she said.

'And that too, that way you have of picking what you want from what people have said and ignoring the rest. You cannot like living in the way that you do. I understand that circumstances have forced you into it but there is a way out. I've come here to ask you once again to marry me.'

She was astonished. Afterwards she knew that he could have had no other object in coming here but at the time she did not believe it. He wasn't looking at her. He looked ashamed but that was for what had gone before.

'I've spoken to my father and mother and they have agreed to our marriage.'

She couldn't think of anything to say. For a few moments she didn't understand.

'We can go back?'

'As soon as you like.'

She thought of what her life would be, married to Tom, all the things she had cared for, the parties, the dresses, the champagne, the people she had known, having someone to see to her every whim, not having to work—

'That would be wonderful, Tom.'

'You will?' His eyes lit.

'Of course I will but—' She spoke without thinking because it was what she had wanted to hear from him as soon as she found out who she was after her father had died but when he drew her into his arms and kissed her she was confused.

She had almost forgotten what she had felt about him. When she had first got here she would lie in bed and try to recall the feelings but she had never come close to the real thing, but something about it was not right and she immediately regretted having spoken so hastily, her time here was not over yet, she knew it.

'My father will buy us a house of our own anywhere you choose and you will be its only mistress so that you don't have to see your mother every day and—'

She drew back from him, the word 'mother' reminding her of what she and Ned had talked about. She told Tom about the idea for the article which they thought might help in the search for her mother. The expression on his face changed.

'You can't do that,' he said. 'Let all the world know about your affairs and have them gossiping and asking questions.'

'But that's the whole point. Who knows where it would lead. It's the only thing we could think of and it was Ned's idea.'

'From a vulgar fellow like Fleming I should expect no more.'

Annabel took a deep breath and then another. 'You still don't understand how important this is to me.'

'Before all this you were happy. We can go back there. Your father made a mistake but he was a gentleman. You seem to have forgotten such things since you came here and lived among common people.'

'Is it gentlemanly to behave in the way that he behaved towards my mother?'

'That's not the same thing at all. Don't be naive. You know how things are. You can't stay here for such a reason.'

'I have to find her.'

'Why? She obviously didn't care for you. She left you behind.'

'I want to settle this in my mind before I do anything else.'

There was silence on the street so deep that she could hear someone laughing in the bar.

'You haven't been able to sort it out this far,' he said. 'It could be that there is nothing else to know.'

'I can't believe that.'

'Isn't it more important to be who you are, to come back to London and get on with your life? Surely that matters.'

She didn't answer, she couldn't think.

'You're in danger of becoming obsessed by this,' he said.

'Perhaps I am but I didn't begin it, that was other people. They put me into an intolerable situation and I'm determined to make an end to it.'

'You could do that by giving up and coming home.'

'And when it happens again?'

'How could it?'

'People would always know.'

There was another silence, longer than the first.

'You can't want to publish such a thing in a newspaper. Think about it overnight. I'll see you tomorrow,' and he turned around and walked abruptly away before she could say anything else.

Annabel walked slowly into the hotel. When she went up to her room Millie was already in her bed but waiting.

'Well? What did he say?'

'He asked me to marry him again.'

'Oh, that's wonderful, marvellous.' There was a false note in Millie's voice which Annabel didn't understand but she thought of how much progress Millie had made into becoming an independent and mature woman instead of the light-hearted girl she was before their father died. She had always loved her sister but now she respected the way she had met the difficulties they had encountered.

Annabel sank down on to her own bed. 'Do you want to stay here?'

'No, of course not, but . . .' Millie gazed past her, trying to think. 'I would never have dared to contradict a man when Father was alive. I'm not the person I used to be and I won't pretend either to Tom or to my mother that I am. I won't go back and have things be like before and I'm not sure I can face the fight. What about you?'

'I don't feel that I can leave here until I know whether my mother is still alive.'

Millie thought for a few seconds. 'That's how I would feel.'

'Is it?' Annabel was pleased that Millie thought the same way.

She explained what Ned had suggested and Millie thought that too was a good idea. 'Then you can get on with your life,' she said.

Ned wrote what Annabel thought was a very good article about her 'quest for her family after a childhood in the south' and after that she looked up every time the outside door opened. Everybody in the town knew who she was by now, at least everybody who read the newspaper, and people came into the office and talked to her about the problem. Gossip, she thought, worrying slightly, travelled quickly in such a small city but the days went by and not one person came in with any useful information.

After a whole week when the next newspaper came out and still nothing had happened Tom said, as they sat outside the County Hotel by the river one warm evening drinking gin and tonic, 'Are you ready to give up yet and come back to London with me?'

Annabel looked across the table at Millie, hesitating. Millie was changing her mind, she thought. She had asked Tom that evening about her friends and he had described various social gatherings he had been to and Annabel had watched the hungry look on her sister's face. Millie was ready to go home but she didn't like to say so.

Annabel had felt that all that week as day followed day without anything more Millie had been disappointed and then frustrated and was convinced there was nothing more to be found, Annabel knew, and she was disappointed at having to acknowledge this. Her sister was loyal and did not want to go back without her.

'I'm not ready to give up,' Annabel confessed, only just realizing it.

Tom looked patiently at her. 'I cannot stay here forever,' he said.

'Then take Millie back with you.'

'I'm not going without Bel,' Millie said instantly, as Annabel had known she would.

'What is the point in going on?' Tom said. 'What difference can it possibly make now? You've agreed to marry me, my parents want it, your mother—'

'Will you stop calling her that?' Annabel said.

'What else am I supposed to call her in front of you?' Tom pointed out. 'Things are back to where they were before last Christmas, before your father died and everything went wrong. I don't understand why you won't come back with me.'

It wasn't the same. She didn't want to point out the obvious to him but she had changed, everything in her life was different.

When she didn't answer him immediately Tom said, and he looked hard at her as he spoke, 'Unless you have another reason for staying.'

She didn't understand. 'What?'

'Fleming,' Tom said heavily.

She stared at him but he continued to look at her as though he had given this a lot of thought and believed it and Millie said, 'Don't be silly, Tom.'

'That's ridiculous,' Annabel said, but she could feel her face begin to burn at the idea and she remembered Ned's bruised body and the way that he had pulled her to him for comfort. No man had ever needed her in such a way, she liked that Ned was apparently vulnerable while still trying to do his best in so many ways, he was a man of the people as his father and her father and Tom would never be.

'Is it?'

'He's far beneath her,' Millie said.

'That doesn't stop some women. I know friends of my mother's who . . .' and then he seemed to recall his company and fell silent.

Annabel thought about it. Ned was her best friend. That was unusual. She relied on him – but love? Love was about finding a beautiful house in London so that she could live with Tom and they could spend time with like-minded people, it was about taking her place as his wife in society and hosting wonderful parties for the top politicians and well-known figures of the day, even royalty on occasion. It was exciting, even adventurous in its way. Who would not want that? It was about house parties and hunting and foreign holidays. He had promised that they would go to Italy for their honeymoon and to other places which she had only dreamed of.

It was ridiculous to think that she would rather stay in a backwater like this to work in a dark little office with a man who stayed up most of the night on Wednesdays to ensure his newspaper was on the streets early. She had never thought romantically about Ned. What woman would? Presumably Jane Baker had but that was when he had prospects. He didn't have those now. What he had was the affection of the people here and their regard. He was their champion in a way and they liked him for it.

And then there was Bert. She couldn't imagine never seeing him again. He had become like a father or like the father she had never had and wanted. He was nothing like her own father, who spent his days amusing himself and his nights – she was ready to admit it to herself now – with other women. He was not scholarly or in parliament though he had friends there.

Bert had worked all his life and spent his time in the back of the newspaper premises making sure that the newspaper looked right, that the whole thing came together in all the ways that it could. She had watched him going home and there was nobody in his house, he had nobody to go back to. Most nights he went to one of the local pubs and had something to eat and a couple of pints before he went to bed and it was all the leisure he had.

There was something so vital, something which looked uncomplicated but was not about him. He had stood by a wife he did not love and other people might call that stupid but there was a reliable quality about him which she had not seen before in anybody until she got here. Bert would be there for her just as Ned would. Could she turn her back on them now?

Just at that moment a figure appeared in the doorway and she turned to one side slightly. It was Ned. She was aware that Tom had not asked him to come with them any of the evenings they had spent at this hotel. She had told herself that he would not want to come, that he did not have time, that he liked being in his office, but she was also rather sorry that she did not have his company though she knew very well that Tom would not have stood for it.

He came over and said without preamble, 'A woman came into the office with news of your mother.'

Tom looked wearily at him, she could see, but she could not have dragged her gaze from Ned's face once it settled there.

'Must we have more of this?' Tom said.

'What did she say? Sit down. Tom—'

'I don't want a drink, thanks,' Ned said immediately but he sat down. 'She says there is a woman who was called Sarah Reid who lives at Deerness Law. Her husband is a pitman there.'

'Was she sure?'

'Quite certain. Her sister lives in the same street. She had red hair though it's losing its colour now and blue eyes, most unusual.'

'Where is this?' Tom interrupted.

'It's a little town several miles away up on the moors.'

'And this woman's husband works down a pit?'

'Yes.'

'You seriously want to take Annabel to such a place?'

'Why not?'

'Among common people?'

Oh dear, Annabel thought, amid her joy and excitement, Ned would not stand for that. He didn't.

'Common people?' he said softly. 'As opposed to what? The likes of you?'

'Don't talk to me like that, Fleming, I'm a gentleman.'

'You're a piece of shit,' Ned said so swiftly that Annabel couldn't help gaping. Millie went pink with embarrassment, no man could ever in their presence before have said such a word.

'Ned, don't say things like that,' Annabel said, appalled.

Tom was red in the face and on his feet. 'You take that back, you insolent fellow.'

'Like hell I will.'

And then she too was on her feet because Ned had got up and she stood in front of him and she said, 'That's enough. Come back to the office with me.'

'He's not going anywhere until he apologizes,' Tom said but she pushed Ned through the doorway into the hotel and, after hesitating, he let her. Tom couldn't get close without getting between them and she closed the door swiftly and then she saw Millie in front of Tom.

By the time she had got Ned out of the front door of the hotel and into the street she was furious. She turned on him. He stood with his head down, still she could tell very angry but managing to control it.

'What on earth were you doing?'

'Are you seriously going to marry that idiot? You want your head examining,' he said and strode away up the street.

She took several deep breaths before she followed him but by the time they got back to the office she wanted to hear every detail about what had been said and she ignored the quarrel and asked him questions, what the woman had looked like, where the town was, what the street was called.

'It's the middle of nowhere. It has several pits, this one's the biggest in the area and it produces good coking coal. The pit is called Catherine.'

'She told you all this?'

'I already knew some of it. I've worked there. It's one of my father's pits, the first he started by himself. It was named after my mother.'

No wonder, she thought, he had been so angry. He saw her expression and said softly, 'I'm sorry, I didn't mean to say things like that in front of you and Millie.'

'Tom's angry,' she said, 'he thinks—'

'What?'

'Nothing. When can we go?'

'How about first thing in the morning?'

'Don't we have a busy day tomorrow?'

'I'll rearrange things.'

He really wanted to do this, she thought, and soon.

'You know the place well, then?'

'I was born there,' he said.

Fourteen

It seemed a strange place for him to have been born though she couldn't think why. He was right, it was desolate, high up on the moors at the edge of the Durham coalfield. It was one long main street and little terraces went off it at right angles. It was ugly and at the same time its very desolation was its beauty because there was no wind that day, the sun shone brightly and as they came through the countryside by train the little pit villages were scarred with pit heaps and mine heads and folded around them were farming communities with grey houses up on the moors. The sky was a clear blue and the day took advantage of any grace the little town had but it was the look on Ned's face which made it lovely. His eyes shone on the wide main street and when they got off at the station the station master came along, smiling.

'Why, lad,' he said, 'how long has it been?' and shook Ned's hand.

Annabel thought it was one of the best greetings she had ever heard. They walked the distance up the winding hill which was called Dan's Castle. She thought it a strange name and the pit they were searching for came in sight as the little town petered out and when they reached the pit yard and the offices

Ned was greeted afresh by other men and one of them said, 'Your dad's here.'

Ned's face told her how unwelcome this news was but it seemed he had no alternative but to go down the short corridor to the closed door and knock, and then, hearing a reply, open it. Annabel remembered Mr Fleming and recognized him instantly. He was sitting behind the desk frowning, not at the interruption, she thought, but at the work he was doing as though he had had enough already that day and then perhaps he recognized the tread of feet because he stopped and looked up. His expression was half pleasure and half irritation and it seemed to her that he deliberately held the irritation on his face and then he saw her and got up and came over and took her hand and said, 'Miss Reid, how nice,' and she thought he was the kind of man who knew everything which went on around him and that he knew as much about her as anyone else in Durham.

'How do you do?' she said.

'I read the piece you wrote about the pit accident. It was well done.'

'Thank you.'

'Do you know why we're here?' Ned asked.

'Not exactly. Do sit down and tell me.'

Ned explained. His father frowned but it was because he was thinking, and when the explanation was over he sat back in his chair and said:

'Yes, I know the woman you mean. I had heard you were trying to find your mother, and I did try to think what I might do to help but I didn't know that we should start right here. She married Ellison, Ned, you know, Walter. They live on Castle Bank, or they did. No, that's his brother.' He went to the door and roared down the passage, 'Featherstone!' and when a man appeared almost instantly he said, 'Find me the address for Ellison, not Fred, the other one.'

'Pearce.'

'Aye, that's right.'

He came back inside and Mr Featherstone went off into the outer office. Annabel could barely sit still. She could not imagine she was about to find her mother. She had to find her, she felt as though she was very close now and some small voice was whispering inside her that it was another false lead, that it would lead nowhere, that she should have gone back to London, that if it did not help now she would feel obliged to go back. To be so close and to feel lost was such an awful feeling and she went dizzy and felt sick and was horribly afraid that she would pass out like any stupid miss.

It was a hundred years before Mr Featherstone came back. The clock behind Mr Fleming ticked loudly and nobody spoke as though the men did not like to make small talk or were uncomfortable or did not feel the need, she could not make out which and she longed to get up and pace the room or to go outside in search of fresh air. There was plenty of that here beyond the little town.

Mr Featherstone did not hurry, it appeared to her. She wanted to shout at him that it was vitally important, that she could not bear to hear that Mr Ellison had moved, or much worse that

Mrs Ellison had died or— She wanted to shout and scream as Mr Featherstone went through his papers and she realized that he was a much older man than she had at first supposed and that he was moving as fast as he could and his hands shook over the papers. Everybody waited patiently. She tried not to look as Mr Featherstone went down the list, and finding nothing, said infuriatingly, 'It is here somewhere, it is up to date,' and then he stopped his finger and put it down towards the bottom of the page and he said, 'Oh, here it is. Pearce Ellison. He lives along Ellison Street.'

At first she thought Mr Featherstone was having some kind of game because he smiled, or was old enough to mix things up and the address was something quite different and then Mr Featherstone looked somewhat apologetically at his employer and said, 'I ought to have known. His father built the street. Old Man Ellison.'

Mr Fleming thought nothing of joining in this game of remembrance and furrowed his brow. 'What was he called? Oh, yes, I remember. Tobias.'

'You have the right of it, Mr Fleming. And his wife was called Edie.'

'And the present Mr Ellison's wife?' Ned asked gently.

'I believe her name is Sarah,' Mr Featherstone said and Annabel sat forward on her chair and hid her face, she did not want anybody to see the emotions which were there, doubt and certainty, impatience and worry and a small beam of happiness which she was anxious about because she did not want it destroyed.

She was so afraid to try for this but nothing would have stopped her and she thought even if it came to nothing she was so glad that they had come here. She wanted to reach for Ned's hand but couldn't and he reached for her hand and squeezed her fingers gently in reassurance and he smiled at her.

'Goodness, you will think me incompetent,' Mr Featherstone said, 'I haven't told you which number it is,' and he glanced again at his paper and screwed up his eyes against either the lack of light or his failing sight and he said, 'Five. Five is my lucky number,' and he seemed happy with that and went out into the corridor pleased with his achievement.

'I don't know what we keep him on for,' Mr Fleming said, shaking his head, 'he's an old ditherer.'

Ned got to his feet. 'Thank you, Father.'

His father got up too. 'Not at all,' he said, with fine sarcasm, 'any time I can be of help.'

They went outside.

'Is it far?'

'Nowhere's far here.'

'Now I'm afraid.'

The sun beat down and she stood there in the hot sunshine and wished herself back in Durham.

'You want to know?'

'Beyond anything,' and he began to walk but she didn't and he stopped and came back to her.

'What if it's her? What if it is her and she doesn't like me? What if—'

'No,' he said. 'Come on,' and he took her by the hand and

walked her back down the hill towards the station and over the level crossing and up past the Golden Lion public house and up to the top of another though slight hill and then along the main street where there were various shops and houses all intermingled and she could see the parish church across to the left at the end of a long narrow unmade road and she could see the vicarage, it was very big, and then they reached the far end of the street and by then a dozen people had said good morning to him and they would have stopped him except that she kept tugging at his hand like a child, she could not bear to wait much longer.

Finally they reached the top of the street and the road there went two ways. They took the road past the Presbyterian church which led down towards the country and into Weardale and there he turned left just before the town petered out in this direction and there was a street of about fifteen houses.

They started, for some reason, at the wrong end so that number five was almost into the country and from it there was a fine view of fields as the hill wound down gently towards the dale, and further over rather less beautifully, though admittedly off to the right and nearer the town, was the slag works.

They stopped at number five, it had a blue door. She couldn't knock on the door, her hands shook and she was so afraid that her instinct was to turn and run the way that they had come and she remembered what Bert had said about finding things out and making it worse.

Ned was the person who knocked on the door and then they waited a small eternity until she heard footsteps behind it and then the door opened and people had been right, the woman was tall and had blue eyes and the kind of red hair which went dull in middle age. Was this her mother? There was no recognition on the hard-worked face, it was lined and told of difficult times and she was skinny, not slender like Etta was, her face was shrunk slightly and Annabel could not help but pity her.

'Are you Sarah Reid?' she managed to ask.

'I was Sarah Reid,' she said.

Annabel went on watching the face and her look had turned into a stare.

'Would it be possible for us to come in?' Ned said. 'I'm—'

'I know who you are, Mr Fleming, and of course you can come in.'

Annabel could not help admiring her soft local accent and the way that she walked, almost a glide. They followed her down the narrow hall. It was a small dark house as many of them were, Annabel thought, but its windows reflected the huge light which came from the sky above the dale. The valley plunged away there and the blue and white of the openness flooded the dark walls. It was a clean house, orderly, Annabel was glad of that, thinking of her first excursion to find her family at the dirty house under the viaduct in Durham. She didn't know what to say and then she managed, 'I'm Annabel Reid.'

'Really? You don't sound local,' the woman said.

'No, I'm from London.'

'Related to the Reids, though? Do have a seat,' she offered and Ned and Annabel sat down together on the overstuffed sofa.

'I think I may be . . . I think you may be . . .' She gathered her breath. 'I've been looking for you. I think you could be my mother.'

The woman looked at her, puzzled for a long time.

'Whatever makes you think such a thing?' she said.

'Because of my circumstances,' and Annabel began to tell the long tale which had brought her from London to this country hillside and the woman did not interrupt, she just watched until it was all done, until every detail was covered and then she said, slowly and with deliberation.

'I'm afraid this is going to come as something of a shock to you, my dear, but I'm not your mother.'

Annabel found her voice as well as her hands trembling. 'You must be,' she said, 'all the evidence leads to it, all this time, all these months, all the – the problems that I have faced. How can you not be when I've come so very far? We even look alike. It may not be something you are willing to admit, indeed I think you've done everything you can to deny it but surely now, seeing me, you must see that it's true, that we are closely related, that we are mother and daughter.'

The woman was shaking her head. 'I'm sorry,' she said, 'it's not to do with anything as complicated as that. It's very simple. You cannot be my daughter because the only child I ever bore was a boy, and he died.'

Annabel thought she had never felt so despondent in her life. She had by now been through many hard times but it seemed to her that she had just lost her mother for the second time.

'I tried to drown myself after my baby died, I was so grieved.

I was rescued and went to Jasper Fleming's house and stayed there until I was myself again. It took some doing after what that – that man had treated me to. I never forgave him for the way that he had behaved so badly to me, like I was nothing.'

'Your son was his child?' Ned asked and it was only at that moment that Annabel realized she had now lost her father. She had nobody and she and Millie were no kin to one another, she had no claim to the family at all, she had unwittingly been living a lie. She felt sick and then she felt dizzy and was only glad that she was sitting down.

'Yes, he was. He never had a son, then, did he? I'm glad of it. He didn't deserve one. He didn't deserve a child at all.'

'There must be a connection,' Ned was saying. 'Why would he take Annabel with him, he must have thought she was his child.'

'I dare say. I lodged with a woman called Stella Smith. I can only assume that she gave him her baby. She never wanted it. Quite funny really, to think she took him for a fool like that. That was Stella all over.'

Annabel was beginning to feel sick. 'And my father?'

The woman looked pityingly at her. 'Stella was a whore. It could have been anybody.'

Now she felt really sick, she thought she might pass out, the room was not as substantial around her as it had been.

'Is she still alive?' Ned asked.

The pity took him in too.

'Whores lead short lives,' she said.

Fifteen

Standing outside in the sunlight it seemed to Annabel that the lovely view from the house was as dark now as the sitting room had been. Nobody spoke. The door was long since shut on them, with relief, she thought, on the woman's part. She had felt left out when she had left London but it was nothing compared to this. Now there was nowhere to go.

She waited for expressions of sympathy, understanding, even bafflement from Ned. Infuriatingly he seemed to be looking towards the distant valley for inspiration. She blinked.

'I think I'm going to faint.'

He turned around quickly. He said, 'No, you aren't. Just breathe.' He steadied her by the arm while Annabel took deep breaths and had to wait for several seconds before she could trust her voice.

'I can't believe I've come all this way for nothing and for such – such awful things to happen.'

He didn't react for a few seconds and then he said, 'I wonder what she's so afraid of?'

Afraid of? What was this?

'You believed her?' he said.

'Well—'

'You look like her.'

For some ridiculous reason that didn't please Annabel either. She looked like that scrawny middle-aged woman? And then she understood and her heart flooded with gladness and with rejection and she choked but she understood.

'You think she was lying?'

Ned took her arm and moved her further away from the terrace of houses.

'It was a story,' he said, 'I've heard enough of them to know one. She made it up, all that stuff.'

Confused, Annabel did not want to walk further away but the dizziness was gone and something close to euphoria was taking its place and she loved the sound of his voice, flat and northern and confident, and she wanted to hug him.

'But how could she deny her own child and so blatantly?'

'It must have seemed that she did the best thing originally and why wouldn't it? Mightn't you have done the same?'

'But being confronted with me now?'

He didn't say anything for a few seconds and then replied softly, 'Looking at you now she must be glad she took the chance. What other girl from such a start could have had your opportunities?'

'And lost them?'

'You haven't lost your refined upbringing, your cut-glass accent, your blooming health, your education, the good food you had all those years, the beautiful clothes – and all those other things you used to talk about so freely, the parties and the fun and the joy of having Millie as your sister. You can't lose any of that—'

He was right, she decided. 'Could she be afraid of her husband?'

'Perhaps she's afraid of you,' he suggested.

Annabel frowned. 'Why—'

'Who would want to acknowledge a mother in such a humble place, cast out from her family, almost hiding here in this wind-swept little town in the middle of nowhere, what good could it possibly do you and she knows that, she knows it better than you and she doesn't want that—'

'You don't think we should go back?'

'I think we should respect her enough to leave her alone,' he said.

'But the story about the whore?'

'People defend themselves however they can,' he said. 'Come on.'

He drew her away and Annabel let herself be drawn though she wanted to go back to the poor little house and bang on the door for entrance as she had wanted to do when she left London. Was she never to have anywhere to call home? Would nobody ever want her? Just to have someone acknowledge her, to have somebody say, 'Yes, you are mine,' would mean the whole world to her.

It seemed like such a long journey back to Durham and trying not to break down she thought her face might just as well have turned to wood. She felt as though she had come to the finish of her quest and it had ended badly. Would she have felt any worse if she had found out that her mother was dead? You could weave such stories around dead people, you could have it exactly how you wanted. Living relatives were turning out to be such uncomfortable things, nobody would conform, nobody would leave her thoughts she could bear to go to sleep with.

She did not want to tell Millie and Tom about it but Tom asked so many questions that it would have been impossible to have hidden the truth. She was only afraid that Ned would not come to the Royal County Hotel, he didn't seem to like the place or was it just being there with them that he didn't like but for once she didn't have to ask, they enquired at the newspaper office and Bert said that Millie and Tom had gone there so she felt she had to follow them.

They had dinner together. She didn't like to say that she could eat nothing. Ned didn't seem to fancy anything either and spent time fiddling around with a bread roll in a way which reduced it to crumbs. He let her tell the story without inter-rupting though she would rather he had done it. He didn't offer to and she took a sideways glance at him and found him with his gaze on his soup which he kept stirring round and round.

The main course came and she watched Tom eating his dinner with apparent relish and her sister, too involved in the story to do more than eat mouthfuls without knowing, Annabel felt sure, what it was she ate. Millie hated carrots but ate three forkfuls and didn't realize.

When the story was finished it looked to Annabel as though she had more on her plate than she had started with and all she wanted was to run back to Mrs Hatty's, the only home she seemed to have, she thought with sudden bitterness, and hide under the bedclothes. Thankfully the plates were taken away and it was only then she knew Ned had not said a single word throughout the meal.

Tom ordered chocolate sponge pudding and then turned his attention to her.

'How do you know she was lying?'

Annabel looked at him. 'What do you mean?'

'She knows that you come from a wealthy family. Why would she not want to claim something?'

'Like what?'

'I don't know. People do things like that when they find out they are related to people so prosperous. Surely, she being so poor, if she had been your mother she would have wanted to claim you for all sorts of reasons, not least because of who you are, unless she had a very good reason.'

Tom shifted in his seat. Nobody said anything for what felt to her like a long time and then Ned spoke for the first time.

'He means unless your mother isn't sure who your father was.'

'I don't care for the implication,' Annabel said.

'That isn't what I meant,' Tom blustered.

'What, then?'

'Why shouldn't she want to know you? I think she might have been telling the truth.'

'That my mother was a whore and my father was paying her?'

Tom, hearing the bald statement, looked about him in case anyone else should overhear. 'Isn't it possible?'

'Ned says she looks like me.'

'Fleming would say such a thing,' Tom said as though Ned wasn't in the room.

'You mean he was being kind?'

Even this didn't needle Ned into speech, he sat dumb and gazed across at other diners as though their meal might be more interesting than his own.

'If you call it that.'

'That's exactly what I call it,' Annabel said and she got up. 'I think I would like to go home now.'

'So would I,' Millie said and it was the first time that Annabel had noticed how upset her sister was, white-faced and glassy-eyed.

Tom tried to insist on going with them but when she said she wanted nobody else Ned asked the hotel for the carriage and she and Millie went back to Mrs Hatty's. Thankfully they met nobody in the hall and it was only when they reached their bedroom that Millie said in trembling tones, 'I don't care who you were or are and I don't care who I am either but you will always be my sister and I think Tom is hateful.'

'He doesn't mean to be,' Annabel said but when they went to bed which was very shortly afterwards she lay there thankful of the darkness and she thought of the woman standing in the doorway of the dark little house up on the fell which looked down into what appeared to be paradise and she thought that in a way they had both been kept out of such places as though they were not fit to inhabit them. She was grateful to have anything in common with the woman.

Ned was about to leave the hotel and walk back to the office because he didn't really want to go home but Tom called his name and so he stopped and Tom came up to him and said right in his face, 'Why did you let her go on believing that woman was her mother? There was no evidence of it. And you call yourself a newspaper man?'

Ned stopped, took a deep breath and then looked at the red-faced and rather out of breath young man before him. He didn't like Tom and he wondered whether if the circumstances had been different they would ever have been friends and then he looked down at Tom's white hands and perfectly kept nails and at his expensive three-piece very fashionable suit and thought, No, it could never have been so.

'What would you have me tell her?'

'Raising false hopes?'

Ned sighed. To be as cosseted as Tom was no advantage to a man once he got out into the world but then Tom would probably never go out into the world such as it was, his family and background would see to that.

'Would you rather she believed her mother was a whore and her father one of a dozen she had serviced that week? And you would marry such a woman?'

Tom hesitated just for a split-second. 'I love her.'

Ah yes, love. He remembered it. He remembered also that the girl he loved was to be married that week. He had even debated, cool newspaper man that he was, whether to send Annabel to cover the wedding, he was sure that all his new enthusiastic woman readers would relish hearing exactly what the bride wore and who the special guests were and whether it rained. He wished it would. He wished there would be such a downpour that the bride would reach the church in satin shoes that squelched and that the bridegroom, the fat little git, would slip and land in an enormous puddle and then he thought, Yes, I am reduced to such ridiculous strategies, like a bluebottle buzzing angrily against glass, nobody taking any notice of it.

'Do you indeed and do you imagine even for a second that your parents would allow you to marry someone of such parentage?'

Tom stared at him, cheeks reddening. He said nothing.

'So, you have been lying all along and they don't know that you're here. You've asked her to marry you, knowing that you can't?'

'In the first place it's none of your business and in the second when I take her back to London they will accept her because I care for her.'

'You sad misguided idiot,' Ned said and then he turned and began walking once again in the direction of his office.

Sixteen

The following day Ned saw the heavy dark shadows under Annabel's eyes but said nothing, only that he had a story to cover and would be out of the office all day. He never did such things but nobody questioned it so once again he found himself taking the train out of the city and into the countryside. He walked again to the little house on the edge of the pit town and it was as he half suspected, he banged on the front door several times but nothing happened and eventually a neighbour, hearing him, came outside and told him that she had gone.

'Fearful row there was last night and when he was off to work she left.'

Ned, walking back towards the town, tried to tell himself that if she had left it was not his fault, that it had been nothing to do with the visit the previous day, but he felt as stupid as he had thought Tom was, how could he have blundered quite so badly? He called in at the offices for no good reason other than it felt comforting to do so only to find his father there.

'What on earth are you doing here?' he could not help saying as he entered his father's office. His father was rarely at the same pit for more than one day at a time and Ned felt a sudden pang of guilt because his father looked tired. Had his father been looking forward to sharing the business equally once Ned became twenty-one?

His father looked patiently at him. 'It has probably escaped your notice but I own the place. You are spending a lot of time here for somebody who said he didn't want anything to do with mining.'

Ned slumped into the nearest chair. 'I'm making a mess of things.'

He didn't believe he had just said that, he never admitted doubt to his father, but for once he needed sympathy and somehow here in this office he felt closer to his father than at any time in the house where they had lived so distantly all these years.

'Well, what a surprise,' his father said. 'Jane is getting married on Saturday. No doubt you'll be telling all your readers whether she carried roses and wore a silk dress.'

This was so close to the truth that it hurt.

'Sarah Ellison left.'

His father looked at him. 'Really, Ned, you're turning into the kind of bumbling fool I always thought you might when you went off into the newspaper business. Did it not occur to you that she would? She has been several steps ahead of you all the way, you could hardly imagine she was going to sit here now while you told the entire universe who she is. She's kept her secret for twenty years, it must have been a nightmare to have a woman claiming to be her daughter turning up on her doorstep with a journalist.'

'She said that Annabel wasn't her child, that she belonged to a prostitute.'

His father looked at him even more sceptically than before. 'Dear God,' he said, 'and you believed her? You're going to make a wonderful editor.'

This acknowledgement of his status meant a lot to Ned despite the insult. 'Did Ellison go with her?'

'He belongs here. Even the very streets are named after his family.'

'Maybe she will come back, then.'

He got up to go but his father was going to say something else he could tell by the way he shifted slightly on his chair so he hesitated when he was on his feet.

'You like this girl?'

Ned was surprised. He didn't say anything. When the silence had gone on for some time his father said, 'I've never seen you go to so much trouble over anything.'

'And does it bother you?'

His father fairly bristled. 'I would like you to have made a good marriage. I would like you to have done a good many things and so far you haven't done a single thing I wanted you to do. I will say this, though. I think Miss Reid has class, manners, education and a pretty speaking voice. Her questionable parentage, however—'

'She's as good as anybody else,' Ned said hotly and then wished he hadn't since his father sat there with a sweet smile on his face.

Ned pushed his temper away and called himself names.

'Don't worry, I'm not going to marry anyone just at the moment,' he said and he left the office.

Annabel had not been able to concentrate on the various tasks she was supposed to do that day and when Ned came back into the office towards the end of the afternoon she followed him into the back and had to wait because he was talking to Bert. It was a good ten minutes before she was able to follow him into his own office and even then he seemed reluctant to speak. He fussed with the papers on his desk and didn't look at her.

'You went back?' she guessed, and her voice trembled because she wasn't certain he had but so grateful.

'She'd run.'

Annabel badly wanted to sit down at that point but the look of self-blame on his face stopped her. 'It proves that she is my mother and no, I don't want to go after her, I don't want to hound her now she's made it clear she wants absolutely nothing to do with me.' She tried hard to concentrate on the other thing she wanted to say to him and after a few seconds remembered what it was. 'I thought I might go to the church for the big wedding. Everybody's talking about it.'

He nodded and somehow Annabel got herself out of the office without breaking down.

'I want to go back to London,' Millie said when Annabel had told her. 'You've found out who she is, you know she doesn't want you, what is the point in us staying here?'

Annabel could see that Millie had made up her mind but was so confused now that she no longer knew what she wanted.

'I've had enough of the life here,' Millie said, 'I want to go back to the life I had before. I know it seems shallow but I'm tired of Mrs Hatty's lumpy beds and being nice to people I'm not really interested in. I'm not like you, I don't want to spend my life doing this and if I go back perhaps Mother will see that I don't want to marry some old man and even if she does I feel as though I can take her now, I think after coming here I can do anything I choose, I just have to want to sufficiently.'

'You always had plenty of admirers.'

'It's time for me to marry. I need to go back. A little more time here and I'd lose my looks and be sure to be an old maid,' Millie said and smiled and Annabel smiled too since her sister tried to defuse the situation with a little humour. She didn't want Millie to go.

She wanted to protest, she wanted to say that she could not manage here without her beloved sister but it was not fair, if Millie really wanted to go and was prepared to leave her to do it then she must be very homesick indeed or did Millie think she could be persuaded to go with her? Indeed her sister was looking hopefully at her.

'I'm not coming, not yet.'

'What about Tom?'

'I don't know. I'm not sure he's being altogether honest with me when he says his parents would welcome me. What if I get back there and nobody wants to know me and I've given up whatever life I have here? I've worked so hard. Then what would I do?'

'I don't want to go back and leave you here,' Millie said.

Ned worked in his office on the Friday evening. He had no inclination to go home, he could not stop thinking about Jane and the awful fat old man she was about to marry. Annabel had come into his office sooner and stood, hesitating, in the doorway.

'Wouldn't you like to come to the County with us for dinner?' she said.

He didn't even look up, his mood was so awful.

'Don't you ever get tired of that place?'

'It's the only place Tom will eat.'

Still she hesitated and it was only when he looked at her that she said, 'Millie is ready to go back to London.'

'I'm surprised she lasted this long,' he said, 'coming from her kind of background. She'll be a big miss. The people here have a lot of affection for her.'

'Thank you,' she said.

'And you?'

'What?'

'Are you going back with Tom?'

'I'm not sure. May I have a little time to decide?'

He sat back in his chair.

'Take all the time you need,' he said.

*

She went. He was glad that she did. He couldn't concentrate on what he was doing and many times lately thought of how he found himself only going back to the little house in Sutton Street when he could stand no more. The house seemed full of other people's memories, of Jasper living there when his brother lived in a huge house and one which had been his home. How could he not resent his successful brother while despising him for giving up his freedom for the bondage of a business which was unrelenting in its problems and demands?

Quietness settled on Saddler Street and yet he didn't move. Mid-evening he thought he heard the outside door and cursed himself for not locking it. He always forgot. Usually there were other people in the premises but tonight he was alone. He listened to the footsteps as they made their way from the door, very light like a woman's but not Annabel's. He hadn't realized until then that he knew her tread. The footsteps came on until they reached his office door and there in the dim light from the hall stood Jane. He stared.

As she moved into the room he could see that she was crying and, possibly for the first time in her life, that she was dishevelled. Her hair was untidy, the hem of her skirt was dirty from the streets as though she had walked all the way from her house and it was a good three miles, and there were streaks of dirt on her face probably from where she had brushed her hands up to her cheeks. She also looked angry, there were red spots on those cheeks.

'I knew you would be here,' she said. 'I knew that no matter how late it was. I saw your father yesterday and he told me that you had somebody else, somebody beautiful and educated, from London.'

Ned silently cursed his father. Would he never be done, making mischief?

'It isn't true,' he said. 'He's talking about the girl I employ.' He was, he knew, making Annabel sound like she was polishing the floors. 'Actually there are two.'

'I'm sure I've seen one of them in the front office, blonde and very pretty.'

'That's Millie,' he said. Did he sound like a brothel-keeper? He wanted to laugh.

'He wants you to go back home, how could you do this to your father? You're his only child.'

'I shall never go back,' he said. 'This is my life and I love it. I'm going to start a daily newspaper soon.' He was astonished at himself. He had not actually known until this second that he would do so but he had been thinking about it for some time. To tell it first to Jane seemed odd but once it was said he was sure of it and already excited about what he would name it and how he would organize it and how he wished that Annabel would stay here because she always had such good ideas and she would love to be part of it. She had not said whether or not she was going back to London and he wanted her to make up her mind because her not doing so was beginning to frustrate him, he felt he couldn't go forward until she made her decision about staying or not.

Jane stood there for a few moments longer and then burst out, 'I don't want to marry Cedric. I never wanted to marry him.

I love you. You were the only man I ever wanted to marry but you made it impossible. My mother told me you would come to heel if I agreed to marry Cedric so I did and then I waited and waited and somehow the whole thing gathered momentum and here I am on the eve of my wedding day and unless something happens I shall be obliged to marry him tomorrow afternoon and it's all your fault.'

Ned had thought many times that if she should come into his office like this and say she wanted him that he would do whatever was necessary, might even agree to her previous demands about his work so that he could marry her, have her in his bed with her mouth and body warm beneath his hands. He had missed her so much at the beginning, had thought about what it would be like to go home to her at the end of the day, to a lovely house and find her there by the fire in the winter and have dinner with her and talk and then later have children and—

He could not imagine any of it now. He did not want her. How astonishing. He had thought the poor little house in Sutton Street was as bad as things could get but the truth was quite different. He didn't care about houses and he no longer wanted to go back to a big house having spent the day overseeing the huge responsibilities which his father and her father had. He had what he wanted right here, where in his way he would fight for the rights of the people, having them enjoy his newspapers, where Bert and the others worked and talked in the back room and Wednesday nights had become the focus of his life.

He was surprised to think he could ever have loved anybody who was so determined to have what she wanted beyond everything else, and that made him want to smile because that was exactly what he had done. If only Jane had wanted what he had wanted but there were other things, she wanted status and money and the company of people whom he could not bear because they did not care about anybody beyond themselves, people like Tom Grant.

Jane was spoiled and petulant and fond of blaming other people and just like her mother would use everything at her command to obtain her desires. Annabel would have said that men had left women no choice but to do so, he could hear her saying it and he found that he was smiling.

'Is something about this amusing?' Jane said with a small quiver in her voice.

A year ago he would have stopped that quiver, been sympathetic, treated her like the little girl she had always been. Would Jane ever grow up? Perhaps she didn't need to, perhaps like Tom there was always money and indulgent parents and even that they were afraid to grow up because they had seen what it did to people. He wasn't afraid, he was relishing it.

'You aren't obliged to marry anyone and it isn't my fault. You didn't have to do anything but accept that you and I will not agree on so many things that it would be foolish for us to marry. If you don't want Cedric then go ahead and tell him.'

The silence went on, the tears slipped over on to her cheeks but he was unmoved. He was starting to get bored. He didn't like himself for it but he couldn't help it, he wanted to get back to the article he had been composing on the state of housing in some areas of Durham and how it should be pulled down and the people re-housed.

'It's all arranged,' she said, 'how could I tell my mother?'

'How could you not tell her? She will think less of you if in six months' time you tell her then.'

'She wants Cedric for me now. He's rich and responsible and will make a good husband.'

'A poor bedfellow, though.' Ned didn't mean to say that, he knew it wasn't fair.

She looked at him and her eyes were huge and shining with tears.

'The only person I ever wanted was you.'

'I don't think so,' he said. 'You wanted me as you thought I was and not as I am. I don't think you would like the man I am now and I have no intention of giving up everything I care about to be your husband.'

'How can you say that to me?'

'What else should I say?'

'That you love me, that you have always loved me, because it's true. I know you hated the idea of me marrying him, I was glad to let you think it for a while. We are meant to be together and you will come to understand that I can only accept a successful man, a man who can give me everything I want.'

'Pattison can give you that.'

'Do let's stop playing games, Ned, come home and we'll be married.'

'I can't do that,' he said.

'You will. You have to. I can't live without you, Ned. If you don't agree that we will be married I will go home and kill myself.'

Ned didn't mean to do it but he started to laugh. It was very brief and he quashed it but he could see how offended she was.

'You'll never do anything of the sort,' he said. 'You're too fond of all the little games you can devise right here.'

She came across the room and smacked his face and he was too astonished at the action to move back so it hurt.

'You,' she said slowly and with venom, 'are low and vulgar,' and she turned around and swept out of the building.

Ned could only think how upset his father would be that he had been called 'vulgar'. It was something his father had done everything he could to avoid. The trouble was that it was true to some extent he would never be a gentleman like Tom, eating chocolate pudding with relish and keeping his hands clean.

He loved the smell of newsprint and the feel of the newly printed paper in his hands and the sound of the machinery in the back and to watch when the first copies of that week's newspaper came off the press. He loved the way people would buy it from the shops and the street corners and come into the office and he was proud of what he had achieved. He could do more, he knew he could. He wanted to fill the whole area with the kind of newspapers which people could not help but read.

He liked this office, it was his favourite place. He sat down and began writing again and nothing else interrupted and the evening was very late when he was finally happy with what he had done and then he locked up the office and went home.

Seventeen

Annabel had not intended going back to the newspaper office. Somehow she felt as though she should, there was a great deal to do. The door wasn't locked, it never was when Ned was there. Bert was always telling him to lock up when it was dark or when there was nobody in the front office but somehow he didn't. Either he felt safe or he just forgot about it. She couldn't quite work it out.

She heard voices and stopped inside the door, closed it as quietly as she could and then waited. She meant to mind her own business but she couldn't. She found herself tiptoeing through into the passage which separated the different offices before you reached the back of the building where the works lay and Ned's office was lit and the door was ajar. Somebody was crying.

She listened, even though she felt guilty. It was a woman's voice and she was telling the man and it could be nobody but Ned how much she loved him so it had to be Jane Baker. She implored him to take her back so that she wouldn't have to marry Cedric Pattison. Annabel retreated, cheeks burning. She couldn't possibly listen to any more. She walked out and made herself not slam the door behind her.

Ned loved this woman in spite of the fact, or possibly because of it, she thought with bitterness, that she was stupid and affected and capable of emotional blackmail. Men like Ned always married dreadful women, they somehow couldn't help themselves. She thought of how soft his voice had sounded and she hurried away back towards Mrs Hatty's as though the sound of that woman's voice would ease the hurt she felt.

The following afternoon at a quarter past one Ned happened to pass by her office. He glanced in.

'Aren't you covering the wedding?' he said.

She looked at him and said nothing.

'Baker–Pattison, at the cathedral. If you don't get a move on you won't be able to describe the dress and all our devoted readers would be very upset.'

He sounded so unconcerned, as though nothing had happened, so she picked up her notebook and put it into her bag, got her jacket and left. She was not going to be late of course, it was only five minutes' walk from their office up the winding street and on to Palace Green where the cathedral stood amidst the rain.

She searched in her handbag for her umbrella when it started, gave a sigh of exasperation because she had left it in one of her office drawers and began to hurry towards the main door where the sanctuary knocker had been giving people entrance for seven hundred years.

The guests soon began to arrive and since both families were so important the women were wearing gorgeous outfits and one of the joys of having a prosperous young life was that she knew a great deal about fabrics and cut and general fashion. Her readers were sure to want to hear about these so she made rapid notes.

She sat about halfway back. The cathedral was so big that no wedding party could ever fill it so she was quite safe there.

The bouquets at the front below the altar were pink and white roses, the flowers were lovely, just coming into full bloom, and at the end of the pews there were pink and white ribbons among the flowers. She wrote as the rain stopped and the sun came out about how the stained-glass windows made the sunbeams coloured against the pale stone.

More and more people came in and the organ played. She noted the hymns and was given a big white card telling her the order of service and what the organist would play when the bride came in and when the couple left.

It was ten minutes to two when the prospective bridegroom came in with the best man. She thought he looked too old to marry somebody as young as Jane and she thought back to what she had overheard. Ned had been no different this morning, he seemed certain that the wedding would go ahead, but what of Jane Baker? How did she feel? If she was determined to have Ned then perhaps she had agreed to whatever he wanted.

Women often did such things though Annabel would not have done so. Surely Jane would have called off the wedding in such circumstances. Annabel could not think that he might have given in, Ned was not the sort who gave in over anything.

It was both his strength of character and his weakness, she thought.

Cedric Pattison's children were there at the front, a boy and a girl, half grown. Annabel was so glad it was not her marrying a widower. She thought it must be awful to take on children who weren't yours and then she thought with a guilty pang of Etta.

People continued to file in and they knelt down to pray and there was a respectful silence until it got to two o'clock. Annabel could hardly contain her anxiety by then and kept looking towards the door. Surely she would not let him down now? Something must have been resolved between Jane and Ned. Was she the kind of woman who would jilt a man at the altar? It was such a horrible thing to do to anybody, even a man like this.

At five past two people were turning in their seats to see if the bride was arriving. By ten past two everybody was patiently waiting. Within another five minutes whispering began and very soon Annabel could see the bridegroom shifting in his seat and he and his best man had their heads close together. Eventually the best man got up and walked the full length of the cathedral aisle, looking neither to the right nor to the left.

It seemed to Annabel a very long time and was in fact almost fifteen minutes before he came back and stood over the groom and after a lot of whispering the groom stood up, ushered his children from the front and made his way out of the cathedral. Annabel did everything short of following him to see what was happening. She half-expected to see a glimpse of white, to hear a rustle of skirts, but nothing happened. There was not even a bridesmaid in sight.

The best man stood at the front and he said briefly, 'Mr Pattison is very sorry to have to tell you that there will be no wedding today,' and then he followed the groom and the children and disappeared into the gloom at the back of the cathedral.

People sat in silence. The silence went on and on and then the whispering started and it grew louder. They started getting to their feet and standing in small groups in the aisle and then began to walk slowly out of the church. The organist had stopped playing so the noise of the talk and their feet and the odd brush against the flowers and ribbons of the pews seemed louder than ever against the way that the sound floated off into the ceiling of the cathedral way above their heads.

Annabel waited until everybody had gone and then she hurried out. People were still standing about outside, women holding on to their hats in the breeze or unpinning them and holding them in their gloved fingers. Children were running about on the grass, glad of the freedom to shout and play after the confines of the church.

She walked slowly back to the office. Ned was out. She couldn't remember where he had gone. It was quiet, being mid-Saturday afternoon. It was only about fifteen minutes before he came back, went past her with nothing but a nod until she called his name. Then he stopped and came back.

'Shouldn't you be still at the cathedral, or was it one of these very brief ceremonies?' he said.

She couldn't help staring at him. Did he not think that Jane would not turn up?

'It was the briefest wedding I ever attended,' she said. 'The bride didn't turn up.'

He didn't react at all, he was like a statue, standing in the doorway.

'I thought you might have known something about it,' Annabel said.

He didn't offer anything to that. Annabel didn't like to say that he was so clearly the cause of it. Did he still love Jane? Would he marry her now? Annabel didn't mind, she didn't care, but as soon as he had gone back to his office she discovered that she was in a very bad mood. She was frustrated because she had thought she would enjoy the wedding and be able to write it up well as she tried to do with everything. It would leave a gap now, which must be filled with something else, only she couldn't just at that moment, think what.

After an hour or so, writing up reports from various organizations in the city such as the tennis club and the cricket club, she was still in a bad temper. Millie had been out, going to the various shops about advertising. She attended to the few customers who ventured in as the afternoon progressèd and then they were alone in the front office and she turned and said to her sister, 'What on earth's wrong with you?'

Annabel said that it was nothing but that was when she understood. It was not the wedding, it was not the work, it was because so obviously Jane had walked out on her wedding because she still cared for Ned and that mattered and now she had the feeling that there was a distinct possibility he would marry her.

Annabel sat, stunned, for several minutes, pretending that she was working, and for the rest of the afternoon she waited either for Ned to leave the office to go and see Jane or for Jane herself to step into the front office. It was ridiculous to imagine either happening, especially the latter, yet the few times that the outside door did open she looked up and was relieved to see that it was not Jane. Ned went nowhere. She did not realize until the late evening that she was glad he appeared to have so much to do that he stayed in his office.

Later, however, when she and Millie were alone in their room and getting ready for bed Millie said, into the silence, 'You care for him, don't you?'

She wanted to act surprised and to say 'Who?' but Millie would know it for subterfuge so she didn't. What she did was to tell Millie about Jane's visit to the office and the wedding not happening and Millie merely nodded as though she had suspected something like that would occur.

'Do you think he'll marry Jane?'

Millie hesitated and then she said, 'What about Tom?'

That was another problem. The thing was that Tom was everything Ned was not, well bred, well dressed, well connected, rich, elegant and well spoken, and Ned was – she was not sure what it was about Ned which affected her so much, it was only that she could not bear he should go to Jane but there was nothing she could do about that and it was nothing to do with her either. He must do what he thought was right for him.

*

Ned put off going home for as long as he could but when he had walked slowly back to Sutton Street in the darkness the neighbours were standing in the road in small groups. There was a fire engine and there was smoke coming from one of the houses and water in the road and running into the gutters and then he could see the fire, flames leaping out of the windows. To his dismay it was his house but at least he knew there was nobody in it, if it had been any of half a dozen other houses families would have been in there.

As he stood a policeman came up to him. He knew the policeman, his father worked at one of Tranter's pits.

'Mr Fleming? I'm sorry, sir, I understand this is your house.' His voice held a note of amazement, that Ned would choose to live in a small terraced house instead of with his father with a small army of servants and every comfort there was.

Ned's first thought was that he must get back to the office, he wasn't sure why, but just in case something happened there. The policeman, Jim Hindmarch, seemed to agree with him. He said that one of the neighbours, Mr Fencombe, had seen men running away from the house though it was too dark to identify them.

So it was with a kind of police escort that Ned arrived back at the office in time to witness men throwing bricks and something lit through the newspaper-office windows. The policemen this time gave chase. Ned hurried inside with PC Hindmarch. Bert was lying on the floor in the front office, obviously caught by something, presumably as he came in having heard some noise outside.

Other policemen rapidly put out the two small fires which had started in the office. Ned got down, calling Bert's name. The side of his head poured blood and he was unconscious. Ned was so afraid that he should be badly hurt and blamed himself. He had the awful feeling that this was his fault somehow. If anything should happen to Bert he would give up the newspaper business altogether, he thought.

It was strange spending the rest of the night in the room which Bert was given at the hospital. Ned had insisted – God, he thought, I really am turning into my father – on Bert having a small room to himself because he did not regain consciousness and Ned was convinced – as were the doctors – that what he needed most was peace and quiet. It seemed ironic that beyond the window Ned could see what was left of his own little house.

The fire had been put out but was still smoking and debris littered the street. As the dawn finally arrived the smoke dwindled away to nothing and he was so glad to see the dawn. He had never thought that the beginning of another day was such a hopeful thing, the chance of another start, an attempt at something better but with the light he could see the smoke-blackened rooms below him across the street from the hospital. He was tired by then and couldn't sleep, shock kept him awake and vigilant.

The door opened but he didn't turn, thinking it was only the nurse, come to check how Bert was doing. There was a polite cough behind him and then his father said his name and he spun round and there stood Tranter, wearing a polite, expensive summer suit as though he was going to a garden party. Ned couldn't help smiling just a little at the incongruity of his father's immaculate attire and the state of his own.

There was blood, dirt and smoke on his clothes and hands and face, he knew, in spite of his hasty attempt to wash it away earlier. He had been too concerned for Bert to care much. He had looked in the mirror at the gashes beneath his eyes and known they were strain and could not get all the grime away either and had given up. He half thought his father would comment on it but all his father said was, 'How is he doing?'

'He hasn't come round. They haven't told me anything.' He was frustrated at this.

'They never do,' his father said, looking around for and finding a chair and pulling it to the bedside. He added unexpectedly, 'I was in here for days before your mother died. Godforsaken hole.' He said it with sad affection and Ned had not thought of his mother dying here somehow or how hard it would be for his father to talk about it even now.

'They got the men,' his father said. 'I met Hindmarch as I came in. They work for Cedric Pattison.'

It was, Ned thought, probably the closest his father would ever come to an apology. They sat down, one at either side of the bed. Neither of them slept but when the summer sunshine began making its way in through the windows there was a stirring from the bed and Bert opened his eyes to find Ned's father looking down at him.

Bert focused slowly. Nobody said anything and then Bert turned slightly and saw Ned and then he smiled wryly.

'Thank God,' he said, 'I thought I'd died and gone to hell.'

Before the morning ended Annabel was there, hugging Bert and looking relieved, and Millie, wet-eyed and fearful. Ned's father left, saying abruptly, 'I'll send the carriage for you later. You'll have to come and stay with me for now.'

'Father—'

'Oh, don't argue,' his father said wearily as he walked out.

Later they went back to the office to assess the damage and to Ned's relief it was slight. The other men had already spent the day clearing up. Ned thought he would get the paper out that week as usual. His house was a different matter, though. When he went back to it a dozen workmen had been employed by his father, the road and pavement were empty of debris and they had already begun sorting out the inside.

'It's typical of him,' Ned fumed, 'he couldn't even leave me to sort this out.'

'He probably wanted you out of his house as soon as possible,' Annabel said, 'the mood you're in. No doubt he realizes this was all your fault in the first place,' and she wandered into the house to see how things were going.

Ned followed her. The sitting room was tidy and smoke-blackened walls were being cleaned. There was no sign of any of his uncle's furniture, which had perished. Some of it had been old and valuable, Ned's grandmother's, and he was sorry.

'My fault?' he said.

'You and Jane,' Annabel said, picking her way through the littered hall and saying behind her in a disappointed voice as though it was her first concern, 'Your kitchen's ruined.'

She was right. He gazed at the mess and then followed her back out into the hall.

'What about Jane and me?'

'She left him for you.'

'She did nothing of the sort. She left him because he was old and disgusting.'

'He was old and disgusting when she got engaged to him,' Annabel said.

They didn't go upstairs, the stairs had burned away and there was nothing but a gaping hole. They went back out into the summer sunshine.

'I don't think she ever intended marrying him,' Ned said. 'I think the whole thing just got out of hand.'

'You could say so. He seems to think it was your fault and you had snatched away his bride.'

'I didn't snatch anybody,' Ned said heatedly.

'Maybe you should have called around and told him, it would have saved a lot of expense and trouble, to say nothing of poor Bert's injuries. Does it occur to you that she told him she was going to marry you instead?'

'Whatever do you mean by that?'

'That she punished him by leaving him there and then telling him afterwards that she was getting married to you.'

'What took you to that conclusion?'

'Any decent newspaper person would have reached it hours ago,' she said and walked off.

Tom was horrified at what had happened. 'So, are you coming back with us?'

They were sitting on the balcony outside the County Hotel, watching the ducks paddling about at the side of the river and people walking on the towpath as it was a fine day.

'I want to stay here and help with the Miners' Gala Day. I told Ned I would write a special piece about it so I can hardly leave now. I don't think I have anything more to stay here for after that. We could go on the Sunday,' she said.

This was not altogether true. She hadn't known what to say to Bert and unfortunately she was now better with words on paper than on her lips and she was so nervous that she just said it there in the hospital room with the rain falling steadily beyond the window. 'I'm thinking I might go back to London next week with Tom and Millie when the gala is over.'

'Aye,' Bert said, looking out of the window too, 'I thought you might. Yon gentleman's well-to-do and can look after you. I know you think by now that you don't need looking after but everybody does in the end.'

'I will miss you so much.'

She leaned over and kissed him. Bert mumbled that he would miss her too and then Ned came in so she had an excuse to leave before she became emotional and upset Bert further.

Ned sat down in the same chair. 'The doctor says you can go home after he's seen you providing everything looks all right.'

'I can't wait to get back to work,' Bert said. 'I'm bored silly sitting here.'

'I thought I might come and stay and look after you for a few days and I don't think you should come back to the office straight away.'

'What good would I do at home? I would just fret knowing what a mess you're making of it while I'm not there,' Bert said and Ned smiled.

'All right, then, but you mustn't do too much.'

'You just want to come and stay with me because you don't want to go on staying with your dad.'

It was true. A couple of nights at his father's house had convinced Ned he had done the best thing by moving out. Left alone they had nothing to say to one another and his father insisted on dressing for dinner and had made the housekeeper find appropriate clothing for Ned. He had tried to avoid being there but his father had insisted and Ned had shouted and he thought it was no better than it had ever been. 'I work in the evenings.'

'If I can be here to sit down like any civilized being and eat a meal then so can you,' his father said but afterwards Ned would change again and go back to the office even if he couldn't find anything which had to be done immediately. He began to think longingly of the little house in Sutton Street but he could hardly complain since his father had sent workmen there every day to repair it and even shamefacedly offered Ned some furniture.

'Annabel was right, you can't wait to be rid of me,' he said with a grin.

'And Jane?'

Ned had been dreading talking to his father about her and could think of nothing to say. It was late now, he had had to come back through the drizzle, he was beginning to think it would be wet for Gala Day and that would be a shame when it was only on once a year.

He stood there in the library where his father was drinking brandy as he always did before bed. He said it helped him sleep. Ned had refused the brandy.

When he didn't say anything his father became impatient and waved the brandy glass in the air.

'Do sit down, boy, you're making the place untidy.'

'I don't want to talk about Jane.'

Ned slid into a leather chair which was so soft it almost enveloped him.

'Annabel Reid doesn't even have a proper name,' his father said.

'I know.'

'And very dubious background.'

'Her mother is Sarah Ellison and her father was Fergus Seaton, I don't know whether you'd call that dubious.'

'He was a bastard,' his father said.

Ned was surprised, his father rarely swore.

'You knew him?'

'Everybody knew him. He couldn't leave women alone. These men, they call themselves gentlemen because they have money and position and power, but they have no integrity and no restraint and no care of anyone else. A real gentleman would never behave in such a way. The Reids were fine, good-living people but their children chose so poorly and they were hurt and humiliated and did the wrong thing. So,' he looked across the room at Ned, 'are you making choices here?'

Ned didn't say anything. His father waved the brandy glass at him.

'Any woman who leaves a man at the altar like that is despicable. You were right, she wanted you for all the wrong reasons. I shouldn't have tried to manoeuvre things like that but I thought it would serve, that you had enough in common for it to work.'

'I don't want to live like that. I'm going to start a daily newspaper.'

There was a short silence during which his father considered the small amount of brandy left in his glass as though he wished it was a little more.

'Something told me you would. And it wouldn't be good business if you didn't. All that new machinery would hardly be a good investment if it was left standing idle most of the time.'

'I had it in mind when I bought it,' Ned confessed.

He had told Bert before this but he wasn't going to tell his father that. He had enjoyed the glint in Bert's eyes, the joy.

'Think of all the fun we'll have, lad,' he had said.

His father looked narrowly at him across the fireplace and said slowly, 'And what about Miss Reid?'

Ned acknowledged this and then he said, 'I think Annabel is going back to London.'

'She's a disappointed woman. Her father was an idiot, her mother doesn't want to know her.' His father paused there and then said quickly, 'And you haven't asked her to marry you.'

'How can I?'

His father considered. 'He has a lot more money than you and he lives in the city, where men like him make powerful decisions, where the most important of them behave like the king, sleeping with ladies one night and whores the next and they shoot and fish and go to parties. They also rule the country and have tremendous influence so your Miss Reid could become a very powerful woman when she marries because she would have social sway and give huge parties and have the ear of politicians and courtiers. It's a heady mixture. Why wouldn't any intelligent charming beautiful woman like she is want it?'

'Precisely,' Ned said.

Nobody spoke and the warm summer day died beyond the shadows and his father eventually looked gently at him and said, 'The house is nearly ready and I could give you your mother's bureau.'

Ned laughed. 'I would be proud to have it,' he said.

'You can't stand the bureau there, Ned,' said a voice from the doorway.

He turned around and Annabel was standing with the sun streaming in through the open doorway just behind her. It made his heart move to see her. Whatever would he do when she was gone?

He covered the feelings by saying, 'There's nowhere else it could go and in any case what would you know about it?'

She gestured impatiently and then she said, 'It's obvious, idiot, it goes in the alcove.'

'The alcove isn't big enough.'

She threw him a look and went over and began to lift the bureau to move it so he helped. She was right, it fitted perfectly there.

'It's very pretty,' she said, standing back to admire it.

'My father gave it to me. It was my mother's.'

'It's too good for you with all your papers and much too small. It's a woman's piece of furniture.'

'I couldn't say that. He was being so nice to me and I'm not used to it.'

She laughed at that.

'It's meant for a beautiful sitting room,' she said and wandered through back into the hall and then he heard a squeal of joyful surprise. 'The kitchen is lovely. Your father had one of those new stoves put in. Come and look.'

He had seen it but went through, smiling because of her delight.

'You know nothing about stoves,' he said but she wasn't listening, she had bent down and was now saying excitedly:

'It's got two ovens. It's exactly right for somebody to learn to—' and then she stopped and after a few very long moments she got up, face rather flushed.

To dispel the confusion he offered to show her the rest of the house and then realized what a mistake it was because the moment they entered the bedroom she saw the double bed. She could hardly miss it, it was sitting in the middle of the floor and had been another present from the big house. It was rather handsome with twisted delicate fruit and flowers in some kind of metal at both the head and at the foot of the bed and his father's housekeeper had made it up and she had put in little tables at either side and flowers and there was an elegant dressing table and even a writing desk.

Annabel went straight to the bay window to see the view of the other side of the street where the hospital rose up comfortingly somehow and little children played singing, skipping games on the pavement.

'How strange,' she said, 'that children play the same games as we used to. I must go,' and instead of telling him why she must or what indeed she had come for she brushed past him and was gone and he listened to her footsteps on the stairs and tried to remember them in case he never heard them there again.

Eighteen

Ned did not go and see Jane, he felt he had nothing more to say and never wanted to see her again after what had happened and he did not need to see Cedric Pattison. The police would deal with it, he would keep out so Ned didn't know what sent him away from the city that morning, only that he felt obliged to go.

He fought it but it was an unequal battle from the beginning. He told himself that he had too much to do, that he could not leave, he was needed, that he had made several appointments and this was true. He was obliged to foist these on to Annabel and since she already had some of her own – though thankfully at different times – he felt slightly guilty. She was very quiet and he was glad, all he wanted was to get away.

Nobody asked him where he was going though probably several people wished they could and he found himself taking the train beyond the little pit villages and into Weardale, trying not to call himself stupid and ridiculous. All the way there he told himself it was a whim, that it was mad and misdirected and would come to nothing and he would have wasted his time when he should have spent the day in the city where all kinds of commitments awaited him.

He got off the train and then he walked. It was a hot day and the walk was all uphill. It was the kind of walk where every time you got to what you thought was the top of the hill there was another hill, another bend in the road and every time the view from where he was standing got better and better until the little farms were grey oblongs below, the sheep tiny cream dots and the fields made up a green quilt beneath him.

Through the little village of Rookhope he strode, walking as swiftly as he could, imagining that his goal would soon be reached and after that he could go home because there was no chance that this was going to work out. He cursed himself for wasting his day, for letting his imagination get the better of him, for deciding overnight that he had to do this.

He was at the far side of the village now, he was at the very place to where he had brought Annabel. He stopped. Nobody was there among the ruins of the old house, just rabbit droppings. A sheep pulled at the grass nearby.

He told himself that he had known all along nobody would be there. What about his strong conviction now? He looked up at the land at either side of the narrow road, he looked about at the stream which ran out from the hillside. There was nothing and nobody.

He trudged to where the sign was. It still said 'Paradise' and whatever had come after it was still broken off, as though it could be anything more. What had he expected? A miracle? He had not imagined it thus somehow. He had thought of the house roofed, smoke coming from the chimney. He had thought of the tidy garden, the glassed windows, the stout doors at either side, children playing in the heather, a woman hanging out washing so that it could blow in the warm breeze which assailed the land and at the end of the day would watch for her husband coming home to her but nothing moved up here.

And then behind him as if from nowhere, like a magician had waved a wand and conjured her from the air a woman's voice said tentatively, 'Mr Fleming?' and when he turned Sarah Ellison was standing behind him.

She stared at him from her lovely though mystified blue eyes and she looked to him as Annabel would look in middle age if no one helped or looked after her, the look of bewilderment, resignation and sorrow.

He didn't speak, he was so taken aback.

'What are you doing here?' she said.

'I came to find you.'

'But how did you know I was here?'

'Where else might you be?'

'I ran,' she said, 'I always run when things go wrong. An old habit. My husband . . . he gets upset. He says I need to stop running sometime but it seems I can't. I don't know how. I would like to, I'm getting so very tired you see and every now and then I can't stay even at the little house with the husband I care for so much and the view which leads me away. It leads me to here sometimes and other places beyond. He usually comes after me but he was angry this time and swore he wouldn't.'

'It's beautiful here. Were you happy when you lived here?'

'I tried to be. You see I could never forget the bairn I'd left. I didn't have another. She's such a bonny lass too.'

'Why don't you come to Durham and see her?'

'How would I ever ask her to forgive me?'

Ned hesitated for a few moments and then he said, 'I think Annabel is going back to London. I thought you should know. I don't think she'll be coming back here.'

'Leaving?'

'Yes. She's going to marry the man she was once engaged to. It's a different world and the place she thinks she belongs. If she goes back there without seeing you—' He couldn't manage any more. He hadn't realized how much it meant to him that she should see her mother one last time, be sure of something, anything in her life. He wanted that much for her. 'Please come and see her before she leaves.'

The day of the Big Meeting, as the local people called it, was a Saturday in July and it was warm and sunny. Annabel had heard people speak of it but she knew very little, that the miners and their families would arrive in their thousands and it was exciting to be in the middle of such happenings, especially since the newspaper office was just above the route of the march.

The miners did not have many holidays and even from the early start of the day she could feel the excitement. All the pubs and hotels expected to make a lot of money from it and Bert informed her that many of the collieries paid the men to be there, so it was doubly important to them.

Women had come into the newspaper offices that week and told her of all the preparations they made, of the baking and the packing of the picnics, of how they had made new clothes for the bairns, of how much they were looking forward to coming in on the train and how proud the men were to follow the parade of banners through the streets of the city they loved so much.

The streets were thronged with people early. There was a buzz of excitement in the newspaper office and she was determined that the piece she wrote for the day would be the best she had ever done because it would be her last. The parade was something wonderful, she thought. The miners paraded with their lodge banners, those who had had deaths down the pit that year draped across the top in black, each accompanied by their own brass band so they moved slowly down North Road, across Framwellgate Bridge, up the winding cobbles of Silver Street and into the Market Place. From there they turned right into Saddler Street and down on to Elvet Bridge.

Tom had been interested to note that politicians and leaders were staying at the County Hotel and stood on the balcony to acknowledge the men and their banners and followers and bands as they marched past and then on to the racecourse. If the collieries were from the villages above Durham they marched down Claypath bank and met up with the others in the Market Place.

Annabel saw it all and made notes as swiftly as she could of how it felt and how it looked, the colours and the tunes and the noise and how people were so deep on the pavement that it was almost impossible to move. She had to apologize as she pushed through, she must miss nothing.

When they reached the racecourse each lodge – the organizations of the workers who carried the banners – had its own spot, she was told it was the same each year and there they would play the miners' hymn, 'Gresford', and then the speeches began.

Ned joined her when she got there and lots of people knew him and came across to him and he introduced her and they all seemed to know her work from the newspapers, at least the women did and how grateful they were to her for this and how much they enjoyed what she wrote and the children's corner which was puzzles which kept the bairns busy many an hour and wasn't it grand that Mr Fleming had employed a woman, they had not heard of such things before, they thought she was very enterprising and clever and they made Annabel feel awful because she did not think she could tell them or should on their special day which they were so obviously enjoying so much that she would be leaving the following day.

There were amusements, there were gypsies telling fortunes and food and drink which could be bought and the families sat down together and had picnics and the sun shone and Millie and Bert brought food from the office and it was good for them all to sit together. Even Tom was there and she had not thought he would but there was little else went on in Durham that day so how could he refuse?

Later she wandered among the crowds alone. Millie and Tom had already gone and she wanted to think about the very last piece she would ever write for the *Chronicle*. She wanted it to be the best she had ever written and she must think and be among the crowds and eventually find somewhere quiet to make notes. She already had several pages of ideas which she had made throughout the day. She paused at that point and thought she should find somewhere to sit down and run through them and see what she had left out and she turned to find a quiet spot and then she saw somebody she thought she recognized.

The woman was coming through the crowd towards her, Annabel saw her from a long way off, even though there were thousands of people down by the river. There was something about the way she moved which was familiar and yet in that same moment Annabel knew that she had not seen the woman move like this. She walked with her head down but not as though she was contemplative and not as though she did not know where she was going.

There was a sadness about her drooping head which Annabel understood immediately. She could see the top of that head and the parting and the red-white hair, neither one nor the other and yet somehow both. She was not going quickly as though she was reluctant to reach her goal, yet reach it she must. The grace of her long limbs and the confident way in which she walked reminded Annabel of something but she could not think of it and then she understood. It was her own reflection, that was how she moved but she had never before thought it graceful or womanly and yet it was.

She didn't move. She couldn't have moved and she didn't want to, she just wanted to wait there for however long it took for the woman to reach her because she had never before seen her own mother picking her way across a field by the river or indeed anywhere, making her way to where Annabel stood. She wished that she could hold those moments because they were more dear to her than anything on earth.

By the time the woman reached her some of the neat red-white hair had worked free of whatever grips confined it and blew about at the sides of her face, softening it and making her look younger and also the way that she gazed so softly upon Annabel meant that for several moments, having seen what she wanted more than anything on earth, stupidly Annabel could not see for the tears which filled her eyes. She scrubbed at them with impatient fingers and she knew that she had begun to smile back at Sarah Ellison and that nothing would ever be so bad again.

She didn't know who moved first, she only knew that down there on the racecourse in the little city which had not yet betrayed her she became enfolded in her mother's close embrace for the first time and she felt safe there on the sunny day, the most important day in the miners' year, and that it would always now be her most important day too with a brass band somewhere across the field playing a tune she did not know but would thereafter never forget, while Sarah Ellison said into her ear, 'Oh, my bonny bairn.'

Nobody had said such a thing to her before and said to her like that in the language of her family, her ancestors, it meant the whole world.

*

It was late when she got back, she should have been at the office long since, composing her report of the day and as it was she got back there mid-evening and she ran into the office and Ned was not there so she ran all the way to Sutton Street – through the Market Place and down the winding Silver Street to the river and across Framwellgate Bridge and up North Road and it was only when she banged on the door of the little house that she stopped, flushed, she knew from the exertion of running so far and breathless. He opened the door and there was a tentative look on his face as though he had been worried all day or even, she thought, as if he had been worried for a great deal longer.

'It was you,' she said.

He gazed at her, his brow furrowed and then said in the throwaway attitude she realized she had come to rely on, 'Where have you been, you were supposed to write up the report of the day. I bet you haven't done it.'

'You found her,' she said, gulping down the tears so that they would not show. 'How did you know?'

'You'd better come in,' he said, opening the door wider.

The house was flooded with evening sunlight, the shadows were long across the city and the little sitting room wherein sat the lovely bureau was warm and welcoming.

'There weren't many places she could be,' he said.

'There were a hundred places.'

'Not that I knew of.'

'You're so prosaic,' she said.

'Nice word,' he said, grinning suddenly and that was when

she crossed the distance between them and put both arms around him.

She intended planting a kiss on his cheek however awkward it should prove and then retreating but somehow it didn't end up like that. When she got close enough he put his arms around her. He made her feel safe, smaller. She had never felt like that she knew except in his presence. When she was with him she always felt safe. She knew it for illusion, she had experienced the vulnerability of loneliness and not knowing where she belonged and although she should have backed away and gone on thanking him she couldn't do it.

There in the little house beside the viaduct she felt happiness and contentment as though there was nowhere else to be, her day was complete. She could hear a train rattling across the viaduct and she thought how noisy it would be living here and she wondered how he looked after sleep in the early morning and whether the sun crept its way beyond the bedroom curtains and she watched him close his eyes before he kissed her.

She knew afterwards that she should not have done it, that she felt like her mother must have felt when Fergus kissed her, as though the world ended beyond him. She had kissed Tom and he had kissed her and it had been good. This was on an entirely different level, it turned people into idiots and sinners.

He began to tighten his arms around her but she had just enough sanity to say, 'No,' and he stopped in a split second and released her as though she had spoken half a dozen sentences of reproach.

He didn't say that he was sorry, he didn't say anything.

'Why did you do it?' she said, to make words fill the distance between them.

He looked confused. 'I just—'

'Why did you go looking for her?'

'I knew you couldn't leave if you didn't see her again.'

'She introduced me to her husband. He's a good man.'

'Aye, I know,' he said, sounding very like Bert and thinking of Bert made her feel miserable so she tried to say something more and failed.

'The Ellisons have been there since the town began. They were pit sinkers,' Ned offered.

She liked the way he said the words that let her move towards the door.

'I'm leaving in the morning.'

'I'll come to the station.'

She said, 'No—' and then wished she hadn't. 'I hate good-byes,' and then she was out of the door taking very fast breaths as though she had run a long way.

When she had gone Ned was restless. He didn't want to go back to the office so he walked into Elvet and out towards the edge of town to where Bert lived in Church Street, near St Oswald's. Bert had insisted on going back there to be by himself and Ned knew he needed rest and might already have gone to bed but when he knocked on the door Bert answered it almost immediately, looked relieved to see him.

'Tell me all about the day,' Bert said, 'I wish I'd been better.'

Ned sat down in a worn comfortable armchair and related everything he could remember and then Bert said, 'Did Miss Annabel do a piece?'

'I don't think she got to it. She's leaving in the morning. I offered to go to the station but I don't think she wanted me there.'

Bert was looking hard at him.

'What?' Ned said.

'You haven't said anything to her, have you?'

'About what?'

Bert gave him what they called 'an old-fashioned look'.

'You've always had a lot of guts,' he said, 'so—'

'I'm not right for her.'

'She's the only one who can decide that, not you. You have to say it, you have to take the risk. You've lost nothing because you've got nowt now.'

'I cannot.' Ned got to his feet, suddenly unable to stay still. 'She would achieve a great deal as the wife of a rich influential man. His family are important.'

'Achieve. Well, that's a new word for it,' Bert said. 'So you're going to let her go, are you?'

'Of course I am.'

'That's what I did and look what it did to me.'

'It isn't the same.'

'It's exactly the bloody same!' Bert said and he was almost shouting. 'What do you think's going to happen, that another lass will come along? It may work like that for some men, lad, but it's not like that for people like you and me. When you're reaching up to take the stars out the heavens you don't settle for less.'

Ned didn't say anything.

'You should give her the choice,' Bert said, 'it isn't up to you, it's up to her to decide what she wants and if you're half the lad I thought you were you'll tell her so.'

In the bedroom with everything she possessed on the little put-up bed Annabel could stand it no more.

'I'm not going,' she said.

Millie had arms full of underwear but she put the clothing down in a heap and her voice quivered when she said, 'I knew you wouldn't. I wouldn't either, if it was me. How can you leave your mother when you've just found her and—'

There seemed so much more to say but nobody knew how to say it somehow so they didn't talk after that because Annabel didn't want Millie to go but knew she must and knew that she would not change her mind now. Millie went about her packing silently and Annabel did not get in the way. Only when the suitcase was closed did Millie turn to her with more resolution in her face than Annabel had seen before and she said steadily, 'I love Tom. I've always loved him, I just didn't want to get in the way because I cared so much about you.'

Annabel was not astonished. She felt she should have been but she remembered how there had always been the three of them and how when she and Tom were engaged Millie had seemed so glad yet so upset. Millie was turning out to be so much like her that perhaps it would put him off or perhaps not. It would be so different when they got back to London.

When Tom arrived she went downstairs to see him by her-self. He never looked comfortable at the Garden House, he stood there with his bowler hat in both hands in the middle of the sitting room as she walked in.

'Is everything ready?' he asked.

There was no point in putting it off.

'I'm not going back with you,' she said.

Tom stared at her. She blamed his incomprehension on her-self, she had changed her mind so many times and he was not to blame though she could not prevent the thought that if he had cared so very much about her in the beginning nothing would have made him give her up. It had been too difficult for him. In a similar position what might she have done?

And then she thought about Ned and that was different, Ned had had nothing to lose by the time he met her, he had already sacrificed everything but his integrity for what he had wanted and what he wanted was worthwhile. Tom was not to blame for that either, he had been brought up as a rich indolent young man and that was what he was, what his parents had intended he should be. He had had to fight for nothing. He had tried to fight for her by coming north but the trouble was too well advanced by then.

'I have found my mother and my place here,' Annabel said.

Tom still said nothing, he had clearly not expected this, he looked shocked and taken aback.

'You haven't really told your parents about me, have you?' she guessed.

He looked away. 'I couldn't.'

'Well, then, nothing is lost. You can go back to London and marry the right kind of girl and make them proud of you. I was never the right kind of girl.'

'Yes, you were. You are . . . you just put obstacles in the way, perhaps on purpose. It's Fleming, isn't it? It's just for what he's done, it can't be love.'

She smiled. 'For a man good with words he moves well,' she said, 'but it isn't just that. I want the newspaper and my mother and him. I want the city. This is my city, I love every stone of it. I could never own London like I own Durham, it doesn't give itself the same, it's too big—'

'Our part of it is wonderful,' he said.

'I know. I know you care about it, that to you it's home but I've found so much here.'

'It would be different if you came back.'

'I don't think it would. I could never overcome the way Etta feels about me and I don't think your parents would ever forgive me if I married you or indeed allow it at all.'

'What about Millie?'

'She's ready to go home.' She didn't say 'She's ready for you to take her home' because she didn't think he was anywhere near the time that he might be ready to accept Millie as his wife but once they were back in London she thought – she hoped – that it would work out. Perhaps it was too neat a solution, she did not dare to think. Relationships were never neat, they were always a mess.

'I wish I'd never come here,' Tom said.

'And not sampled Mrs Hatty's black pudding?'

He looked appealingly at her as she smiled.

'You can't really want to stay here,' he said. 'You'll grow tired of such a life.'

'I'll have to wait and see.'

'Has he asked you to marry him?'

'No. How could he? He thinks the little house in Sutton Street isn't good enough and anyway I think in the end he will probably marry Jane.'

'Well then,' Tom said stiffly, 'I'm wasting my time.'

'You could carry Millie's luggage down for her,' Annabel said, 'that would be a big help.'

In the morning she went with them to the station. She didn't want to go but she didn't feel as if she had any choice, she did not want to bid her sister goodbye and she must be brave enough to leave it to the very last moment so she went with them in the carriage, half afraid that she had made the wrong decision and half glad that at least she had made some kind of a decision that felt more right than wrong.

They were early and it was awkward, standing about on the platform. Tom always did everything too early and they couldn't look at one another or she knew that she and Millie would cry and then she heard somebody say her name and when she turned around Ned was coming on to the platform. He didn't even acknowledge the other two. He said:

'I know you told me not to come here but I couldn't help it—'

She took a deep breath, told herself to talk straight, looked him in the eyes and said, 'I'm not going. I haven't finished my piece about the gala.'

He stared. He didn't say anything and her stomach fluttered so much that she couldn't think of anything to say either. Her hands shook so that she could scarcely hug Millie and there was a betraying part of her which was desperate to get on to the train and run away.

The train came in and then she had to say goodbye to Millie and they both started to cry and Tom pressed a chaste kiss on her cheek and then he handed Millie inside and Millie said, 'If you don't come back to London soon I shall be back here. Promise me.'

She promised and then everybody was on the train and the doors were closed and she stood there, waving until it was out of sight and then she felt she had made the wrong decision and she didn't know what to do. She stood. She felt she would never move again, that she had become a statue on the station platform.

'Are you going back to the office to do the piece?' Ned asked.

'Yes, I thought I would,' and she strode off out of the station and began walking down the steep hill which led to the city and it had the view of the whole town below with the castle and the cathedral in front of her and she thought, how could she ever have left this place?

'Bert's threatening to come in on Monday,' Ned said, falling into step with her.

'Didn't you tell him it's too soon?'

'I tried. Will you stop a minute?'

She stopped and turned to him.

'I'm upset about my sister leaving. I don't want to talk. I feel now as though I should have gone.' She couldn't look at him and fiddled with her gloves.

'I'm so glad you didn't. I've been thinking about you all night and trying to think of the right thing to say to stop you from going and then you made the decision without me.'

'I don't need you to make my decisions for me,' she said. 'I don't want to leave this place now. I've just found my mother, what is the point in my going away? All I have in London is Millie and she will marry soon and then where would I be?' Her voice was becoming more and more unsteady so that she feared for it and for her composure.

'With Tom?'

'No.'

She started walking again and after a moment he followed her.

'Annabel, will you stop for a minute?'

They paused just where the steep hill encountered the bend and the city beneath them glinted in the summer sunshine.

'Look, I don't know how to say this because I'm frightened of what you're going to say but I want you to stay here not just because of your mother and for Bert but for me too. I want you to stay here because I want us to get married. There, now.' He let go of his breath. 'I can't tell you what men usually do and say I've got a nice house by the river because you know only too well that I haven't. You know what I've got, the newspaper and that's it really. I should be able to afford something better than Sutton Street in time but I can't at the moment.'

'What about Jane?'

He looked uncomprehendingly at her.

'I don't want Jane. I can't think why I ever did want her. I think I was trying for the first time in my life to do something my father wanted me to do. I tried to please him.'

'Well, you've certainly made up for it since,' she said.

He half smiled and shook his head and looked away.

'I never loved Jane like I love you. I didn't realize it was like that. I thought it was all about other people and families and such but the way I feel about you isn't like that.'

'That's what scares me,' she said.

He looked at her then. 'What do you mean?'

'When you kissed me I felt like I thought my mother must have felt when Fergus kissed her. I felt like I would do anything for you and being like that – it seemed so dangerous. It made me want to run to Tom and go back to London and settle for less. My love for Tom was something safe, something I could rely on.'

'You can rely on me. I want us to get married, I want us to be together in the little house in Sutton Street. We may not get this right but I do think we should try – if you want me.'

'What would your father say?'

'I don't care and besides I think he already knows and he likes you but we'll be married regardless of what anybody else says or thinks. Just say you will.'

'All right then, but I still have to go back to the office to write up my piece about the gala. We could go to Mrs Hatty's after that and tell her and then your father and then I want to go to Deerness Law and tell my mother.' My mother, she thought, the sweetest words ever except possibly everything which he had said to her in the past few minutes.

'You do know I want to start a daily newspaper,' he said.

'What do you think we should call it?' and they began to walk slowly down the hill unable to agree on the name for the new venture because neither of them could manage anything else.

She didn't like to tell him that she had already dreamt of being with him in Sutton Street, that she was already rearranging what furniture he possessed and thinking what else they might need. She loved the way that the trains roared across the viaduct to Edinburgh and to London. It made you feel that nowhere was far away and you could go if you wanted but you didn't have to. You could sit in front of the fire with a man who would do anything for you and talk about when you would visit your mother in the windy little hilltop town which was about to become so dear to you.

And she planned to get to know Ned's father. Maybe one of these days they would name a pit for her as Tranter had done with Catherine. If they did she thought she would want to call it Sarah for everything she had lost and for all that she had found. The little city in the north with the Norman cathedral was indeed her paradise. She would never forget the moment her mother walked across the grass to her on the racecourse down by the river. Gala Day would always be the best day of the year to her or perhaps not, perhaps there would be better.

It could be that she and Ned would have many happy days at the newspaper office and at the little house and she dreamed that she would have a child and she would be able to knock on the door of her mother's house on one of those windy days in May when the trees were so green that it hurt your eyes to look at them, when the lambs were crying in the fields below the house and the sky was so blue that the sun glinted off the roofs of the little farmhouses in Weardale.

Her mother would come to the door and take the baby from her and into her arms and the cycle of life, she thought, would be complete. That was what she wanted. It was a great deal to want, it could be that it was too much but it was not too much to try for, it was how things were meant to be.

She wanted to have a little girl so that the little girl should grow up as she was meant to with a mother and father who loved her and a grandmother who doted on her, so that she would feel so safe that eventually she would do the things that she wanted and not the things that life had tried to force her into. It may be a great deal to want but there was nothing wrong with ambition, she knew it now.

Acknowledgements

I would like to thank all the librarians at Clayport Library here in Durham for their help, patience and friendliness, and the librarians in the reference section who entered wholeheartedly into the quest for northern newspapers in general and Durham newspapers in particular.

Elizabeth Gill was born in Newcastle upon Tyne and as a child lived in Tow Law in County Durham where her family owned a steelworks. She has spent all her life in Durham but recently moved to North West Wales to be near her family. She can see the sea from her windows and spends a lot of time eating seafood, drinking orange wine and walking the family Labrador, Izzie, on the beautiful beaches.